MRS. BLOOD

ALSO BY AUDREY CALLAHAN THOMAS:

Ten Green Bottles

Mrs. Blood

AUDREY CALLAHAN THOMAS

The Bobbs-Merrill Company, Inc.
Indianapolis · New York

Acknowledgements
This book was written with the help of a Canada Council
grant. I would also like to thank Tom Meikle for his
help with some language difficulties.

The Bobbs-Merrill Company, Inc.
A Subsidiary of Howard W. Sams & Co., Inc., Publishers
Indianapolis/New York/Kansas City

Book design by Dorothy S. Kaiser

To Lori Whitehead
Walter Goresky
and J. A. S. Macdonald

—The Listeners

"But I don't want to go among mad people," Alice remarked.

"Oh, you can't help that," said the Cat: "we're all mad here. I'm mad. You're mad."

"How do you know I'm mad?" said Alice.

"You must be," said the Cat, "or you wouldn't have come here."

Alice's Adventures in Wonderland

MRS. BLOOD

PART ONE

Mrs. Thing

Some days my name is Mrs. Blood; some days it's Mrs. Thing.
Today it's Mrs. Thing. I came to this place sitting straight up on
a kitchen chair (you know the kind) in the back of what professes to be an ambulance. I say "professes," or, better still, "pur-
ports," because things here aren't always what they seem to be and
one must behave accordingly. Or try to. Take the matter of the
ambulance, for instance. When Jason came back and said, "They
think you ought to go to town," I was sitting up in bed wearing one
of my new striped nighties. I have six of them, six different "flavors"
you might say: lemon-lime, raspberry, candied violets, orange, chocolate and Fox's Glacier mint (blue, really, but I was trying to think
of something blue and cool that you could suck like peppermint-
striped candy and the nearest is a Fox's Glacier mint, although
they're not blue of course). We got them all (or Jason did) at
Woodward's bargain basement; only it isn't a basement but six
floors up, which is very confusing to anyone brought up on bargain basements which you went down to. (I remember one where
we used to go and get our pants and socks and have our shoes re-
paired. It was in a large department store and you went down the
steps from the main floor and past the ladies' washroom which
was very cold and smelled of Lysol so that somehow you knew
even then that a bargain basement lower even than that cold,
foul-smelling place was something not quite nice. For Lysol was
something Mr. Ironside used in school if somebody threw up and
what Mama used when the puppy did his business on the rug. So
I can't get used to the idea of a bargain basement being six floors

1

up. But that's where Jason got the nighties. I wanted lots and I wanted cotton so it would be cool and of course they had to button down the front.) And there I was sitting up and wishing I could see out of the windows and sort of nervously running my fingers along the mend in the nightie (they were all seconds which is why they were so cheap) because I'd already recognized the sound of Jason's car (you can hear him shift down getting ready to turn off the road) and was afraid of what, in fact, he'd come to say. And feeling very sorry for myself, you know, with all the new sounds coming in from outside and the new kind of brightness and the whole new thing that was out there and I couldn't get at— like Alice and her garden. And also very frightened, for that's one thing you'll have to accept about me, the fear. I can't remember a time when I wasn't afraid; and now I felt the hour had come round at last—and time has proved me right—and whatever it was that I had felt behind me, stalking me, for all those years was nearly on me and I could almost smell it. Somebody had brought me some *Markovitch Black and White,* which at six shillings a packet (or more maybe, by now) was a gesture in the grand manner, let me tell you, and I tried to light the match to smoke one and picked up a book so he wouldn't know how scared I was. But I dropped the match and burned a little tiny hole in the bedspread, so I knew, right then, it wasn't any use and things were just about as bad as they could be. And I cried when he told me and said I didn't want to go; he stood there very uncomfortable and worried and said it was rotten luck and English-y phrases like that which he never uses anymore except when he's embarrassed (now if he'd said it was a "bad show" at least I might have summoned up a laugh). And when he said "ambulance" I cried some more because it seemed so official and I knew right then I was going to die, because why else send an ambulance? But I didn't put on any clothes—just a very thin cotton dressing gown over my stripes and a clean pair of pants and we sat there smoking and waiting for the ambulance to come. I hoped the school bus wouldn't come before the ambulance, not only because I didn't know what I would say to the children (when I was little, ambulances seemed to me like wild things fleeing through our city streets, looking for someone to eat, looking for me) but because the legendary Mrs. M. would also be there, sitting at the back, as she does with her goodness and concern and *bravery* (for hadn't she driven twelve miles with Benjamin's tongue bitten off and lying there on the car seat; and hadn't she held him while Dr. Biswas stitched it back in place and she all the time placating the other four who were weeping out of fear and empathy?) And now they bring me tales, like offerings, of how she copes with mine as well as hers. They use the word "cope" a lot. "Oh, Mary can always cope." "Oh, Jason's coping very well." "Oh, we'll just have to cope." I see them all invested with a bishop's mantle or the conical cap of the Archbishop of Canterbury. Yet I'm not sure what a cope is. I must ask for a dictionary. I have no cope, I cannot cope. I have no hope! Skip rope. My doctor gives a little hop and skip, a sort of shy little dance as he advances into the ward each morning.

Anyway, as it turned out the ambulance came first. No siren, just the sound of gravel in the drive and Joseph's voice calling something to the driver. I waited while Jason went down the stairs to meet them He came back looking rather harried.

"There's no stretcher."

"No stretcher?"

"No."

And I felt lighter—a commuted sentence—almost gay. "It doesn't matter. I can walk."

So we walked together down the stairs (I remembered to put on my sandals, thank the Lord) and I felt as though I were being given away in some bizarre marriage parody—me in my peppermint-striped nightie and my peekaboo cotton gown, leaning on Jason's arm, and Joseph at the bottom of the stairs looking up. The groom, maybe, or the preacher in his torn undershirt and the oven cloth still in his hand (for the house was filled with the smell of Joseph's bread). He looked worried and embarrassed, for he knows (who doesn't?) what's the matter.

"Eh! Madame."

"Look after the children, Joseph."

"Yes, Madame."

And Jason leads me across the drive to the ambulance (the sun striking across my back like a whip), and the nurse, her mouth full of groundnuts, takes my arm and helps me up the step and into the back of the van.

3

Mrs. Blood

I am here because I bleed. I came in the back of a converted diesel truck, sitting very tall on a straight-backed chair which was chained to the floor like the chairs on a ship in a gale. The nurse was very square and solid and reassuring and I willed myself to neither faint nor cry but to observe what might be the strangest (if not the ultimate) journey of my life. I did not look back at Jason or Joseph when we left. I'm like that. They had not ceased to exist but they existed, once I stepped inside the van (or "ambulance," if we want to use hyperbole), on another dimension altogether, like figures in an old daguerrotype or relatives they told me had gone to heaven. Sometimes, now, I wonder what they are doing at a specific moment. While I am waiting, buttocks tensed, for the iron shot, is Joseph relaxing on the back stoop, smoking *Tusker For Men,* not aware of his buttocks at all, but only aware of the silent, ordered house behind him, maybe the smell of the bread baking, and the feel of the first drag on his cigarette or a mosquito bite on his arm? And while I am tensing and Joseph is relaxing, what is Jason doing, or Nicholas or Mary or the ladies who will come to see me this afternoon? We are all in the same time zone and more or less in the same place and yet we do not exist at this tense/relaxing moment for anyone other than ourselves. Pain, pleasure—can they really exist in group relationships? It is difficult to make love with your eyes wide open or crap in an open field. Or cry on a bus. Although men can pee together, and talk while they are peeing, women find it difficult to ask their friend to pass them toilet paper underneath the door. I have pale blue plastic curtains around my bed to keep my pain in. I am bathed behind these curtains and I roll on my side so they can take the bloody sheets away behind these curtains. I pee behind them. And when they are removed I am sitting up, swabbed and scrubbed and clean-toothed, too, having brushed and spat into what Alexandria ("Is that really your name, Alexandria?") insists on referring to as the Nemesis basin. Perhaps she is right. "All the perfumes of Arabia could not sweeten . . ." And the masquerade of order has begun. Soon the two men who clean the floors will wander in with their tins of turpentine and Mansion Polish and we will inhale the perfume

4

of their labors. It is difficult to tell how old they are (these people age in a different way from us), but one is certainly a lot older than the other. They wear cut-off, ragged khaki trousers, like grotesque parodies of U.S. college boys on holiday, and the inevitable ragged undershirts. The nurses treat them very badly ("Staff" in particular, but I hate her on other grounds than these). I smile at them in my egalitarian way and once in a while the younger one acknowledges my greeting with a solemn nod. Would he believe it if I told him I had a job like that once in order to get summer money? "Yes, Madame!" he would say, but he would not understand. They also bring the food on trays from somewhere rather far away because it's cold by the time it comes around. My food is terrible and tasteless. "European-bland" it says on a piece of paper which is planted, like a flag, on top of my cold porridge. I cannot sit up to see what the others get but it smells delicious—spicy and full of sunlight and color. And throughout the morning, although visiting hours aren't 'til three, friends of the women here will come with pans of stew and papaws and sliced oranges, and they will talk together in their high, nasal, rather bee-like voices, and eat; and the nurses will call greetings and stop to chat and pay no attention to the many rules which are being broken. This is a very pungent place by half past ten, with the smells from the turpentine and Mansion Polish and the smells from the peripatetic "breakfasts" brought in by the "Aunties." ("Eh, Auntie," calls Alexandria, *"Ma che, who ho te se?"* Good morning, how are you? They are teaching me to say it.) And the smell of the flowers and the earth outside. The fans are on but they do not shift the smell or the gathering heat. They simply force it into the corners where it will creep out again and lie against our faces, like a cat, while we are sleeping. What is Jason doing, or Nicholas? I can't remember the smell of Joseph's bread, only the smells of this place and the smell of blood.

Mrs. Thing

And then they put me in this bed. After the ride in the so-called ambulance, sitting straight up on a chair like some queen, my buttocks tense under the billowing robe because I was sitting

on my fear. *"Hysterio passio,* down."* I had put some phenobarb
in my purse, along with my toothbrush and toothpaste and a
photograph of the children. But I didn't really want to take it
in case they gave me something else when we got there and the
combination killed me or killed the baby. Pills never used to
bother me, but now I hate to take them—they're so irretrievable
once they're down. Without a stomach pump at any rate. So I
just hung onto the chair and tensed for all I was worth and
watched the nurse who was sitting on the campbed where I was
sure I was supposed to be and thought how strange it seemed
to see a nurse with bare legs and sandals on. Like a nurse on
holiday or something. (Or once I saw my dentist in a sport shirt
in the Hudson's Bay store.) She wasn't very pretty, rather moon-
faced and stocky for such a young girl, and she just sat there
shelling groundnuts and eating them as though she were on her
way to the amusement park or taking a bus ride to nowhere in
particular on a lazy afternoon. (These are all "back home" similes
but they'll have to do.) Shuck. Chew. Shuck. Chew. They are not
stupid or bovine. It is simply a different philosophical state. We
hate to wait or to "waste time" or to be trapped into anything
we might consider boring. We put magazines in doctors' offices,
and comics for the children. We chatter endlessly. We fidget.
We pick at our noses or our fingernails. We talk when we make
love. (Do you like that? That? Tell me what you like.) This
is not to say they never chatter. Esther and Grace and Alexandria
giggle as they make the beds and bathe us and talk over our heads
(or mine) about subjects which surely must be as banal and as
interesting as the subjects of young girls' talk in any land. But
they do not waste their words on strangers. (But that's not true
either, if you're white. "Hey, Madame, you give me shilling?"
"Hey, are you from Chicago, Illinois?" What is it that I mean to
say?) I was nothing to this girl. We were to take a ride together
to the city. Then she would come back without me. We might
meet again; we might not. The ride itself was not a topic for
conversation. Nor my illness. We shared a silence. I doubt if she
thought anything.

After the second roundabout we turned off away from the main
road into town and climbed a hill. My lifelong habits made me
break the silence. "Are we nearly there?"

"Nearly. A few minutes only."

We turned into the gates and drew up by the entrance. The driver came around and opened up the back of the van. The nurse got down and she and the driver went off and left me sitting there. "Please. One moment." There was the sound of many voices, like a waterfall, and the sound of the crying of babies, and the sight of many people walking in or out the gates. I opened my purse and put my hand around the bottle of phenobarb. Two little children sucking shilling tins of sweetened condensed milk climbed in and sat down near me on the floor of the van. The floor was covered with groundnut shells. "Hello," I said.

They just looked at me and went on sucking at their tins. I thought of Nicholas, just then, particularly of him, and wondered what Jason had told him when the school bus brought them home. Nicholas doesn't like it when I go away from him and it is very important to him that I remain standing at the front door while he walks down the drive with Joseph and turns to wave good-bye to me. Tomorrow I wouldn't be there. Or the next. Or the next. Or maybe never. (That was maudlin.) I felt the two here beside me would accept things as they were, and I begrudged my son his bland European babyhood. We are too important to our children.

Then the nurse came back and shooed them away. "Please," she said. "Can you walk?"

"I guess so." And she helped me out into the blazing sun. And there I was at the hospital, only with all that sunlight and my weakness I went giddy for a minute and couldn't see. And when my sight cleared it still didn't make much sense. So I looked up at the blue sky and tried not to be afraid. Only there were vultures wheeling in the sky and vultures sitting like gargoyles all along the roofs. But where could I run in my nightie and peekaboo robe, and if I knew where, then how far in a sun like that?"

"Please," said the nurse. "This way."

Mrs. Thing

All the signs were there from the beginning if only we had stopped to think. A dead man on each boat.

"Which one was he?"

"Sat over by the wall there," says Waldo. (Even had Waldo's

7

name, now that I come to think of it. Why weren't we thinking then?) "Second night out it was, in his cabin. That's his wife there." And we look discreetly over our Coupe St. Jacques at the back of the woman whose husband died on the second night out. It seemed wrong, somehow, that she was there in the cabin class with us, all alone except for her self-important steward. Surely death was distinction enough to move her up one class and on to the Captain's Table. "Put 'im in the deep freeze," says Waldo, watching to see what effect this will have on his captive audience.

"That will do." I glance at Nicholas and Mary. Waldo shrugs.

"Just thought you might like to know. The milk will go off before we reach Cobh." He winks at Mary. "Better drink up while it's fresh." And in the fog the widow and the ambulance men who had come on with the pilot walk slowly down the gangway while we hang over the rail and watch.

"Are we getting off here, Daddy?"

"No, a little longer."

And at Le Havre a rope snapped off a capstan with a terrible *crack*. That too. (And again we are all leaning over and watching and listening to the voices of the local people who have come down to watch us, sounds which ring as exotic in our ears as the sound of unfamiliar birds.) When the rope snapped there were louder cries and some laughter and bilingual curses as the ship swung awkwardly out away from the quay and had to be lassoed in again. Someone was wearing a beret, which struck a responsive chord in Mary's ordered mind. In her books the Frenchmen often wore berets. She knew she was in France. Just as I "knew" (but why?) that we were really in Africa when I saw the vultures circling above the river when we stopped at Bathurst. So, first a dead man and then a broken rope. And then another dead man—from another class as well. How could we have been so stupid? And somebody said—I think it was the Judge's wife—"The milk will go off now, worse luck," and I wanted to turn around and ask if this was really so, or only an old wives' tale; but right then it was my hand and she was at another table. But in this case, because of the location of the kitchens, the dead man would have come up in the world, and I stood and looked down at the deck passengers and wondered whether he was married or had children and whether they'd

8

take him off at Takoradi or leave him until Lagos. People were singing down there and there were torches set up on the tarpaulins stretched across the hold, but I couldn't see anyone visibly grieving or off by herself like the woman on the *Britannia*. I never saw them take him off either, but we were so excited by this time that six or seven dead men might have been carried by right under our noses and we wouldn't have turned an eye. Once you're well and truly down the rabbit hole nothing seems incredible. It wasn't that we really wanted to identify with the sudden deaths, the way one might when one comes across a really bad auto accident, with red lights flashing and policemen waving you on, and you think "Oh, my God, another one" and "It might have been me" and feel slightly sick. Strangely enough, the worst accident I ever saw, myself, involved a milk truck, and maybe that was a portent way back then. I must have been seven or eight and we were coming back from a drive along the old Lackawanna Canal. There's a hill at one point which has a blind curve on it, and everyone called it Dippy Hill. I thought, as a very small child, that it was because you went up and up and then, suddenly, after this curve, dipped back down into the valley. I didn't know it was called Dippy Hill because there used to be a state asylum at the top. Anyway, my father was a really nervous driver, constantly putting on his brakes and swearing and telling us kids to be quiet while he passed this goddamn truck, can't see a damn thing, etc., etc. He hated this hill and simply crawled up it, staying as far over to the side of the road as he dared (which wasn't too far, because he not only hated driving, he also hated heights). It was getting dark and it had been raining for some time. Just as we got near the top a policeman stopped us and said we'd have to wait a minute: there'd been a really bad accident and they wanted to get the vehicle off the road, because of the blind curve and all. (I remember it was the first time I realized what "vehicle" meant, really took it in, I mean. Just as I was ten before I discovered that the "catastrophés" I kept hearing about on the radio were the "catastró-phes" of my mispronunciation.) So there we were *teetering*, almost, on the brink of this hill with the rain coming down and the police car blocking our view of what had actually happened, my father cursing under his breath all the while because he was sure the emergency brake wouldn't hold and also because he hated anything to do with death or physical disaster. We heard the ambulance come up the other side of the hill and heard the sirens stop, and then the policeman waved us on. Quite suddenly, so that my father stalled the car in his nervousness and had to start it up again. I still don't know why they didn't have us wait a little longer. Maybe because it was such a dangerous hill and they didn't like to hold up traffic with dark coming on. I don't know. Anyway, there was the milk truck on its side and another car smashed underneath it and blood and milk together running all across the road. The rain wasn't heavy enough to wash it all away and there must have been hundreds of gallons of milk in the truck. The driver of the milk truck had been decapitated as the truck went over and all this blood had run out of him and onto the road before the ambulance men had got there. My mother shouted at us not to look—"Don't look!"—but of course we did, and the head was just there in the road as we went by. My father didn't see it—he was staring straight ahead and cursing—but I saw it and so did my sister and of course my mother. The ambulance men, who'd been putting the body in the ambulance, I guess, were coming back, presumably to get the head, for they had a blanket or a bag with them and looked startled and furtive as my father drove by, like somebody caught doing something he shouldn't. Poaching or something like that. My father was in a really bad state about the hill and the blood and milk and my mother kept saying "You'd think they would have had us wait a few more minutes," and my sister and I just looked at each other in excitement and horror. The next week I had trouble swallowing and they said it was my tonsils but I know it had something to do with the way that man's throat felt when he died like that; and I can still see that milk and blood and my father's hands just glued on the steering wheel.

But we didn't identify with the two dead men at sea. It was simply part of the romance and mystery of the whole adventure. Even though Mary and Nicholas went around telling everyone how there'd been a dead man on the *Britannia* and now a dead man on this boat. But it was just another thrill—like seeing porpoises off the stern one day or watching the purser move the little magnetic ship each morning closer and closer to our goal.

Maybe if the milk had really gone off we would have paid attention.

Mrs. Blood

I stink therefore I am. This is the bloody and bawd of Christ which was riven for thee. Take this in remembrance of me. And we stick out our tongues and wish the carpet didn't itch so. Hold out your tongue and close your eyes. It was only a game and the adults made sure that we all got something. Open your mouth. How strange to have your tongue cut right off in that instant, all the words and gentle murmurs gone in an instant, quivering on the carpet by the altar. Red on red. Was the carpet red for blood—"This is my blood"? (But the blood was purple because he was of the city of David and also a king. And the blood was also purple because it was Welch's grape juice.) I keep a red washcloth in my purse in case the children fall or have a nosebleed. Red on red—it doesn't show. I shall steal out early and gather flowers and bleed to death on a carpet of hibiscus. And from the garage where I am hiding with the boy from down the street I watch his sister mince along in last year's first communion dress.

They have broken my body and the wine dries sticky on the sheets and in the secret places and the hibiscus shrinks against the clumsy fingers of the sun.

Mrs. Thing

They brought in a woman this afternoon who cried and screamed until just now.

"Auntie!" the nurses would call. "Hey, Auntie," and then something in the vernacular, but she would only scream louder. She must be a very big woman, possibly a mammy. I don't know why I think that except the mammys are big and often have deep voices like this woman. I can't see her, of course, because she is beyond the partition. The other women became uneasy because she carried on so—all except "I-am-the-daughter-of-a chief," who is still barely conscious and the Lebanese girl who is listening to her transistor radio and eating a box of chocolates, one right after the other. The woman screamed, the nurses called out from time to time and the other women muttered amongst themselves. Finally Dr. Shankar came pounding in wearing his white rubber boots. The first time—years ago—that I saw a doctor in white rubber boots I couldn't believe my eyes. I still think it looks vaguely gay and at the same time sinister, as though they work in a slaughterhouse. Dr. Biswas, even when he has just come from the operating room always finds the time to change back into shoes. But not our Dr. Shankar. I think he likes the sound they make as he comes along the hall. They announce him: "Here is Dr. Shankar. He has just come from surgery and he is a very busy man. See? He has not even time to change his boots." But to me he sounds like rainy days at school and wet boots along the corridor outside the classrooms. They must be very hot as well.

Anyway, in he came and went over to the woman's bed. The nurses hurried to join. (He is very bad-tempered.) "Here, now, my good woman, you'll have to stop this noise. You're disturbing all the other ladies. Let me see her folder then, hmm?" And the woman screamed louder while Elizabeth explained what was the matter. (I still hadn't any idea.) Then I heard him say, "The best thing is probably to humor her until her doctor comes. Who did you say it was? Oh yes. Well, if she gets too noisy get the matron to authorize some morphine. No, I will *not* do it. Dr. Ho may come at any moment." And then in a loud voice, the way one talks to the deaf or to a foreigner, "You'll be all right soon, my dear. These ladies will look after you." And slish, slosh, slish, slosh, leaving rubber heelprints on the waxy floor, back the way he had come, Elizabeth running after him with unfinished business and he brushing her aside. "Tomorrow. Get someone else to do it. I'm busy. Figure it out for yourselves." His contempt for all but the staff nurse is really quite incredible and I am glad he is not my doctor even if Roger M. did say he's a "dashed fine 'gynie' and we're lucky to have him here."

I called to Elizabeth as she came back, laughing. "What's the matter with her?"

"She thinks she's being electrocuted. She thinks her bed is plugged into a certain electrical machine and that we are going to kill her."

"Why does she think that? Fever?"

"Yes. Malaria. It has gone to her head."

"Will she get better?"

Elizabeth shrugs and soon I can hear the sound of Alexandria and Grace chattering together as they move the woman's bed out into the center of the ward. I can see only the foot of the bed and the heaving bedclothes.

"There, Auntie," says Alexandria. "We have disconnected you." And the woman is quiet for a few minutes, muttering to herself and sobbing. Then she begins to scream again.

The staff nurse, back from her afternoon off, shouts at the others and then gives the woman a shot, presumably without permission. The woman is quiet now and they are about to put down the nets.

To be driven mad by a mosquito bite. It is terrible but fitting for this rabbit hole. Alexandria says the woman will surely die.

Mrs. Blood

I made love once in the Japanese gardens at the university, where everything is dainty and on tiptoe and the students come to talk and walk along the clean, well-ordered paths. Across and beyond are the woods which is really where it happened; up against a tree and rough and clumsy and violent. Necessary—like a sneeze. And only the tree saw us.

Afterwards we stood on a little bridge and looked at the huge goldfish—more dull white than gold. "Ugh," he said. "They look like blood-soaked bandages." I thought he was pretentious.

"What d'you know of blood-soaked bandages?" I asked and spoiled his poetry.

But it was strange there, in the trees, so close to all that order and those swollen fish and with my skirt hiked up above my waist like someone wading.

Mrs. Thing

Dr. Biswas is learning French through the Alliance Française in town. *"Bonjour,"* he says, frowning slightly as he paddles against the current of his native intonation. *"Comment va-t'il?"*

13

He is very proud of himself because he has done a year's course in six months and has been advanced to the *deuxième étage* ahead of all the others. I can see him giving his little nervous skip at the door of the classroom and shyly taking his seat. I know quite a bit about him now. At first I think he talked to put me at ease and now it has become a habit—a kind of mid-morning pick-me-up. After all, he and I are "white," relatively speaking, and thrown together in a strange country. And his wife is English. Therefore we are "connected," as it were. He wants to go back to England to become a licensed gynecologist like Dr. Shankar, but he is afraid and unhappy about taking his family back. He says there was no prejudice while he was on his own, but after he was married he noticed the hostility of the people. They went to India, then, in a wave of sentimentality and ethical idealism (he admits this shyly, his long, girl's eyelashes dark against his cheeks) and hated it. There was little money; the baby didn't like the food; his wife was unnerved to find that his family considered her inferior (it is one thing to consider the darkskinned races our equals; quite another to see them as they might see themselves—as our superiors) ; the heat bothered even him. There was little money. His idealism evaporated and he began to resent his wife's pale skin and the baby's diarrhea and longed for the cool hostility of England once again. Then they saw the ad in the paper and wrote off quickly. "Suddenly everything seemed all right again." (And I feel that they made love that night, perhaps for the first time in months, but I can't really picture him in bed. Perhaps she takes the initiative.) Here he gets an expatriate salary and he and his wife are accepted as one out of many mixed couples. Jason says that he has seen them occasionally at the swimming pool and that Dr. Biswas always wears a thin white rubber bathing cap and nose plugs and his wife usually sits in the cafe with the daughter, although sometimes the daughter goes in the pool as well. Then he holds her very carefully while she kicks and shrieks and tries to swim. But she is very spoiled and cries easily and soon goes back to the cafe to drink Fanta and watch the other children. Jason says that in spite of the wife's pale skin the child is completely Indian. I am disappointed when I learn that she is spoiled. I thought

14

his daughter would be shy and gentle, as he is. Did he spoil her because he felt sorry that she would have to face problems he was only just beginning to be aware of (in anything other than a theoretical way), or does his wife spoil the child because unconsciously she resents the dark skin which binds the father and the daughter in a closer union, perhaps, than anything that he and she will ever attain? Perhaps Jason is wrong—he is very strict.

Today Dr. Biswas had a new phrase, *boîte de nuit*. As he examined me he made me try to guess its meaning.

"Privy?" I said.

"I beg your pardon?"

"Outdoor toilet."

"Oh. No. Very good." He gave a little giggle of pleasure. "Turn on your side, please. Thank you. Try again."

"Parcel that arrives at night. Like a 'night letter' only a box instead."

"No, not at all. Do you give up?"

"I give up."

"Nightclub. In France a nightclub is a *boîte de nuit*."

"Did you guess it?" I ask him teasingly.

"Oh, no. I didn't. But it's a good phrase, yes?"

"Very clever."

He peels off his glove and throws it on the tray.

"What do you think?"

"I think everything is pretty much the same."

I can feel the coarse sheets, already damp with sweat.

"If it stops can I go home?"

He teases me now. "Don't you like us?"

And my eyes fill so quickly I don't have time to turn away. He is embarrassed. "I will be in tomorrow."

"Of course." There are barriers we must not cross and we toss the old safe words back and forth like worn tennis balls. I call to him as he reaches the door.

"Dr. Biswas!"

"Yes."

"I have another definition for your *boîte de nuit*."

"Yes?" He smiles because we are playing games again.

"Coffin."

15

Mrs. Blood

I put a sign on my breast, "Eat me," and on my lips a notice, "Drink me," but only the mosquitoes came. "Take this," I said, "in remembrance of me," and they flew away without speaking.

. . . .

The fans are enormous insects or flowers growing downwards toward my head. They hum as they spin—like insects. But they have petals, or are they wings? I am sure they are getting lower every day. When I am sleeping they will hover over me and plunge into my body, taking what little is left of growth and nourishment. Thus I must sleep always with my hands across my belly—to protect the child, my nutmeat, my center, my dying darling, oh my dear. Some nights when they forget about the nets I fight to stay awake, and lie on my back, my hands across the child. And yet there's always the possibility, if they are insects, not flowers, that they will attack my eyes. Is there fluid in the eyes? I remember a hot day and a sheep's eyeball and the color and texture of mother-of-pearl or opals. But was there fluid (and hence refreshment for the fan bugs), or was it hollow like a dime store Easter egg? If hollow, then my eyes are safe—if the fan bugs know this. Perhaps I should sleep with one hand on my belly and the other on my eyes. They would only think that I was praying.

Mrs. Thing

A girl from the compound came in on Tuesday. She is on the other side of the partition, so I can't see her, of course. But I can hear her crying. "Come, come," says the voice of Dr. Shankar. "You won't help things by crying. The sister says you tell her you are not in pain. Is that correct—you are not in any pain? We can give you a little something for pain, you know." She mumbles a reply.

"So. Sometimes life is sad and maybe a little bit unpleasant. You will not improve it by crying."

Again, I cannot hear what she is saying.

"I'll be along tomorrow."

Slip. Slap. Slip. Slap. Exit Dr. Shankar into the maternity

ward. Does he have contempt for all women or only for African women because he considers them inferior and European women because he thinks them weak? One could speculate that a man from India, a gynecologist particularly, might eventually become so saddened by the suffering and stupidity of his own women and so indifferent to the suffering of others more fortunate by reason of birth or economics that he could no longer understand or even tolerate the psychology of pain or mental anguish. And does he limit his contempt to the African women on this ward, Senior Officials—3? How does he act toward the women on the general wards, for instance? But no, it's too complicated. Look at his attitude (an attitude which Dr. Biswas shares) toward Elizabeth and Alexandria and Grace Abounding. Africans are inferiors, poor or rich. Which of us, black or white, does he dislike least, I wonder? We have no tolerance for uncertainty and possible disaster—the Indian and the African are more stoic. But so are the British usually, and the girl is British. I have not asked about her because voices carry and I would not want her to think I am simply curious about her distress. But it is strange to listen to her crying there on the other side of the partition. A tall thin man with glasses comes to visit her, also a flashy Lebanese. But never at the same time. When my ladies come to visit I am sure they will tell all.

Mrs. Blood

That spring it was unusually hot and Jason laughed and said, "You know what happens to girls who don't wear any nightgown, don't you?"
And I said, "If you get me pregnant I won't go with you."
"Tell me to stop then."
"Stop?"
"Tell me again."
And that spring I noticed for the first time that the streetlamps looked like onions growing the wrong way up and wilting in the sun. Or chive plants gone to seed.

Mrs. Thing

After we make love I cannot bear him to touch me and I shrink. I can feel myself shrinking and imagine I look like

17

fingers which have been too long in the bath. And it flashes through my mind the old joke we used to tell at college: "The Duke's a long time coming," said the Duchess, stirring her tea with the other hand. And my friend Marie at school who told me she had an orgasm when she had her first internal examination. Slow. Slow. Quick. Quick. We foxtrot around the bed.

"What's the matter?"

"Nothing." (Will he never come?) But in the end he does and is completely spent. Even as lovers it was never more than once a night. He has no joy in him and I remember the sound of his mother's voice: "I'd do anything for the people I love."

But out of love? When I get out (if I get out), with or without the child, it is time for me to go.

Mrs. Thing

The phenomenon of being "horizontal man" for such a long time is—I am convinced of it—beginning to affect me. I gaze up at the ladies like some enormous baby in a cot and I'm sure their faces look quite other than if I were communicating with them face to face. I used to lean on my elbow—the left one on Monday, the right one on Tuesday, the left one on Wednesday, etc., when visitors came to see me, but the skin on my elbows got very red and raw so finally I gave that up. And these women, even little Mrs. Hare, look so enormous to me, so full of Brobdingnagian strength and vitality, I feel quite helpless and am often much more peevish than I intended to be at the outset of the visit. Mrs. X asks me how I find the food.

"Horrible. Tough turkeys in congealing gravy and peas that taste like pills. Jason brings me in fruit, though, when he comes."

"Oh? When I had Mark" (or Matthew or Luke or John) "I thought the food was really very good indeed. What did you think, Sabina?"

"Oh, no complaints whatsoever." Then, to soften my obvious fussiness, "But that was two years ago, of course."

"Well, maybe by comparison to English hospital food. I remember being in hospital in Birmingham and all I seemed to get was great thick mutton chops and greens. The nurse said you had to be diabetic to get anything out of the regular diet."

And they gaze at me with what can only be described as "adult" sympathy. I am a child kicking the rock on which she has stubbed her toe—"Yes, darling, we know. Naughty old rock. Poor you." They tell me how wonderfully Jason is coping with the children. What a hit he was at so-and-so's dinner party. How beautiful the children are. "Quite like storybook children really." And I feel (most probably wrongly) that it is not quite *comme il faut* to have such pretty children. They should have regulation hair-cuts (short) and braces on their teeth. Everything they say conspires to make me feel that I am not one of them ("She's not really one of us, you know") and that they find me puzzling and a bit decadent lying here and bleeding the afternoon away. I remember one of Jason's mother's friends who came up to see me just before we sailed.

"Oh, well, if it happens, it happens. I had a miscarriage at nine o'clock one New Year's Eve and went to a supper party later in the evening."

And Jason's mother, after her morning tea in bed: "Well, this will never do. I must get on."

By the time they all leave I feel both angry and somehow humiliated. They are like the vultures who gather over dying or helpless things. And the vultures who sit above this hospital. Vultures in terylene dresses they have "run up" themselves, the same way they "run up" curtains for each successive house they live in. Vultures who look in the mirror and see only fresh English-y faces with no-fuss hairdos and the merest touch of lipstick. I hate them and I want to be like them. I want to be brave and competent and healthy. And I want to be a hardy annual, not something wilting on a too thin and bloody stalk.

Mrs. Blood

When I got out of the truck I nearly lost my balance because of the old rucksack and I thudded against the side. I shrugged my shoulders to readjust the weight and he said, "Did you drop something?"

"I don't think so. Why?"

He held up my change purse and a pair of bloody underpants.

"No. They're not mine. Ugh!" I said, and began walking away, very quickly, along the side of the road. And I could feel him laughing at me as the truck went by. And the worst of it was there was about three pounds in change in that goddamn purse. Still, it hadn't been my wallet and what would you have done? After that I was afraid to accept any rides from truck drivers until I'd crossed the border. He might have told them and I couldn't take that chance. The fact that he could speak English only made it more awful. I kept imagining him telling not only his buddies but maybe some of the other students from the university.

"Say, I know you. You're the girl who . . ." It was like a nightmare. When I reached Cologne it was everything I could do not to buy a railway ticket the rest of the way. I can hardly remember what the cathedral looked like, but I could still describe to you that truck driver and find the place on that road where it happened.

Mrs. Blood

I know the smell of death and I know the feel of death too. Listen. When the mad die alone and unclaimed they cannot be laid on the city walls as an offering to the birds and the insects. And nobody had claimed her and the thirty days were up. So I went down to prepare her for her pauper's grave and dress her in her black crepe-paper nightie. And she was very heavy—a lot of them are, you know—and very cold of course and Mrs. Karensky said, "Does it bother you, love?" and I said no, why should it; but I slitted my eyes the way I did when there was something scary in the movies and told myself I was only propping up a lump of ice and tried to remember what it felt like in the back of the iceman's truck: cool and the smell of sawdust and the big chunks of ice wrapped up in burlap. And was perfectly all right in spite of the smell of formaldehyde and I listened with real interest while Mrs. K. chattered on about "The poor old soul— you'd think she was going to a fancy dress." And how the RC's have to keep every bit, even fingers and amputated legs (but of course she was ignorant and it made a good story).

And then as she was doing up the ties at the back she let go a minute when I wasn't prepared. And my hand, which had been flat against the back, reached out like a claw to grab the corpse, and long strips of her skin came away beneath my fingernails.

"Oh, sweet lord-lifting Jesus," shouted Mrs. K. and grabbed the thing as it toppled sideways off the table.

"I didn't know which of the two to go for," she said afterwards. "Poor little buttercup here or Big Ann. But Jesus, what a thing to happen. I just hope to God they don't turn her over when they drop her in or somebody's going to wonder what we're running here."

And I quit the next day and couldn't stop washing my hands. I still wear my nails cut down almost to the quick.

Mrs. Thing

If I die here and Jason and the children go back home, who will bring flowers or water my grave with their tears? Mary M. would probably come for the first year, but they aren't coming back when Roger's contract is up. Perhaps she could pass me along to someone else—a kind of heirloom or chain letter. Imagine some poor unsuspecting wife in one of the other departments. Second day on the compound, sorting out the hand luggage (for of course the trunks won't have arrived although she won't have begun to worry—yet). "Hello? Mrs. Makepeace? I'm Jean or Jane or Josie McPherson. Could I come in a minute?"

And the poor girl, thinking it's a social call, delighted to have someone to chat to (compare children, houses, get all the "gen" as the English say), rather self-consciously asks the steward to make a pot of tea and then sits down to hear not where to buy gingham or whether to join the club but the sad tale of me and my all-but-forsaken grave.

"Could we put you down for January perhaps? The harmattan blows then and the poor cemetery gets terribly dry and brown. We try to get the boys from St. George's to water it but it's a bit of a bind, you know. Anyway, just a few flowers would brighten it up. We have a rota system so that somebody pops up there at least once a month. And Sue Chamberlain [or Sue Bumble or Mumble or Fumble] our 'January girl,' so to speak, will be on leave this year. Would you? That's awfully kind. It may seem rather a superfluous gesture—none of us really knew her, but

21

maybe that's why. Anyway, Mary M.—you would have *loved* Mary, such a dear—asked us to keep it up when she left and keep it up we shall, so long as there's someone to 'pass the torch along,' so to speak."

And after her visitor is gone, the new girl pours herself another, more thoughtful, cup of tea and thinks of my story, gazing blindly at the hibiscus hedge with its flowers orange-red, like blood.

Mrs. Blood

We came up out of the Holland Park Tube Station and into the fog.

"Look," I said softly. And three old ladies with three violins appeared and disappeared while we stood still and watched them softly come and go.

"Three old ladies with three violins
Appeared one night by the Holland Park Station.

I'm going to write a poem about them. Wasn't it strange? Like the three graces or something." And I held his hand very tightly, for suddenly fear ran over me like wind on a field of wheat. He stopped me at the corner.

"Look. There is no nice way of saying this."

But he said it nicely anyway and then nicely left me.

"Call any time. You know I'll think about you and wonder how you are." I stood in a shroud of fog and watched him quickly dissolve in the opposite direction. And I thought to myself, "There goes the only person I have ever loved," and stood there watching him dissolve.

That night I thought the house was on fire because I woke up choking. But my roommate said, "Go back to sleep—it's only the fog." And all night long I could hear the ambulances going, taking people to the hospitals. The newspapers said it was a bad November for the very old and very young, and it was a bad November for other people too.

Mrs. Blood

The funny thing is he wrote me once that he was trying for a job in Freetown, "and you know who I want to go out there with me." I wonder if he went and if he still breaks hearts and if he

22

admires that beautiful silk-cotton tree and drinks imported beer and says his nice things to the circuit judges' wives.

I have memories preserved intact, like men in peat, to be found by a later me. That is what happened this morning with this memory.

Mrs. Blood

The smell of death I know too, with the old ladies screaming and cursing and Nurse Primrose and Mrs. Karensky and myself, handkerchiefs soaked in Old Spice cologne, making the rounds each morning to swab out the bedsores and paint them with gentian violet. Some of the bedsores went right down to the bone and the old things would lie there and curse us and scream and the others mutter to themselves or play with the filth we hadn't had time to clean off yet, for we simply started at the top right-hand corner and worked our way down and up. I carried a pail of green soap and water and a sponge, Nurse Primrose had the swabs and gentian violet and the powder, and Mrs. K. went ahead with the piles of sheets and drawsheets and pillowcases. When we got to Eleanor La Duce she always pointed at me and screamed, "You're a whore. You ride the beast with seven heads." And one day Mrs. Karensky said, "I don't like to be a buttinski, love, but I think your skirt upsets her."

And Nurse Primrose looked up from her compact and snorted. "How could it? She can't tell her ass from a hole in the ground. Jesus, Karensky, you're soppy."

But I went to Penney's and bought another one, just the same, and watched Nurse Primrose put on her "told-you-so" face when Eleanor did it again.

Mrs. Thing

The drive down had been uneventful, me sitting on a pillow and Pa driving quite slowly, for him, out of deference to me. We stopped and had a picnic in a field just before the Mersey Tunnel. I wanted to run through the familiar wheat like Mary and Nicholas but instead sat like a good girl on the car rug and tried to take the afternoon inside me—the very blue sky, the gentle English heat, the silence, the taste of the wheat stalk Mary gave me to suck. "Remember this," I thought, and sought to make it a part of me, like a song or an equation. *Something* $= \ldots$; but see, I cannot even remember what the something is, or whether there were michaelmas daisies growing along the ditch or whether that was some other place and time. Our heads become crowded and details fall away.

Just afterwards we ran across a herd of cattle and Pa sat there cursing and swearing and afraid we'd miss the boat. But also afraid of the cows. He made us roll the windows up and we sat there floating on a sea of dust and cows and the good smell came right in to us through the cracks. And then a bull mounted a cow right in front of us and Jason and I started to laugh, first at Pa's discomfort, but also because somehow it was so unself-conscious and right and I said to Jason—"Perhaps it was not so bad to be Europa," but he had started talking to the children. I see the tunnel now for what it really was—and yet I thought then it was really the beginning.

"Damn nuisance," said Pa. "I wanted to stop at a little pub before we went down to the docks. Shan't be time now." And he fled from all that splendor.

Mrs. Blood

"You know what I'd do with people like that?" he said. "Line 'em up against a wall and shoot 'em."

"It isn't the Communists we have to fear, love, d'you know that? It's the Yellow Peril."

The street of the woodcarvers is called Odum Street and odum is a very hard wood. And the hard street of death is called Pain.

Mrs. Thing

Mrs. Maté, who is now the lady next to me, offered me some of her cologne this morning. I envy her because she is allowed to get up and wash and because she has friends who come to see her all day long. Today I thought I smelled a familiar smell, and when they pulled back my screen she said, "Please, would you like some cologne?" and proffered me an enormous bottle of Avon toilet water. I thanked her and dabbed a little on my wrists.

"Can you buy this here?"

"Not at all." She smiled proudly. "My husband was recently in the United States and he brought it back for me. You can buy nothing like this here." And she put the bottle carefully back on her night table.

Mrs. Maté's husband is an official in the office of the Town Council—I am not quite sure what he does but it must be something rather big. In the afternoon she told me that her husband had also brought her back a wig.

"Does it fit? Do you like it?"

"It is very nice. But it is not a perfect fit. I am having a stand made for it and will place it in the hall."

I try to imagine the thoughts of the woodcarver when Mrs. Maté describes her specifications for a wig stand and how the finished set will look—wig and stand—in its place of honor in the hall.

Many women here wear wigs of straight lacquered jet-black hair, particularly the younger, "modern" ones. I didn't recognize our charming staff nurse when she first appeared without her uniform and in her shining wig.

Mrs. Blood

I took the boat across to the public campsite and left it there. Trigger came down to meet me and we pulled it up on the beach and he put his robe and megaphone in it so nobody would mess around with it, and then we got in the Landrover and drove to Tic-Tac, only I ducked down as we went through the village in case somebody should recognize me and tell the folks. I had on a pale green two-piece Jantzen which I had chosen because of the little diver which told everybody else you were wearing a Jantzen and not some old thing picked up at J. C. Penney's or someplace like that.

We left the Landrover down at the bottom of the trail and started walking. It was still very cool in the woods and the pine needles were lovely under my feet, not hot and prickly, just a kind of interesting tactile experience, like walking the ribs of a beach when the tide is out. My whole body was happy that morning, even though I was afraid of Trigger and thought he looked like an anthropoid ape. We passed along the trout stream and crossed to the other side on some flat rocks. They were cool as well and part of me wanted to sit on a rock and just wait for the fish to jump, the way I did with Daddy.

And then when we got far enough in on the other side he kissed me and took off my top and looked at me carefully. "You've got big nipples," he said. "You'll be able to nurse a baby really well."

And I was flattered, you know, because I remembered Jessica Ash at camp and how somebody said she wore an undershirt even though she was seventeen, and anyway her tits were like rat bites—hadn't I ever spied on her in the shower?

But I didn't feel anything else and after that he said, "Put on your top," and we went back down the mountain and through the village and back to the public campsite where I got in the boat and went on home. I could hear the bell ringing when I was only halfway there.

And I was really hungry at lunchtime and enjoyed my food. Mae-Love had made fried chicken and blueberry grunt from the berries we had picked the day before. Only all the time I could feel my big nipples growing there underneath my shirt and got kind of frightened they might suddenly show through like a spreading stain.

Mrs. Thing

There was an open cupboard full of bandages and tongue depressors and manila folders and small metal files and a broken wall clock (I didn't know it was broken at first) and across from me an identical green bench where several ladies were sitting. But at first, coming in from the sunshine, it was just a dark box of coolness, smelling strongly of Dettol and faintly of urine and alcohol. And because my nurse had disappeared so suddenly and so (I thought) definitively, the tears which must have been there all along backed up behind my eyes and when I did see the other objects of the room they were blurred and indistinct, Eliot's "shape without form," and I told myself I mustn't cry, not really because I was white and therefore vulnerable (though

26

that, too, I am sure), but because once started I knew I would be carried screaming to a place far worse than this. And Jason, who had shaken his head so often at my vague fears and various minor aches, would shake his head for this ultimate disgrace and maybe even leave me.

So I waited quietly and wiped my face with the cool cloth I always carry for emergencies (and a red one for the children in case there's blood). And I waited and waited and more women came in, smoothing their long skirts as they took up a place on one bench or the other, and the hands of the clock never moved. I looked at a poster which told me what to eat to have a fine, fine child like the baby being held up proudly by his smiling Mama; I read a notice asking me if I remembered my Sunday-Sunday medicine; I thought of the women sitting with me and wondered if any of them were pregnant out of love or desire for children and how they made love and how often; for someone had told me years ago that in primitive cultures the women are mounted from behind, like animals. If so, at what stages does this pattern change and why? Does a missionary's wife scream at two retrograde students she has literally stumbled upon in the bush— "Animals!" or some such word and does she tell her husband, "They were doing . . . you know . . . like dogs or cattle. Can't you speak to them about it, dear?" An old Hamish, who feels suddenly and strangely heavy around the thighs, tries to imagine what she has seen and how it would feel to do it that way (and rushes off to the schoolhouse to deliver an impassioned sermon on the wages of sex and demonstrates—maybe on the blackboard —how God intended Adam and Eve to do it and now that they are God's children they must do it that way too—that is to say face to face). And he writes to the home church about this appalling thing that has come to his attention; so that in the year of our Lord eighteen something or other a decree goes out that lectures on "hygiene" must be added to the scholastic diet of English, history, arithmetic and Scripture.

And do the Afro-Americans readopt the old ways or is it all a myth?

I wonder all this and still the hands of the clock say half past two.

Mrs. Thing

Mrs. Maté tells me the head of the Town Council has his food sent from the kitchen by conveyor belt. I am fascinated. From what movie or book or rumor did he get this incredible idea?

As if reading my mind, she adds, "Just like the Queen of England."

"Oh," I say. Then, "I think they only do that in order to keep things hot."

How many points does Mrs. Maté's wig count, against the humming grandeur of the wife of the Chairman of the Town Council's conveyor belts?

Mrs. Thing

The courtyard of the hospital was filled with people then, as it must be now and every day. People on benches, people on the concrete pavement, people talking, eating, sleeping. People with dirty bandages or clean, people with casts and crutches, weeping children, sleeping children, someone vomiting into our path and the smell of oranges and sickness. It was not quiet, like the doctor's waiting room or a hospital corridor back home—I wonder if they have *Quiet, Hospital* posted anywhere—and I thought of Stanley Park Zoo and was ashamed and frightened (one among so many) to think such a cruel nonliberal thought. The big girl who came with me walked in front, quite rapidly, for she was to go back with the driver and I think she wanted to deliver me, like a parcel in which one has no vested interest, and go back to the van and her groundnuts. There was no time to really stop and look, but after I thought "Stanley Park Zoo," I thought "Jason will love this," and then "Where is she taking me?" One or two women glanced at me but without much curiosity, and a thin child called out *Obronie* (white man) and several people looked up as I passed among them, very conscious of my nightgown and my peekaboo dressing gown. Nobody laughed, but nobody smiled either, and I hurried to catch up to my one familiar face—or back. At one point, because there were many nurses passing to and fro and some of them square and broad-backed like my nurse, I was afraid that I had well and truly lost her and hoped that the person I was following wouldn't turn around and prove to have a different face, which is what had happened once when I was little and in a department store with Mama. I had stopped to look at all the fancy boxed sheets and towels and pillowcases, some with little gifts included such as artificial flowers or a salt and pepper shaker or wooden salad bowl. And when I threw my arms around my mother's waist she was no longer my mother but a terrible voice which said, "What on earth," and who wore the face of a stranger. And I began to cry.

So I half ran, half walked through the crowds of people until finally we turned left along a row of benches and open doors and the nurse, who was, after all, *my* nurse, took me in through one of the doors and set me on the end of a bench and thrust a brown envelope in my hand (as though I were a child about to register for kindergarten) and said. "Please. Wait here," and disappeared.

Mrs. Blood

Nearly everyone else had gone down for the Christmas vacation and that night those who were left in the house were out because the two doctors had gone to some party at the Student Union and Morag had gone to Edinburgh to see her mother.

We spent the afternoon walking and talking and window-shopping (and I sneaked in Murchie's and bought him a copy of *Death and Entrances* because I liked it and was pretty sure he would). He asked me to have supper at the Cross-Keys and then we walked back home, very quietly, as though we were carrying something either very young or very delicate between us. It had begun to snow and I said, "I like to squint my eyes and look at the streetlights through the snow." He nodded and smiled but didn't say anything and I thought maybe he was thinking of home. So I said, after a while, "I suppose you're going out to a party or something?"

"I'm supposed to go to a party, yes."

"Don't you want to go?"

"Ah. Christmas is a difficult time to go to other people's homes. This party is at someone's home."

"Listen," I said (but very softly, because of the thing we were carrying between us), "why don't we have a party?"

"But aren't you going out?"

"No. Not any more."

He stopped and put his hand under my chin. "I think your idea is lovely. We shall have a party." And the thing between us grew strong enough to carry itself so we shouted and grabbed hands and ran back to the off-licence for a bottle and then back home and up the stairs. And he lit the gas while I set out all that beautiful food that some kind relative had sent me—melba toast and tinned crab and shrimps and tongue and ripe olives—and he ran down laughing and came back with a huge fruitcake and a cheese.

After we had eaten he gave me a tiny doll made of shells which his mother had sent him from Kingston and he told me a little bit about his life but not much. And then I gave him the poems and got up to wash my face and hands and he reached up and said, "Don't leave even for a minute—you'll break it." And I knew what he meant because now the thing between us was crying to get out and around us both and we lay down right there and then and let it be. Our hands and faces were covered in butter and fish and crumbs and I remember thinking, sort of half-conscious, what a pity it was that grown-ups probably brush their teeth and all that before they get into bed, and how good love tasted with food on your face and fingers.

And Christ, it was beautiful. He just let himself into me as though he were some sort of magic key and then it was slow and full of affection, not passionate, but just two halves of the same thing gently coming together. And I couldn't get over his skin—it was so beautiful in the gaslight—and he laughed at me because I made him find another shilling for the meter so I could look at him while he slept.

And we just lay there for a long time, very drowsy and grinning at each other like two kids—full up on good wine and good food and good love. Then he said, "Hey, I liked your party," and fell asleep. I got up quietly and locked the door and then just sat beside him feeling good and looking at him and remembering what he felt like: like the very edge of a sandy beach, where the water licks it, cool and soft and a pleasure for your feet to walk along.

Mrs. Thing

Mrs. Maté has gone home—still pregnant. So it was the "will of God," as she would express it, that she have another child—probably a son. What a strange mixture she is with her Avon cologne and her knowledge that she belongs to the new money elite because she is the wife of an official. I wanted to ask her about her past, but although she questioned me minutely about myself and my life in Canada, I could not bring myself to reciprocate. Why? Was it because I sensed that she is re-creating herself in some image culled from the American ladies' magazines and the ads in the *Graphic?* And yet she believes sincerely in God, at least in the negative or malevolent power of God, and raised her voice faithfully when the hymn singers came around each Sunday afternoon.

Her nightgowns were fantastic things and must have been brought back from New York with the wig and the cologne: nylon, frilly and very hot, I should think. But lovely bright colors—coral and peacock blue and cerise. My peppermint-striped cotton seemed terribly prim and proper and often I could see her look at me in a rather patronizing way—the kind of look a teen-age girl might give her maiden aunt. Yet she breaks wind loudly and unself-consciously and wears a kerchief even in bed. In short, she is what we would call "incredibly vulgar" but in a fascinating way, not like some of the men at the College who Jason says are so very very careful to be "Western" in all their words and deeds. Utterly materialistic and yet a hymn-singer. A child of nature and of love yet utterly self-conscious about her new toys. Wants you to know right away who she is and has no time for the nurses (who must be fools to work long hours for little pay and whom she treats like servants) but plently of time for the woman who is the daughter of a chief of one of the outlying districts and who chews on her chewing stick right up until they wheel her away for her gallbladder operation.

She came over to my bed just before she left. "You will come and see me?"

"I'd like that."

"Good. And remember" (for the first time she looked at me

as simply one woman to another), "when it is all over don't let him touch you for six weeks."

"Thank you, I'll remember."

And she sauntered off, accompanied by various female relatives who were carrying her bundles for her. Alexandria called to her and she answered something in a contemptuous and sullen voice. Esther and Elizabeth come over to strip her bed, but I don't feel like talking.

Mrs. Blood

In Seville we peered through the black iron grilles at the lush fountains in the courtyards and the heavy sensual flowerpots and jardinieres. One house had paintings in extraordinary gilt frames (so elaborate they looked molten, so heavy one felt the walls might crumble from their weight) at intervals along the walls. And I remember the splash of bougainvillaea against the walls and pastel wash drying along narrow streets, as if by arrangement with the tourist bureau. The orange trees and the smell of old leather as we pushed aside curtains to gaze at paintings and chalices. Old women in black and many blind and one-armed men and beggars in the churches. And everywhere tiny plastic arms and legs and hearts in front of altars and candles, as though the churches were doll hospitals, not houses of God.

And we stayed in a pension for fifty cents a night and thought we were clever, until suppertime, and our crazy friend shouting no, no, *"less jeunes filles n'aime pas l'huile d'olive,"* and the old man worried and a little hurt because Rosemary made such terrible faces and waved the fish around ("Did you *ever see* anything so ghastly?") and this crazy character we'd met on the train shouting at him in French which he didn't seem to understand (although that may have been Charley's accent and the fact that he was stoned as well). And I wanted to die of shame and suddenly knew what it was to hate all Americans who spread their slime across Europe every spring and summer.

And later, at Toledo, a terrible woman who had made the driver back up several times so that she could take pictures stood on a chair and took a flashbulb shot of the *Burial of the Count D'Orgazo* and was red-faced with fury when the monks ejected her.

32

"Hey," she said, "who do they think they are! I traveled with a bunch of Jesuits right through Afghanistan and there was never any trouble."

And Rosemary whispered, "Did you ever *see* anything so ghastly?" And I remembered what she had said about the fish in the pension in Seville.

Mrs. Thing

There are smells here which will always be part of Africa for me; and yet if someone asked later what Africa was like and I said "Mansion Polish," or "Dettol," or "the smell of drying blood," they wouldn't understand. And they would be right not to, for the real Africa (whatever that may mean) is none of these and my Africa is only real for me. I can see this in Jason's face when he comes to visit. He has left me behind, like a friend high on a new drink or drug that I am unable or unwilling to try. This would have been true even if we were not here—the horizontal state is alien to him and once awake (aware) he must get up. To him I am a creature from another planet and sometimes he talks too loudly at me as one does to deaf people or to foreigners DO YOU SPEAK ENGLISH? CAN YOU HEAR ME? And yet his loud words come to me from far away as though I am already dead and buried and he speaks down through the layers of leaves and baked red earth above my head. He has been to hunt bats in caves, and the words "bat" and "cave" conjure up nothing but a sense of horror or uneasiness, like a child misconstruing an adult word or conversation. He swims in the pool each day with Mary and Nicholas. And I want to shout at him, *"How can you be so frivolous where there are people dying and in pain?"* And he shows me the drawings they have made me, which I stare at with the polite disinterest one shows to the accomplishments of other people's children. He brings me books to read and the daily paper, and when he holds my hand I notice how brown he is getting and think (still objectively) that he has never looked so well and that I wish he'd go. And after he has left (extending a greeting to Mrs. Maté, who always looks up from her current round of visitors to smile and acknowledge him) I wish I had been more cheerful and try to hold onto the initial vision that came over me at Bathurst; the muddy river and the heat and the crowds of people laughing and calling to one another. The smell of vegetation and the smell of charcoal burning and the vultures gliding overhead. For Africa moved into focus at that moment and as the gangplank went down I felt an almost irresistible urge to run quickly off the ship and into this strange adventure as one might run into the arms of a waiting lover.

And Jason, with Nicholas on his shoulders and Mary jumping up and down beside him, laughed and said, "My God, it's like all the Humphrey Bogart movies rolled into one." And that's what I *must* remember too, and hang onto when they ask me, "What was Africa like?" But is that not as false a picture as my Africa? And wasn't the stink of the river the important thing? Or was it the crowds of people laughing?

Mrs. Blood

That summer they moved me to the O.R. and I scrubbed and washed things down, only blood this time, not shit, and dirty bandages and instruments lying at the bottom of the green soap. And my God it was hot outside, so hot we had to push our way through the heat as though through crowds in order to get to the dining hall. And the two old dears behind the counter let the sweat run off their hands and down the ladles and some of the regulars said it was a disgrace and Mother Brown who was still on 88 stopped coming at all. Some noons Mrs. Karensky and Nurse Primrose asked me to hop down to the Dairy Queen with them in Mrs. K.'s convertible, and they told me how much they missed me and said poor old Eleanor had nobody to shout at now and filled me in on all the gossip from the wards. But mostly I took 11:20 dinners because Martha always liked 12:30's and somebody had to be there in the O.R. all the time in case the phone rang. And I remember the smell of cottage pudding with chocolate sauce and watching the old dear dip the ladle in and the sweat running down her arm and on to the handle, and taking the plate anyway but leaving it when nobody was looking, and finally giving up eating there altogether because the stews and puddings were just too much in all that heat and I was lonely without Mrs. K. and the fellows from 92 had taken to sitting on the porch and waiting for me to come along so they could speculate out loud whether I was a virgin or not and if so what they were going to do about it.

So finally I just stayed in and ate a sandwich and maybe read (I was fascinated by the names of all the clamps) and washed up the instruments and gloves after Martha and Joy had gone for their break. I had to put the pads in the autoclave as well and turn up the pressure, all of which made me feel kind of important I guess—being alone there with the autoclave going and the distilled water dripping away and in charge of all those exotic instruments.

Only once when I was dreaming away as usual and washing up the stuff from that morning I suddenly sliced the back of my thumb open on a blade some idiot had left attached to the handle, and when I took my hand out of the soapy water it wouldn't stop bleeding and I had to go next door to 92 and knock on the door and ask them to help me, which amused them no end. And they said, "What's the matter, sweetheart, cut yourself, did you?" and they laughed and things like that. Only then I began to feel really funny and they must have seen my face because the senior nurse sat me down quick and pushed my head down and told the others to bugger off and do their work.

Then he put a pressure bandage on and when I felt a little better I went back to the O.R. and Dr. Steinberg was there waiting because he had forgotten his sunglasses and he said, "What happened to your hand?" And when I told him he said, "From this morning?" and I showed him the stuff (the blade was still on and everything was right where I had left it, including some drops of my blood on the drainboard). Then he got really worried and said, "My God, that woman had 4+ syphilis," and I said, "Whatever that means," and he said, "It means we may be in trouble, sweetheart," and I realized he was the one who'd left the blade on and also what he meant by trouble and I was so upset (and my hand was really hurting by then) that I began to cry.

Just then Martha and Joy came back and Joy looked pretty guilty too because she's supposed to check the stuff before it's all dropped in the bucket of green soap and obviously she hadn't.

So they all flapped around and Martha gave me a drink of the brandy they had for the occasional circumcision (they used it with a sugar-tit) and Steinberg called the lab and arranged for me to have a Wassermann every day and left full of apologies. And Martha said, "Goddamn kike" (she was an "RC," as Mother Brown would say).

And Joy said, "What a lawsuit you could bring," but one of them told (I never found out which) and soon it was all over the building.

And O'Brian (the head on 92) said, "Now how're you going to explain *that* to the girls at Smith?"

Mrs. Thing

Elizabeth and Alexandria were washing me today and exclaiming over the whiteness of my skin. "Please, you have very fine skin."

"It has its disadvantages."

"What kind of disadvantages?" (And as they talk they soap my legs and rinse them with a cool cloth and soap my back—very carefully and tenderly as though I were a precious relic or an exotic bit of flotsam washed up on an alien beach.)

"Oh, sunburn. Blemishes. Anything shows up. Look." And I point to the spreading brown stain on each of my thighs.

Elizabeth: "It is only the iron. It will pass." She has a deep voice, unlike the usual high, nasal semiwhining accent of the other girls. Her voice is richer and goes well with her deep brown color. I think too she is older although it's hard to tell. She does not giggle about Mrs. X's boyfriend the way Esther and Alexandria do and she is not a student like them, but a qualified nurse who trained in England.

But she is not pretty like the other two, although prettier than the Staff Nurse who looks like a very well-fed frog (or some illustration of a frog, really, that I must have seen in one of the children's books). I love to hear Elizabeth talk, in much the same way I love the darkest chocolate.

Alexandria: "Are your children light or dark? Your husband is dark."

"Light. Very light. With blonde hair and blue eyes. But they look like him. I will ask him to bring a photograph." And they smooth my ."fine" skin with talcum powder and take away the sheets and nightgown and I prop myself up to comb my hair. They take turns washing out my nighties and bring them back beautifully pressed each day. I wonder if they talk about me in the dormitory or examine my bloodstains for any ethnic difference. It would be impossible to tell what they really think of me because they always treat me like a guest and it is this that embarrasses me and not the fact that they gaze upon my naked body. They do not speak to the others in quite the same way. They say, "Auntie?" if one of the others calls, or joke with them in the vernacular and sometimes get quite bossy with them. Only the Staff Nurse is bossy with me, but that is partly because she doesn't like Dr. Biswas (too gentle and self-contained) and I am his patient and partly because she doesn't like anyone very much.

One afternoon she stopped at my bed and hissed, "So please, who killed Mr. Kennedy?" And when I said I really wasn't sure she gave me a look of such utter cynicism and contempt I felt quite frightened. (The lizards here have the same cynical stare— one needs heavy lids to do it—but they are objective, not contemptuous.)

And I remembered our first trip to the Castle and high on the battlements (after seeing the slave market and the women's quarters and the stairway up to the burgomaster's private quarters) the police officer saying, "Please, what country are you from?"

And I quickly replied, "Canada," because I felt the same thrill of fear and shame go through me then as I felt when Staff asked me who killed John F. Kennedy. And when we got back to the car Jason laughed and said, "You hypocrite."

Mrs. Thing

"You see, what a difference it makes," he said and bent over his calculator to work things out. It was something like a currency changer.

That room was not so cool as the anteroom, in spite of the fan and the louvers fitted to catch any hint of breeze. The sister had a round, kind face, the kind of face that children draw on

37

suns and moons and, except for her eyes, the kind of face one sometimes sees on idiots. She stood by the tiny doctor like some huge and benevolent sergeant-at-arms, never moving unless he told her to.

"So," he said, writing some notes on a piece of paper. "We will have a little look, but I think you should stay here for a while."

"Do I have to?" (and my voice thin and high—the voice of a child at the dentist's).

"It would be better. I will give you something to make you quite sleepy and then perhaps you will not mind so much."

"Can I call my husband?"

(And the voice of the second-grade teacher, "Of course you *can*. What you mean is may I go to the washroom.")

"I will call him."

And we have the little look and when I get down the sister unrolls another lot of paper towel and places it along the table. The smell of Dettol is very strong and I can smell my own body because of the fear and the heat and twist uncomfortably inside my cotton nightgown.

Then a student nurse appears as if by Prospero's summons and we go off together, out through the anteroom and past the waiting ladies—I shamefaced because they have taken me first (but now I know not because I was white and a "European") ahead of all these others who sit so patiently along the hard green benches, some of them with sleeping children tucked against their backs or on their knees. The courtyard is even more crowded, and this little nurse, who is much more talkative than the other, tells me that visiting hours have begun. We walk up two flights of stone steps with the crowds surging around us everywhere and everywhere color and sound—reds, yellows, blues, and the sounds shrill and high too, primary like the colors, and along open verandas past more little doors marked "X-Ray" and "Path" and other things I can't remember, and more green benches with people softly waiting; the smells are primary too, though not so intense as down in the central courtyard—urine and vomit and oranges (not too different now that I think of it, from the smells in the channel boats' washrooms or the smells of third class train cars, except there is no smell of garlic), but sweeter and nastier because of the flowers and the heat.

And still no one laughs or comments on my nightie and my peekaboo cotton robe; but are we not all dressed in long or flowing things—or most of us, so that the important-looking man in the white shirt and European trousers looks quite extraordinary and out of place, as Alice must have looked to the March Hare or the playing cards.

Eventually we stop at the entrance to a ward and I am really surprised and maybe a little disgusted to see two white men sitting in grey cotton dressing gowns playing chess.

"Are the men and women in the same wards here?" And the little nurse stops short and looks down at the slip of paper in her hand and giggles.

"Oh. Not at all. Please. They have written it incorrectly." And she calls out something to a Staff Nurse who has got up from her desk and is starting down the hall. The two nurses laugh good-naturedly and we retreat. The Englishmen do not speak or laugh. (I think they are embarrassed to be seen like that— sick and with their legs so hospital pale.)

We turn down another corridor and this time past a group of little children who have set up a sort of play school in the hall. They are the first to acknowledge that I am different. They giggle and point and run after me so that I enter "Senior Officials, F-3" in a cloud of children and laughter like the Pied Piper of Hamelin entering the hill or the speckledy hen returning to the barnyard.

Mrs. Blood

The name of this street is Rue de la rue and I call to the women, *"Avez-vous du pain?"*

And Jason says, "Do you know what they call those in French?" and he takes one in his hand and smiles at the old woman with the plastic cherries on her hat. *"Pistolets.* See?" And it goes off under the pressure of his fingers. Bang. Bang. And later we sit at a cafe and watch a young man and a girl and a frog which has hopped up on their table. She has on a middy shift and a hairband, but the backs of her legs and her buttocks are not those of a very young girl. Jason begins to sketch her and I watch the young man who has captured the frog in his hands and is offering it to the girl. She squirms and turns herself aside and Jason mutters, "I wish she'd fucking well sit still." But she doesn't and squirms even more, wriggling her buttocks around on the little leatherette-covered chair. The young man laughs and holds the frog up by one leg. Some of the watchers laugh. Then he brings it down hard in the center of the table, upsetting their drinks and squashing the frog with the side of his hand. The girl gets up and runs out, her hand to her mouth, and the young man looks at his hand with wonder. I can feel the insides of the frog on the side of my hand too. The waiter and the young man begin an argument and Jason closes his sketchbook and stands up to go. But I wonder who they were and if that was the end of an affair or only the beginning.

And I forget the name of that street, but the name of this street is Rue de la rue and it only goes one way.

Mrs. Blood

And she refused to help herself at all so Joy practically got on top of her and pushed down regularly shouting, "Come on, Jezebel, give us a little help, won't you." And Martha and the student stood at the other end to help once the head was crowned and even with the airconditioning working Joy was sweating like a pig and so was the girl, who never left off moaning and groaning and calling out somebody's name (Jesus, maybe; it was hard to tell because she wasn't making any real sense at all).

And I thought, "What will happen to it now?" And "Is it always as bad as this?"

And then wham, out he came, "Like a cork out of a bottle," Martha said later, and she cut the cord and gave him to the student to clean up and weigh and make comfortable.

And Joy said, "Christ, I'm beat," and made me come over and massage the girl's belly until the afterbirth came out, and I did it, although I didn't really want to and was feeling pretty sick by that time.

And the girl still hadn't given over moaning and calling out, so Joy said, "Shut up, Jezebel, it's all over," but not really mean because there was something about the baby, you know, and the birth in general which softened her up.

But later she said, "They ought to be sterilized," and told me this was her second and every time they sent her back home she got knocked up by some bum or other and the poor little buggers didn't have much future, did they, when they were wards of the state from the moment they opened their little eyes.

And I called him Jamie and went to see him a couple of times before the Children's Aid came and took him away. And they said the girl wouldn't have anything to do with him and was even worse than before. But I thought to myself that wasn't such a bad thing after all.

Mrs. Thing

I looked around as we approached the docks and I said to Jason this was my first sight of England—the Royal Liver Building in the pouring rain—only it's not raining now. We went into a long building to wait and Pa was very nervous and kept asking questions of the porters and trying to find out from somebody if our trunks were already on board or whether we had to claim them. And we were nervous too, but in a good way, and we wanted to join hands and run past all the barriers and onto the ship at once. But the children had become quite still and sat very upright on the metal folding chairs, and I thought how beautiful they looked but how if they were someone else's children I'd probably be thinking, "Poor dears, I guess they're not allowed to run and play," and try to figure out which one was their mother and finally choose a grim-faced creature who had a military-looking leather shoulder bag and sensible British walkers.

They always get quiet like that, particularly Mary. And I, who talk when I am nervous, find it difficult to understand. And Jason, too, gets quiet.

I said, "I wonder which ones are going to Akwabaa?" and we tried to guess, but the children weren't really very interested, suspended as they were between the past and future.

"When can we get on?"

"After they take our tickets and check our passports, I guess."

"When will that be?"

And Jason, "Just let Mummy be. It won't be long."

And we huddled together ("noe man is an ilande") and watched rather enviously as the arriving cars and cabs deposited families who were greeted with cries of recognition and laughter by other families.

Mary said shyly, "That lady has a pretty dress." And we agreed with her and talked about how the ladies would dress differently out there, and maybe she could have a dress like that someday and felt more and more anxious and excited as the hands on the big old wall clock moved along and nothing happened.

"Do ships ever tip over?" (Mary).

"Sometimes—hardly ever."

"There was a picture on the cereal box of a ship tipping over and people falling into the sea and fire."

"Was there? It must've been during a war."

"Is there a war now?"

"Not anywhere near where we are going."

"Do they ever tip over anyway? Just tip over?"

"Not big passenger ships. I've never heard of it." All this said in a very desultory manner, like people playing a game or holding a conversation on a very hot day. Nothing was real. There was no ship. Soon they would come and tell us it was all a hoax—some sociologist was doing an elaborate experiment in motivation. We would be thanked for our cooperation and given money (candy for the children) and told to go out by another door.

Nicholas: "I want to pee."

And Mary (copying Grandma): "I want to spend a penny." So we separate and head for the toilets and I let Mary put the huge and satisfying English penny in the slot and then of course she can't go.

"You just wanted to put that penny in," and she smiles at me but shakes her head so as not to completely acknowledge that what I say is right.

We spend too long washing our hands and I worry now that the boat has left without us and picture Jason and Nicholas looking sadly at the Royal Liver Building from the deck of the fast-disappearing ship.

"Hurry up." Our moment of shared childhood is over. I want to pick her up and run. There is no one else in the washroom and that seems ominous.

"I *am* hurrying." But she dries her hands finger by finger (or so it seems to me) and finally I grab her arm and almost drag her out. The place seems full of people (thank God, it hasn't gone), but I can't see Jason or Nicholas or Pa (where are they, oh God, where are they?) and then feel clammy with relief when I spot Pa's bald head at the very far end of the room and see the other two right behind him. I wave gaily, like those who have been greeting old friends, and relax my grip on Mary's arm.

"Look, there's Grandpa and Daddy and Nicholas way down there. I guess we better join them." And we push our way toward the back cheerfully and politely and greet each other like long-lost brothers.

"What took you so long?"

"Why are we way back here?"

"We're lining up now to go through embarkation. It's alphabetical."

"Oh, Lord, I wish my name were Apple."

"At least it isn't Xerox or Zebra."

"Trust you to look on the bright side of things."

"What's that, boy, what did you say?"

"It's nothing, Father. We're just fooling."

And we can see him thinking, "It's all very well to fool, but you've got a sick wife and two kids to look after and get on that boat and you should be worried like I am." And I suddenly feel great tenderness for him because part of him wishes he were going too and envies us our youth and opportunity. He feels us moving away from him and he feels old.

"D'you wish you were going too?"

"Well, I don't mind telling you, love, that if I were forty years younger I'd seriously consider it." And we smile at him, but wonder if he really would.

The line moves slowly and he begins to fidget again. "Shan't be a minute, son," and off he goes again to check on God knows what and I look around at all these people ahead of us and behind us and wonder what prompted them to go out or what keeps them there and think of Coward's song and try to imagine what

43

it's really going to be like, all the time wondering why so many old public buildings were painted in such sickly colors that remind one of nasty things like dog poo or vomit and maybe that was so people wouldn't want to linger any more than necessary or maybe because yellow and brown are cheap to make.

"Are yellow and brown cheap colors to produce?"

"I don't know. Why?"

"Oh, all these old buildings, not just here but at home. The colors are so horrible."

"I expect they're cheap."

"I saw where Windsor and Newton aren't making any more Mummy Brown. They've run out of mummies or the world supply is getting low."

"What weird things you know."

"Have you ever seen it?"

"What?"

"Mummy Brown."

"No, I don't think so. Move up, Mary, there's a good girl."

And then Pa comes back, very important, and says we are to go to the head of the line because people with children can get on first.

"*C* for *children*," I say. "That's pretty nearly as good as *A* for *Apple*." And we go back to the top of the room and this time under the barrier rope and out to the embarkation desk. I want to look back at the suddenly safe and familiar room but am afraid it might bring bad luck. And besides, now I can smell the sea.

Mrs. Blood

"An island is a body of land entirely surrounded by water." No man is an island except inside his mother's womb. Macduff was from his mother's womb untimely ripp'd and Caesar too. Render unto Caesar that which is Caesar's and unto Caesar's mother that which was Caesar's mother's and unto God that which was God's. And the wagon got going too fast as we turned the corner onto Johnson Avenue and I, who was always the last one on, went off over the back wheel which caught me as I fell so that for an instant I hung and clung there while the wheel

44

spun angrily into me like a hopped-up insect—whirred zzzzzzz— and then I was off and screaming and holding myself and Mama said, "Well we can't take her to Doctor Howland for that—she's too little," and we went to a lady doctor instead.

And the nurse said, "Did you know little Mrs. McNeil had a lovely baby boy?"

And I said, "Fuck Mrs. McNeil."

And the student laughed, but the midwife said, "Now that's no way to talk."

And the cabdriver brought in a woman who had got drunk and fallen down the stairs. She was screaming, "Oh God, you got to help me—it's comin', it's hangin' out. Oh, give me somethin' for the pain." And rubber-soled shoes were running up and down the corridor and the screaming died off suddenly as though it had been disconnected or turned off by the click of a switch.

And they told me later that when he was born he didn't have a mark on him.

Mrs. Blood

"So there was old Nigel," Jack said, "and old Nigel's wife and way out there all alone so of course they wanted her to go over to the mainland to have the child. Only she had this big thing about giving birth on an island . . . "

"Christ . . . she didn't really!"

"Oh yes she did . . . you know these Americans" (and he gave me a leer and started rubbing my leg up and down while he was talking). "And so the doctor was pretty annoyed with her but said all right and left some kind of tablets if the pain got too bad—only Nigel had got into the spirit of the thing by this time and flushed them down the lav—and made them promise to send up flares or something equally dramatic if anything went wrong."

"I'll bet she loved that."

"Oh, she did, she did. Very dramatic, you know, and sort of like a royal child being born and all the bonfires. Which is what they did, you know."

"What?"

"Set off all the flares when it was over, and had all kinds of boats and a police launch and everything over there in no time, and Nigel gave everybody a glass of rum toddy for their trouble."

"I can just see it."

"Yes. Well, they did all the necessary—Nigel even shaved her himself and he made up big bundles of sterilized sheets, newspapers for her to lie on, and when she got the first twinges they had a few double whiskies and he sterilized scissors and all and then out came the baby just as nice as you please."

"And were they all right?"

"Positively. Except for one thing. The afterbirth never came. The midwife who came over in one of the boats said Louise would have to go to hospital, but they gave her a couple of drinks and talked her around and she finally admitted it would probably come out in a few days by itself and she told them to save it and—"

"Save it?"

"Shut up. That's what I said. To look at, I imagine, and make sure it was all there."

"And did it come out?"

"On the fifth day. Louise was up, actually, and in the kitchen, and she felt it coming so she just squatted down or something and out it plopped. Nigel said it was really slimy—like liver."

"Ugh."

"That's not the end." (He put his hand between my legs.)

"Nigel went to get a plastic bag he'd been saving for it, and Louise went to clean herself up a bit and when they came back the dog had et it."

"Oh, Christ!" They both began to laugh.

"He was just finishing it up as Nigel came around the corner."

"Oh, God—that's beautiful. The dog!"

I said, "I think that's disgusting," and they looked at me as though a glass or the ashtray had spoken.

"Why?"

"I don't know. It just is."

"You mustn't be so squeamish."

"Well I am." They turned away and his hand lay still inside my stocking.

"Where are they now?"

"Still there. Nigel has another six months to go and then he gets two months off."

"Let's go see them."

"Go to Eigg. Christ, man, it's about six hundred miles."

"At least."

"The boat only goes there once a week."

"We'll find another boat."

"What'll we use for money?"

"My brains and your body."

"O.K. Let's go. We haven't seen old Nigel in a long time."

"Have you met Louise?"

"Never. But Richard says she's the most beautiful girl he's ever seen."

"She sounds incredible." They get up.

"Pay the bill, there's a good girl."

"Where are you going?"

"You heard."

"Can I come?"

"You weren't invited."

"You're too squeamish."

"Richard's up there with his new girl."

"I want to go."

"You'll just make everyone uncomfortable. Why humiliate yourself? I'll come around and see you when we get back."

"Please let me go with you?" And the other.

"Oh, Christ, get rid of her, can't you? If we're going, let's go."

And, "Richard," I think, "Richard!" And "I hate the name Louise."

Mrs. Thing

Today Jason brought me a book about the sea. It is a beautiful book and cool—with lots of photographs of birds and water. I find it so difficult to read anything without a pillow (perhaps this is just a habit like eating salt on food), but I have been reading a bit about the starfish "Echinodermata—spiny-skinned animals." Wheel-like, with parts usually occurring in fives or multiples of five. Five stomachs, five sex organs, five arms and five noses. Or maybe fifty or fifty-five of each like the sunflower star. Thus fifty-five orgasms maybe (sunburst not sunflowers) but also fifty-five stomachs to feed. Jason says when I am better he will take me to the sea and I will try to remember what it felt like on top of that fort with the wind blowing and the Atlantic (could it really be?) crayon-blue down below us. It was very hot and we could see a line of fishermen pulling back the nets far away along the beach. Later we went and had a look at their canoes which are dugouts—very big and very beautiful. The waiter at the motel told us all the big trees are used up on the coast and the canoes must be made from wood in the forests 150 miles away, and brought down, finished except for decoration, to the villages here. The canoes had eyes on them and one said, in English, "God looks after tailless animal." Will he then look after this tailless fishy thing which swims inside of me? The children bought a fish for a penny and were awed by the beauty of the fish in the nets—a silent tangle and untangle of silver ribbons, a net full of quicksilver and the palm trees bent right over by the wind, showing the silvery backs of their leaves until in the heat and the glare it seemed somehow that the trees themselves were full of fish and the fish in the nets had dropped down from the sky.

Mrs. Blood

The road, once we passed Sproat Lake, became worse and worse and we drove part of the way in fog. I kept nudging him because I was scared we'd go right over the edge of the cliff and said, "Sound your horn."

Until finally he said, "If you don't stop it I fucking well *will* have an accident," and I was ashamed because the children were back there listening and could tell I was afraid. I really wanted to turn back, but was too ashamed to say so.

And whenever the fog cleared the children looked down at the lake below and called out, "Look, Mummy, look down there," and everything seemed very tiny because we were up so high and I only dared look through squinted eyes.

We stopped up above a trout stream at a picnic table and later on stopped again because they were blasting, and I was afraid again of the men with their hard hats and tough, competent faces and the huge earth movers which made me feel very tiny like the lakes we had passed on our climb. And Mary wanted to know why it said to turn off your radio and Jason said because

48

maybe the blast is set off by radio somehow and Mary asked how and neither of us really knew, which annoyed her. She still doesn't believe we don't always have the answers. And Nicholas wanted to pee but I didn't think he should get out of the car, so we all sat there hot and cross with our own private crossnesses and irritations until finally the man with the flag waved us on and we listened but we never heard a boom.

But once we got there it was all worth it and we drove right onto the beach and started piling out of the car like something from the Crazy Gang (it was that beautiful) and Jason got really manic and started skipping rope with a big piece of kelp and cars whooshed by us out of the fog while the sun burned up above and almost out of sight in the mist like the light of an approaching train seen at the other end of a tunnel.

The next morning we went down early and in the tidal pools were hundreds of starfish and anemones and barnacles laid out before us like a magic garden—pinks and purples and greens and whites, like one of those things you drop the little rocks in and all those colored spires start growing right before your eyes. And Jason said, "Well, was it worth it?"

And I said, "Yes—it was," but was sorry he'd said anything at all because now he'd reminded me that we had to take that road to get back home.

Mrs. Blood

All flesh is glass. This is my body which was riven, my body which was roven—my flesh all scattered and tattered and torn, and Rosie is the riveter who nailed me there as a totem in front of the door. And he said why seek ye a living among the bread. He is not here; he has risen.

And the man at the Home Office opened his mouth and the words came out in little strained bits, "DO YOU SPEAK ENG-LISH?" And when I said yes he told me to get in the other line.

We would hold hands across the beds and listen, "Who knows what evil lurks in the hearts of men? The Shadow knows, Ha-hahahahahaaaa." And because it was advertised by Blue Coal it wasn't long before I was afraid to go down those basement stairs alone.

And when Sally James had to go out West for a few months because of her health, we all said, "oh yes, we know."

And because nobody was paying any attention I said, "I may be stupid but I bet I can tell you what 'fuck' means."

Mrs. Thing

The younger of the two sweepers has not been in for several days. Esther says he has run away.

"Does he live here at the hospital?"

"At all. He lives in town."

"Do they know why he has run away?"

"Because there is talk that some Fantis will be beheaded and he is afraid that he will be beheaded."

I am about to say, "Do they really do such terrible things today?" but realize that Esther is one of "them" and quickly change it. "Why will the Fantis be beheaded?"

She shrugs. "Please. Not just the Fantis. Other tribes as well. Because of the festival. So he has run away and many other boys too."

"When is the festival?"

"In ten days' time. At the Palace. It will be a very fine thing."

I try to imagine this fine festival where heads roll and what else I wonder. And is this really so or just a rumor to brighten the excitement? And where is he now—running or lying quiet somewhere—or perhaps captive and quivering with fear somewhere not far off? When Jason comes I ask him. "Who knows? Apparently this particular festival is only held once in a great while and every time in the past men of alien tribes have been rounded up and beheaded at the four corners of the Palace. Some of the stewards on the compound have run away as well."

I become obsessed by the image of a thousand lonely figures running through the night. Stewards, sweepers, indigents, "foreigners" who came North or South to seek a job in the city. Running now through the hot nights or hiding in half-forgotten pockets of the town. I wish now I had spoken more kindly to this man. The other continues to sow the gobbets of wax and spread the turpentine as though nothing at all has happened.

I who have never been pursued by physical demons cannot

imagine what this man must feel like and I wonder if all the people of Middle Europe who live on the compound are looking at one another with the memory of hostile steps beneath a window or the possibility of hostile eyes peering in through cracks in the door.

And once captured, to have to wait for the inevitable. Are they really more stoic then we? I try to remember everything about this particular man, but discover I had not really looked at him. Tall, thin, khaki trousers and torn vest, some sort of tribal mark along his cheek, his eyes. I see him but I could not describe him so that anyone else would know him. "A sweeper, Senior Officials Ward, F-3." Would I know him at all without the smell of Mansion Polish? Would I know him stripped naked and afraid?

I ask Esther if she and the other girls are going to the festival. She smiles and shrugs. "Perhaps."

Will his be one of the heads she sees?

Mrs. Blood

There is an animal in me straining to get out, like a dog in an empty house.

And there was a flower up there called the red-hot poker and we squeezed the milk from the milkweed pods and spread it on our breasts.

"Listen," said Aunt Hettie, "what would you do if Jesus came in and sat down beside you?"

And the dentist said, "Will you remember to tell your Daddy he'll have to pay something on the bill or you can't come here anymore?" So of course I told him like a fool.

And the next time I went all the fish in the dentist's aquarium were dead and Jane said, "Did you know that marmalade is made from goldfish?"

Mrs. Thing

"So I went down," she said, "and I walked right up to him and said I want you to know what my little boy said to me just now. He said, 'Mummy, is there an animal outside?' And I said 'No, my pet, it's just a poor drunken man who doesn't know he's frightening my little boy.' And he said, 'Mummy, I think there's an animal down there.' So I told my little boy, 'Mummy will go down and tell the poor man he's frightening you.' And the poor mite screamed and held onto me and thought that I would be surely eaten up by this animal he could hear howling and crying out down below his window.

" 'And I came down here to tell you that and say I think you owe my little boy an apology.' And he looked at me very shame-faced and said, 'Yes, Madame,' just as sober as you please, and the very next day he came to the house—I hardly recognized him —and asked to see Madame and the little boy and apologized to us both and gave Trevor a bar of chocolate. And I said, 'You see, Trevor, it wasn't an animal after all.' And do you know what Trevor said? He said, 'Well, he shouldn't behave like one then.' But you have to be firm with these people, you know, and poor Trevor was right, of course."

And she went off to ask the Staff Nurse how I was really getting along. "I'll just have a word with Sister."

Mrs. Blood

When they sent George up noboby was there but the student— I forget his name—and me. O'Brian brought him in. "Here you are, sweetheart, treat him well. He's an old buddy of mine, aren't you, old buddy," and he gave George a great poke in the ribs and left him there. As O'Brian went out I noticed for the first time that he walked with his bum sticking out—like a chicken really or anyway some kind of bird. I wondered if he was queer or if it had something to do with the rubber-soled shoes and tried to imagine what the others had looked like before, going in and out of the building or the store or whatever. But I couldn't so I turned and looked at old George standing there with his big foolish smile on his map and wondered what in hell we were going to do with him until Martha came back. This student— David, I guess his name was, now that I think about it—was looking at old George too.

"I guess we can't really give him a Classic Comic and ask him politely to wait."

"I don't know what to do. I wish O'Brian hadn't left him like that."

"So O'Brian wants his lunch."

"O.K. But what'll we do with him? Martha won't be back for at least half an hour."

"I know how to take blood."

"You're a student—you're not allowed to do it."

"So what?" He had a very bad complexion and now that he was excited all the whiteheads showed up horribly. I began to feel really uneasy alone with these two characters and wished Martha or Joy would get a move on and come back from lunch.

"What d'you say? Want to get it over and done with? I don't much want to spend my lunch hour with this cretin here."

"I don't want anything to do with it. I'm sure you'd get kicked out and I'd probably lose my job. I need the money."

"Oh, Christ. Are all you Smith girls like that?"

"That remark just shows your ignorance," and then he was really mad and I was sorry I said it.

"O.K., Shirley Temple. Go fuck yourself. C'mon, George." And he went off down the hall like a dog behind David—yes, I'm sure that was his name.

What could I do? "Listen, if you're going to do it you'll have to have another person."

"I'll manage."

"I'll help."

So I did; but God I wish I hadn't, because old George had been a donor so many times his veins were as tough as vines and David got so intent on getting the blood out he forgot to loosen the tourniquet and when he took the needle out old George's blood went up, up everywhere and great splashes of blood bloomed like flowers on the green walls and ceiling and we were still washing it off when Joy and Martha came back from lunch.

And later I asked O'Brian what George did—because he was dressed in work clothes, you know—and he said, "Oh hell, he works on the garbage dump—a dollar a day and all you can eat."

They were most of them like that, callous, you know, and full of weird jokes. I didn't really like it there.

Mrs. Thing

The English girl across the partition is crying again. Her boyfriend has just left. Elizabeth will not gossip about her, but the others tell me he is really the father of her child. I do not like his looks, but that may be an ingrained prejudice against Lebanese and men who move as though they were too aware of their buttocks. Also his pants are very tight and he wears a gold wristwatch. I tease Alexandria and Esther as we whisper together. "But he is very rich. Don't you like rich men?"

And they giggle, but Esther (who is a hairbreadth more serious than her friend) says "Tsk. He is a bad man. I do not like him. They are bad people." But I am not quite sure whether he is being condemned because he is an adulterer (Esther was brought up in a mission school) or because he is Lebanese. They look down upon the Lebanese in much the same way we look down on pawnbrokers and Jews. They are here to make money and their prices are too high. Frances Hall who lives on a road where there are several wealthy Lebanese told me that dear Trevor went to a birthday party where he was the only child not wearing a fancy wristwatch. She thinks they are "charming people"—at least the ones she knows. And yet she is Indian and a snob. I am surprised that such ostentation would jibe with her English-oriented upbringing.

"Mrs. Margolian is a very charming lady indeed and she took special pains to see that dear Trevor was included in everything and that the other children spoke English. It was quite delightful —he is so fair, you know—to see him there with all the others and having such a good time."

But Jason says that she is a very strange woman and doesn't seem to be liked by the other women on the compound. And she has invited Nicholas and Mary over to tea several times. I suppose I must be grateful to her for that, but her perfect enunciation and her incredible contempt for the Africans make me shrink away from her. Jason says they are already on their fifth steward because she is so particular. He went to dinner there and she has a little bell she rings when she wants the steward to clear or bring things in and there was a terrible uproar because he dropped a plate of sliced chicken and she caught him kicking some of it under the kitchen table. And Hugh was drunk the whole time. But Jason says he is a terrific teacher and already very popular with the students.

But to get back to my fellow inmate, the English girl. My

"ladies" say she is "quite a nice girl, really, *very* pretty" and has wanted a child for years. But they have a knowing look as though "there is more to the story, but you are not yet one of us, and besides, we do not indulge in *that* kind of gossip at all."

Her crying is very young. I must ask the girls how old she is. I feel no sympathy for her, but have a certain objective interest in her as an "unknown" about whom I may speculate and thus pass some of the time away. I have no sympathy for anyone, anymore, except myself and the half-doomed child inside me.

Mrs. Blood

We sat all afternoon in the Place of the Two Fish, on a cement circle with old-fashioned flowers in it: cornflowers and marguerites and anemones. And he said, "I've been feeling sad all day about your leaving."

And I began to pick at the flowers, just out of nervousness, you know, until a woman came over and said, "Can't you read?"

And I said, "Eh?"

And she said "DO NOT PICK THE FLOWERS" in a loud, slow voice and pointed at the sign, and I shook my head and smiled to show I didn't understand. So she took my hand and gave it a little slap, the way a mother does, and took my flowers away from me and shook her finger. And suddenly I began to cry because of what Richard had said about my leaving, and the cross woman walked away quickly. And Richard picked two soft leaves and wiped my face and led me away.

There was a small revival meeting going on at the other end of the park and they pointed their fingers and shook their heads like the lady about the flowers, crying down sin in both French and English. One of them, later, was in the elevator with us and told Richard she had actually spoken to Jesus several times. You could see the sweat come out on her face when she talked about it. "Have you ever noticed," he said, "people like that have a funny smell?"

"What kind of a smell?"

"Cold and musty. Like death or old people's underclothes."

And later that night when we were dancing I wanted him so much my stomach felt sick and I had to sit down and not touch him at all. And he took me and led me out of that place and up to the room and unbuttoned my dress very carefully and folded it carefully over the chair and then my pants and bra and said all the words in French and then in English and then in the crazy language we had made up for trains and restaurants and he finally got me laughing again, but only for a little while. And I still carry the feel of him around with me like a birthmark or a scar. And that was a long time ago.

Mrs. Blood

All fresh is glass and shatters at the touch of a barbarian finger.

It was terrible to see them all sitting there in the sunroom with the radio going (nobody ever turned it off or changed the station) and most of them playing with themselves off and on during the afternoon. But not really getting any pleasure out of it, just sitting there with their hands going the way a child might suck his thumb when he's asleep. And the nurse would come in every so often and say, "Naughty, naughty," to one or another or maybe take somebody out for treatment or to the baths. But mostly they just sat there listlessly or playing with themselves and there were no pictures on the walls and only a few torn magazines and that awful radio going in the corner. So I was glad when the girl who was sick came back and I could go down to 88. And I kept crying, you know, about the least little thing the whole time I was up there. Because there wasn't any energy there, you see, the way there was on 88. No cursing and no screaming, no violent life at all. Just that damn radio and the sound of those wet fingers rubbing back and forth and the sound of the indifferent voices talking.

Mrs. Thing

Jason has just been and gone and left me some ladies' magazines. What a clean, well-lighted mythology they set forth. An article on the Queen's dogs, one on crewel work, recipes for the best buffet ever and a column at the back on Where to Buy It. And the cheaper ones with their serialized romances set on Skye or in Palma and their agony columns at the back. "Dear Sister, I have a friend who." "Dear Evelyn." "To Miss X. K. of Eastbourne. You have left things rather late. I am sending you some addresses of agencies where you might apply for help." "Dear Mrs. F. If she were my daughter I should tell her that just as we save our best china service for very special visitors, so there are parts of our body which should be saved because they are very special. I do not think the negative approach—you might get pregnant—will work with the younger girls anymore."

Life as it should be lived. Flowers on the dinner table, angostura bitters in the Irish stew ("Sweet tricks with Bitters"), clever things to make your friends for Christmas—"It's never too early to begin." Escape literature. Or is it really? Is it not sadism of a particularly nasty kind? Can you live up to this woman or that dress or this complicated recipe? And of course you can't. And yet Miss X. K. is real (we assume) and desperate and takes her problem to the oracle. And Mrs. F. whose ten-year-old is taking more than an ordinary interest in boys.

What is Miss. X. K. having for supper tonight or Mrs. F., who vaguely suspects that Our Ethel has been mucking about in the lanes. As for me, I will have the "Full European" again and take my pill like a good girl and try not to cry.

Jason's mother, the night before we were married: "He wants such a lot of looking after."

Mrs. Blood

We served the old dears a kind of pap—a faceless democracy of pureed oats or pureed bananas or pureed meat and veg. That was because it made it easier to feed them and anyway a lot of them didn't have any teeth. But they'd slurp it up off the spoon, most of them, and slurp up mugs of sugared tea, and Mrs. Karensky would go around with seconds if there were any and afterwards with a wet cloth to clean them up. And when they smelled the food coming they would yell out all sorts of comical things and sit up (if they could) and Innocent the Third (as Mrs. K. had named her) would sit up very straight and stop playing with her little balls of shit and call out, "Give it to me give it to me give it to me."

And Nurse P. would say, "I'll give it to you all right if you don't stop that racket," and a great murmuring would swell the ward so that we found ourselves hurrying and uneasy until the actual dishing out was over.

And I wished sometimes if they had to have food all mushed up like that if the kitchen couldn't have colored it bright colors for them. For that reason I was always happy for them on the days when they had jello.

Mrs. Blood

We will call this "doing our exorcises." All the others could swim so much better than I and wore green caps if they were intermediates or red if they were advanced, and some of those were also working toward their Lifesaver's. So you must understand that I was the only one with a blue cap in that group and my buddy was a real drip from the East Side whose mother made her wear nose plugs and was always getting out of the water for some reason or other, and of course I couldn't go back in until I found another buddy. I wasn't really afraid of the water (the blue caps swam in a sort of pen, I mean, what was there to be afraid of), but I was afraid of failing, you know, and also I tired very easily and couldn't get the breathing right. Sometimes she had us practice in the washing-up pans and the others would tease me when I got back to the cabin.

But I like the singsongs and learned the new songs much faster than anybody else, which made me feel worse, though, not better, about the swimming. And I especially liked "John Jacob Jingleheimer Smith" and "The Lonely Ash Grove."

And there were snakes in the water there. I never saw one where I was but some of the others did.

Mrs. Blood

And on a program dealing with obscenity we saw a lady in the street (a woman in the street) and she told the interviewer, "People are using four-letter words in my office right now, so what's the difference if you see it on the TV?"

"What sort of four-letter words are they using?"

"Well, — — — —. Oh. — — — damn. Well that's only got three letters." (Laugh. Fade.)

And when they showed the priest the picture of the topless go-go girl he said, "No, I don't think that's offensive. But it belongs in a clinic."

"What kind of a clinic?"

"Oh. A medical clinic."

And the businessman said, "No, I don't think that's offensive."

And the housewife said, "None of these pictures offend me, but when I wonder about their effect on youth. . . . "

And that time Richard's roommate let himself in on tiptoe and came to the door of the bedroom and shouted gleefully, "I smell cunt!"

Mrs. Thing

There are no victims. I said to Jason, "If you get me pregnant I won't come with you."

And he had said, "You know what happens to girls who wear nightgowns like that?" And yet one does not really see Fate as so unoccupied that it will chance to notice what you are doing. Disaster always comes as a surprise. And so, even after the first warnings, we traveled on and even a dead man on each boat could hardly give us pause for contemplation, and the events, being "outside" phenomena—i.e., not directly linked to us as us— we failed to see as analogies or premonitions. We were leaning over the railing, watching a forklift take the dead man's station wagon off at Cobh when Jason turned to me and said, "You look very nice today—the trip has done you good." And it never occurred to me to hook up that remark to the dead man himself, who was carried cold and stiff, like imported meat, into the land which he had set out so eagerly to see.

And when we got to England, doing the twist with Mary in the back garden, and Jason's mother: "I don't know if you should do that."

And I, genuinely surprised, "Oh? No, I guess I shouldn't." And stopping like a good girl but not from anxiety. And so the four of us rocked gently on our painted ocean and laughed and drank a toast to us and to our future and saw the second warning

59

as just an annoyance rather than a message from the gods. And I, who am now so frightened of the unexpected, laughed and sang as I sat on my pillows on the trip down to the boat.

And what I remember as the really important things are going to sleep to the last sight of a wheat field and a telegraph pole and pulling up the shade the next morning to see a wheat field and a telegraph pole and Jason and I laughing and I saying, "I feel for the first time what the word 'prairie' is really all about." And Nicholas losing his red cardigan in the Toronto Station and the deserted airport at Carthage, New York, and the automatic displays switching on and off at the lights, humming away in the ladies' room and nobody there but us.

And going out past the Statue of Liberty for the first time (because always before flying or leaving from Boston), all four of us drinking champagne because there was no one to see us off, and being so glad to be on a ship again and showing Nicholas what the Statue of Liberty looked like through a porthole while Jason took Mary up on deck.

All that night the four of us were so close together it was as though we were growing from a common stem, and Jason, looking at the children sleeping, said, "God, they like it, they really like it." But I couldn't see why he was so surprised since they were part of our collective stem. And yet while we were gently making love a man who was on his way to Ireland was dying in his sleep.

Mrs. Blood

At Halifax Jimmy and Oh Say and the Irish boy Mattie said they'd take us to the flicks, so we said O.K. and it was terribly exciting because we weren't supposed to fraternize with the crew. (That's what they said, "fraternize.") But after all the music the night before and *everybody* down on the crew deck it was probably all right and anyway we were going to make sure we didn't get caught. So at seven-thirty the five of us went off the ship and through the big loading hall and met the fellows when we were a long way from the quay. Rosemary had a big thing going for Jimmy (who was a first-class steward and so we hadn't seen him before last night), but frankly I thought he was too pasty-faced, and besides he had a fat bum. But we were all kind of high just on being out on an adventure and in Canada with the billboards saying "Players Please" and the knowledge that home was now a long way off. There was a suit of armor in the foyer and the fellows thought this was really funny and they also thought the film was funny as well. (It was "Love Is a Many Splendored Thing" and very romantic.) That is, all except Mattie, who said afterwards it was a lovely film, and Oh Say hooted and said, "C'mon, you mother fucker, who you trying to kid" and then," Excuse me, ladies," which made us giggle and feel all right again. Then walking down the hill Oh Say said, "Watch this," and right there he took out his left eye and tossed it up in the air and whirled around facing us as he did it, only somehow I knew it was an eye he had tossed up and closed my eyes so I wouldn't have to look. (But Rosemary said it was awful— just a hole.) Jimmy and Mattie grabbed Oh Say and tried to get him to put it back in.

They were all laughing and shouting and I was sure the police would come so I said, "Let's keep walking." And when they saw us walking away like that they ran after us and Oh Say said he was sorry he scared us and later Jimmy said he'd been in a really nasty accident about four years ago and usually pulled a stunt like that before anybody could get a straight look at him and ask him if he had a glass eye or whatever.

So we felt sort of sorry for him after that, but we didn't really like him because he was so crude and because he made fun of Mattie who was very gentle and used to meet me by the steps down to the crew deck and we'd just sit in a dark corner and talk.

But Rosemary really was getting serious about Jimmy and later he left the ship and came to marry her. Only she'd had second thoughts by then and she said he was really awful and tried to rape her. Only she didn't tell me this until long afterwards. I only knew he'd packed up his job and gone back to Liverpool and she had a new boyfriend about whom she seemed really serious this time.

Mrs. Thing

The man on the ship said, "Say, d'you always have to wait this long?" And we smiled at his eagerness, for there was indeed something childlike and innocent about him with his new mackintosh and his neat plaid shirt and the scrubbed look of his ears and the back of his neck. He had made a record of everything they had eaten all the way across. "Monday, August 19th. Calm sea. Mother: Cheerios, apple juice, ham and eggs, 2 cups of coffee, toast, strawberry jam; Dad: griddle cakes and bacon, orange juice, blueberry muffins, coffee. Lunch. Mother: lamb chops and potato baked in foil, petit pois, apple strudel à la mode; Dad: Madras curry, iced coffee . . ."

"I'm the adventurous sort," he said. "I like to try all sorts of new things. Not like Mother—she's very conservative." On Thursday he had tried blood puddings for breakfast, Cornish game hen for dinner. Mother had stuck to the roast beef au jus and potato baked in foil. We were awed by the meticulous way he had set it all down—quite objectively with no comment on whether he had liked the blood puddings or the Wiener schnitzel, or whether mother had found her roast beef underdone. I tried to imagine his wife, for truly I had never remembered seeing them before either alone or together. What would he write about the Tower of London or the Tate? Did he perhaps collect facts the way other people collected paper bags or bits of string? Had mother saved the colorful menus as well? And yet we couldn't laugh and inwardly blessed him because we were so happy standing there, so young and strong and, like him, on our way to high adventure. He complimented us on Nicholas and Mary and then said, "Say, what d'you think about that fellow dying like that? They kept it quiet, didn't they? We didn't know anything about it until they docked at Ireland. Mother was terribly cut up over it. Somebody told her it was their first trip—just like us. Perfectly all right one minute and dead the next. It seems cruel, don't it?"

And Mary said, "They kept him in the icebox."

And the man looked at her and then at us, and for a moment seemed almost on the point of tears. "Still," he said brightening, "I guess there are worse ways to go."

And we smiled and moved off to rescue Nicholas from the embraces of a group of maiden ladies in the corner.

"Waldo said," remarked Mary, smoothing her new dress, "that if you die on a long trip sometimes they throw you over the side."

When that man looks at his journal now does he remember the empty station wagon being lowered into the mists of Ireland or

62

does he remember the fancy hat he wore at the gala dinner when he tried not one but two entrees—"Sole Ambassadeur, and Filet Mignon and Coq au Vin"—and mother even ventured to try a little of the Cherries Jubilee.

Mrs. Blood

And Richard said, "Look, you've cursed my pajamas."

"I'm sorry. I'll wash them for you."

"Leave them, it doesn't matter. You've cursed me too."

And there was blood all over him and down his thighs.

"I'm not ashamed."

"Nor should you be. I'm not orthodox. I love you for it." He pulled the sheet up over us.

"Shall I take the sheet and ride through the streets to proclaim your chastity? Like the husbands of old?"

"I doubt if the lovers did it."

"Perhaps not. We'll leave the chambermaid to proclaim it, shall we?"

Later, in the shower, he called to me, "You're a funny girl, you know."

"Why?"

"Lots of women wouldn't do what you did. You're very shy about everything but sex."

"I'm shy about sex too, and the curse and all sorts of things."

"Then did it bother you?"

"No. Not at all."

"Why not?"

"Because I know you'd never hurt me."

"Oh, God," he said. "Now I want you all over again and I'm getting hungry as well. What shall we do?"

"Eat."

Mrs. Thing

Jason has told me a story which substantiates Wilde's conclusions about hell even if he was only thinking of sexual perversions.

Some of my ladies were at the regular Thursday coffee morning.

(They have been telling me, "When we get you back on your feet you *must* come to our coffee mornings." How can I tell them that the idea both bores and frightens me?) Dear Sabina was there and Frances who had brought dear Trevor and was complaining about steward number 10 or 11—and about the heat—all the usual rosary of grievances from what I can understand. Anyway, somebody had brought along one of the Polish wives because although she speaks very little English she does speak Spanish, and Eva, the Spanish girl, was going to be there too. One wonders how or why a Polish girl learned Spanish, but somehow no one seems to know, says Jason, that aspect of the story. (Being a romantic I find that part of the narrative, which is really incidental to the tale itself, the subject of much thought and maybe a little pity.) I had seen these Middle European women a few times before I came here. At the swimming pool mainly, and noticed them because most of the women were older and wore unfashionable black bathing suits and had varicose veins or huge vaccination marks, like white brands, on their thighs. I remember noticing those because it made me think of Mama and of being quite frightened of that mark she has when I was very, very young.

And one day there were two very pale little boys playing around in the wading pool with Nicholas and later I saw them in the cafe drinking Fanta and wearing nasty red plastic sandals. Jason says the footwear here is incredible. I must look at the visitors' feet, althought I suppose this variety he talks about wouldn't apply so much to visitors on a Senior Officials Ward. He says in the market one can buy sandals made of old tires—"Dunlop Sandals"—for 2/6. Anyway, as he told me the story I tried to visualize this particular woman, but as he says she is quite young and very pretty I couldn't place her. She must have been, if I ever saw her at all, just another young and pretty face. I only noticed the others because they were so other and I did not need to hear them speak to place them as somehow removed from "us."

Mrs. Maka, I think that was her name, sat in one corner with her little boy and smiled and said nothing. It was all rather awkward as Eva hadn't shown up at all and Ann, who had invited the Polish girl, had assured her that someone would be there who could speak Spanish. I can just imagine how she felt, or at least imagine part of it, for there are times when three or four of the ladies come to see me and fall to discussing curtains (which they "run up," apparently, in about five minutes) or prices at the Kingsway compared to the U.T.C., and why it's almost criminal to buy from the Mammies behind the Kingway: "3/6 for a cauliflower the size of my fist."

"You really should go to the market or send Thomas."

"I don't trust him. He adds on to the prices."

"Mary's right. It's better to do it yourself."

"I like to see what I'm getting."

"Did I tell you what my Enoch did last week?"

I feel my strangeness, my foreignness as much as that girl must have felt it while these healthy, hearty, competent women sat around drinking coffee and uttering sounds which were mostly (to her) meaningless.

Every so often someone would direct a question to her or offer her a sandwich or a cake, but mostly they just smiled at her and wished Eva would hurry up and come.

But Eva never came and Mrs. Maka, her little boy standing quietly by her knee (the other children had run off to play on the veranda), sat quietly for over an hour observing, smiling but not really participating in this little ritual they have.

Mary told Jason that it was Sabina, who of course is always so terribly polite, who finally decided the poor woman really must be dragged into the conversation. They had been discussing flour (or the lack of it) and the annoyance of having to go and beg a pound of butter from the manager of the Kingsway or the U.T.C.

"What do you think, Mrs. Maka?" said Sabina. "Do the shortages bother you?"

Mrs. Maka looked at them and smiled politely. "Shortages," she said. "What shortages?"

And Wilde said hell would be a paradise to those whose natures were suited to it. Read "used" for "suited" and there is something so profound about Mrs. Maka's reply that it takes your breath away.

I wish I could ask Sabina when she comes, "What did you think, just then? Can you describe to me the faces of the other women? Did any of you feel you had had a real epiphany? I want to know all. What you wore, what she wore, what X was wearing." But I can't. I do not "know" these ladies.

Jason only said, "Well, enough for that," when I inquired. "That's all she told me. Mary said, 'I thought we'd die.' "

Mrs. Blood

All that week we lived on oranges and love and spat the pips of laughter in the grass.

Richard said, "Did I ever tell you about the time Jack had a job playing piano in a country pub?"

"No. I didn't even know he played."

"Well, he did and he does." He turned over on his stomach. "Anyhow, this pub was way out past Lincoln somewhere and he had no car, of course, so he used to walk back home across the fields. One night—maybe the music, maybe the beer, maybe just Jack, you know what he is—he felt his clothes were a real affront to all this nature so he simply took them off and made a bundle of them and walked on naked. Only the cool grass tickled him so it gave him an erection and in the end (he had several miles to go) he was so full and so uncomfortable he cut back to a field where he'd seen some cows and went up and rubbed himself against one until he came."

"Do you believe him?"

"Of course. He said the feel of that cow's hide, all cool and smooth in the moonlight, was better than the skin on the inside of the thighs of any woman he'd ever had. I used to try and imagine what it felt like."

"You didn't want to follow his example?"

"No. Because it was obviously not just the cow, but the music he'd been playing and the feel of that grass—well, the whole thing that made him take his clothes off and led up to the cow in the first place. He didn't do it for kicks, you see. He did it because it just happened that way. But I used to try and imagine what it felt like."

"Did you ever come close?"

"Why do you think I'm telling you this? Tonight, just now, I went beyond it."

"I don't know whether to be flattered or insulted."

66

"That just shows your ignorance. Or the fact that you're a female."

"But that cow was just a kind of *deus ex machina*. She didn't participate. She just contributed her flesh."

"That's what you did, just now. You forgot to try and please me like you usually do or move yourself this way or that or to try at all. Maybe because you're tired. You just were there and lying down and I was in pain and you relieved me."

"I would like to be a man sometimes. Women's genitals are mouths and tongues and eyes. Men's are tongues and fingers. One would have to be a man to know what Jack felt and what you say you felt just now."

He turned back over.

"Come and walk with me now. Across this field. Naked. Try not to think about it."

So we walked and it was no good because I wanted him too much and made him stop and lie down again, and afterwards he said, "Madam, you are no philosopher."

And now I have a horse called Nothing and when you ask me where he rides I'll answer, "Nowhere."

Mrs. Thing

The Maternity Ward is next door and you have to go through our ward to get to it. Like the visiting hours here, the visiting hours on that ward seem to be pretty well ignored and there are always people coming and going there, passing through our ward. For the past few days I have been watching a Lebanese and his son, who come twice a day to see someone, presumably the mother. The father holds the child by the elbow and advances steadily past us and through the door to Maternity, but the child—he must be about six or seven, very pretty but with a sulky mouth—looks at us with curiosity and at me in particular. I find it strange to think that maybe twenty years from now he will tell someone how he went twice a day to visit his mother in the General Hospital and there was an Englishwoman there and maybe he will speculate on what I was doing there. Or perhaps he does not see me at all, so caught up as he may be with the wonder and horror of birth and the ward beyond. I assume that he will be like me and hoard all the peripheral details of days that I feel are important. Thus on the way to my grandfather's cottage I would try to memorize the billboards or the number of cows in a field in order to preserve that day more perfectly in my memory. I have taken him in as part of my experience here, why should he not return the compliment? So that under the cedars of Lebanon (I have already created a history for him, in which he returns to his homeland) I may be discussed and re-created as part of the story of his life. We do not know how often we may be picked as details in another person's drama, just as I remember the nameless old ladies with their three violins the night that Richard left me or the color of the check-girl's dress at the Budapest Cafe and Cabaret.

"There was a young Englishwoman there and she smiled at me. I wonder, now, what she was doing there."

And yet if he notices me at all it will be not because I am I, but because I am "the other," like the odd-colored kernels on Indian corn.

Is this why we come—so that already we are unique and will be recognized and singled out? But yes and no. That is why "we" come but it is not a general principle. The one-armed boy in Mary's classroom is unique, but this uniqueness works to his disadvantage. You must have an attribute which is generally recognized as superior and then you are free to travel anywhere. The French have it in their language and their culture. In a broader sense we have it in the color of our skins. Thus the boy looks at me because I am different and maybe already associates me with the superior Englishwomen who frequent his father's shop.

What does he think of Dr. Biswas or Dr. Shankar? Are they inferiors because of race or because they no doubt have less money than his papa does? (The boy wears one of Margolian's gold wrist-watches and his father's suits are shantung and well cut. But to be born white is to be born with a dowry he can never hope to have. How rich must the boy become before it doesn't matter?)

And this afternoon there was a great bustle from that ward and voices calling out so that even Esther and Elizabeth and Alexandria put down what they were doing and ran.

All the visitors came tumbling out en masse, including the

Lebanese father and his son, whose expression had not changed as he was pulled along firmly by the elbow. He and his father left but many of the others thronged our little ward and talked to the other women or among themselves, until Elizabeth came back and told them all to leave. Later I asked her what had happened.

"Tsk. A certain woman died."

"Died of what?"

"She would not eat."

My sense of drama immediately saw it as the Lebanese mother, but Alexandria tells me it was an African woman who had had a Caesarian a few days before.

"Why wouldn't she eat?"

"I don't know."

Why didn't they feed her by force? Where were the doctors? I am frightened again, but tell myself they may have respected the woman's right to die. Cut up the middle like that, perhaps she is now tabu. If she chose to die that is a different thing. Or perhaps they are not telling me the truth. Something went wrong. Why were they all running? Why were the visitors shut out?

And my mind goes back again to the boy. Will he forget me in the wake of this greater "detail" or will he still say, drinking his sweet black coffee after the evening meal, "There was an Englishwoman in that hospital. Very pale and quite young. She used to smile at me as we crossed the ward. I wonder where she is now."

Mrs. Blood

So there I was standing waiting for all this traffic to come out of the little mews and thinking about nothing in particular except that maybe I was hungry or maybe I should just dart in when I saw the chance—only not really in that much of a hurry. And suddenly there was a man on the other side of the drive and he caught my eye, shrugged and smiled the way two strangers do when they're waiting for an elevator or a bus that doesn't seem to ever come. You know, that sort of thing. And then lo and behold the driveway cleared and I walked on.

Only I hadn't gone very far when I heard someone running after me and calling "Pardon me," so I turned around thinking I might have dropped something, and it was this man.

"Pardon me, are you a student?" (I had been writing, you see, and had a couple of notebooks under my arm.)

"No, not really."

"Oh," he said, and looked rather disappointed. "I thought you might be a student and looking for work."

"I'm looking for work, I guess, but I'm not looking very hard."

I smiled at him—he had a pleasant, harmless kind of face, like the fathers in ads for furniture or life insurance.

An average colorless face with average colorless hair and average worker's clothes. His accent was Midland maybe, but not the vulgar "cuppatay" kind of Midland accent.

"Well, I'm looking for someone to work for me. As a matter of fact I was just on my way to place an ad."

"What kind of work? I can't type."

"My dear girl, do I look the sort who would need a typist?"

A stupid remark. A warning. But the donkey took the carrot.

"What d'you do then?"

"I'm a dancer. Come, we can have a cup of tea, anyway, and I'll tell you all about it." Obediently I turned around and we walked back to the Corner House at Marble Arch.

My soul cried, "Adventure, the Royal Ballet, young wardrobe mistress wins praise from principal dancer. 'Couldn't do without her,' he said in an interview on Friday!" My sense dictated that the first encounter should occur in a public place.

We got a tray and he offered me some buns as well as the tea, and I accepted. I was hungry and tired and alone. We sat facing each other and I noticed his hands now—beautifully manicured and the nails a soft, buffed pink. The hands of a dancer.

"Now," he said, "let me explain myself. As I told you before, I'm a dancer. An acrobatic dancer."

I looked at his hands again, curled fernlike around the cup. No. But why not. What was? How? And I? There were only a few lingerers downstairs where we were sitting. Keep asking questions.

"I don't know what that is."

"Of course you don't. Very few people do. They call it vague

70

things like 'modern dance' or 'rhythm and movement.' But strictly speaking it's acrobatic dancing. One doesn't interpret someone else's work, as is the case with ballet, for example—one 'interprets,' if that is the right word, the body itself—the muscles and tendons, the whole great symphony of tension and relaxation. To music, of course, but the music is very much a secondary thing."

"I can't see where I . . . ?" Run. But you want to be a writer. Stay. Why nervous in a clean, well-lighted place? "There are no bad experiences," remember? Take the second bun. Encourage him, the hands gesturing, uncurling, waving softly, pink and white, like sea slugs, too pink and white. (And remember the roses which grew in front of your house. Too pink and too blowsy. You never liked them, never, and the thorns were very bad so that Daddy had to tie them against the house with wire.)

"I can't see where I . . . ?"

"Um." Mouth daintily full. Paper napkin pressed to lips. "Well, it just so happens my assistant has gone away on holiday and I shall need a new assistant for several weeks."

"But I don't play the piano."

"A pity; but not, as you will see, essential. Modern technology being what it is I rarely use anything other than a gramophone. Cheaper, and you don't offend it by doing the same bit over and over."

"Then your assistant?"

"Beryl? Oh, she helps me limber up, you know, helps with the relaxation and breathing."

"How?" Too afraid now. An African man with a flag has come in from Hyde Park Corner. He props his flag (what nation, oh what nation? You could go and speak to him. He looks depressed) against the wall.

"How? Well, there are all sorts of ways, you know. I pay more for the Swedish method. Ten shillings for the ordinary and fifteen for the Swedish. I have a studio in Chelsea, just an upper room, really, but quite comfy!"

The hands go very fast now and the mouth and the little pink tongue. Just say, "I'm not interested," and get up and walk away. The African man is crying quietly with one hand up against his face. Go to him. But what country? And what is the Swedish method? If you leave you will always wonder. Mother used to go on and on about her hatpin in New York. I have the subway fare and a ball-point pen.

"What is the Swedish method?"

"You're interested, aren't you? I knew as soon as I saw you—I believe in Fate, y'know—that we were kindred spirits. It's fabulous. You need new leather shoes absolutely brand-new and preferably with perforations. One breathes very slowly in, out, in, out, like so; and the strength and vitality of the leather enters your body and makes it very strong. There's no other feeling like it on this earth."

"And your assistant?"

"She puts on the other shoe and gently treads my back up and down the entire length of the vertebrae. And all the time I breathe in and out while she's treading up and down. You can't imagine what it's like. Maybe even sixteen shillings. I have costumes."

One pink frond now underneath the table. The African gentleman is slumped over his cup planning revenge or dreaming of glory. Stand up. A few others; but to call out? The explanations, and maybe Court and, "Why did you accompany the accused, my dear, when it must have been obvious . . ." I can hear him underneath the table, buffed fingers working, the sound of cloth against cloth. Get out.

"I really don't think . . ." I stand up. It's easy. Walk away quickly ("Don't pick it up," she called. "Put that thing down right now! Come here!") and forever. Remember he's sick. But he may seek you out. Walk quickly but in the wrong direction.

And as I reach the door I hear him call out, "Now jump on me," and he is on the floor face down, writhing, and the crowd is beginning to run toward its nucleus.

And Jack to Richard: "Is she really stupid or does she just come on stupid?"

And Richard shrugs and laughs at me. "That will teach you to wear a red duffle coat along the Bayswater Road."

I hang onto the fact I told him my name was Rosemary; but I don't wear my duffle coat again until I'm out of London for good.

Mrs. Thing

To prepare myself for the journey I read the *National Geographic* magazine and said, "I'll have to get some cotton nighties." But it was Jason who got them, in the end, because he was down there buying seconds on sheets. I thought they were very pretty, pale summertime colors like snapdragons and ice cream sodas or peppermint candy. Each one is, of course, imperfect; the pink one has a peculiar seam, the mauve a three-cornered tear, and so on. He bought six and I said, "My God, I've never owned six nighties in my life," but they were very cheap, he said, and I know how you are about washing.

And now five nighties are not enough, and Esther and Alexandria, sometimes Elizabeth, take them home to the nurses' quarters and wash and iron some every night. They come back smelling faintly of scorch and charcoal. Do they talk about me with the other girls and say here, look, this is the white woman's blood, so that a crowd gathers around while the charcoal is heating and they pass my bloody garments from hand to brown hand and comment softly, because they are women and maybe because they are nurses, on the universal calamity of pain and birth and blood?

I would like to ask them what they call their periods. I would like very much to be objective and anthropological toward them, as Jason apparently can be when he visits the stool village or the village where the women make the smooth-bellied waterpots. He asks them questions about their craft and about themselves as craftsmen. Why can I not ask these nurses similar questions about themselves as women? What do you call your periods, among yourselves? What do you feel about virginity, sex, contraception? These are the children of the new order—not Elizabeth maybe, but the other two. Sixteen and seventeen, wearing short skirts and working independently of family or of tribe. The pill is available here, I know that. Also, *Delfene*, although, like everything else, not always available. Do they have intercourse at all and with whom and in what position? Yet they are not really quite free from the cocoon. They went to Mission Schools, and Alexandria has a tribal mark across one cheek. And on their days off they do not wear wigs and European skirts, but the traditional long dresses made of mammy cloth. And in their photograph albums, which they brought to show me, I see school pictures which include the earnest white faces of the people from the Basel Mission (or in Esther's case—she is from the North—the more sophisticated smiles of the White Fathers), Church outings, even a Girl Guide Pack. And the houses in Alexandria's village are the square laterite and thatch houses of this small village's region, not the pastel stucco houses of the town of Akwabaa itself. They are still rooted, I guess, in the colonial and tribal past, however free they may seem to an avid reader of the *National Geographic*.

I would like to really know them, but I sense that they are only as verbose as they are because I am a stranger, and they are young and romantic. So I must arrange the snippets of information I gather on a thread of the purest conjecture.

Their laughter is innocent and often uncontrollable, like the laughter of girls anywhere. Therefore I conclude they must be virgins. Their hands are gentle as they wash me and therefore I conclude their reaction to suffering must be the same as mine. Yet they treat the other girl behind the screen with a moralistic contempt that would do credit to my Aunt Hettie and her rigid views on sin and the devil's business. And they have attitudes that may be a result of the fact they are nurses or may be part of their ethnic makeup. Death does not disturb them, or noise, or rebuke from the fat Sister who spends most of her time at the desk.

Are they modern or are they not? Does this brave new world of dams and electricity and independence trouble or thrill them at all? Does it embarrass them to see their leader assuming a role they had traditionally associated with a white man? Does "Uhuru," now that the festivities are over (they would have both been under twelve, still very young), mean anything other than the best highlife band in town?

How many generations will it take before all but remote pockets of the country are converted to the new heaven and new earth of technology?

Jason told me another story. (I am like a child before bedtime—I beg him for stories.) Mary's husband is tutor to one of the halls. He received a message, last year, to come over there in the middle of the night. The rainy season had begun and rain was pouring through the cracks of all the windows along the north side of the hall. One of the students was very violent and said Mr. M must do something immediately about this very bad situation. Roger said he couldn't do anything just then and it would have to wait until morning. Then all of the students became angry and talked about how badly they were treated, etc. So Roger, who of course is never frightened because (a) he is a genuinely tolerant man, and (b) God's always with him, asked the first student, who seemed to be the leader of this little rebellion, what they did at home when the windows leaked. It turned out they had no windows!

But what does this really prove? That the young learn quickly? That the students here are spoiled—a well-subsidized elite who know they will hold the key positions in this new world once they have finished their studies? Yet the propaganda machine in the capital says that neocolonialism is a disease which must be stamped out. Is it not neocolonial to give a few students dormitories with windows? They will come to expect windows, and windows that do not leak even if they *were* put in by native workmen.

And did Roger have any right to ask that question? In a house with no windows the rain outside ceases to be a problem.

Mrs. Blood

And Richard said, "That's the first time I ever drank coffee and left lipstick on the cup," and I thought how pale he looked and wondered if I were that pale too. And I can still remember meeting Jack, who was standing outside the New trying to decide whether the picture would be any good or not, and I didn't want to stop and talk to him because I was so afraid he'd spoil it. And he looked at us and laughed that crazy, almost soundless laugh he had and then asked Richard if he'd ever heard somebody or other's remark about sitting up in bed and eating buttered toast with cunty fingers. Then he began to sing one of his rude songs and we all went off to the Cross Keys to get drunk.

75

And that was not the real Richard, because the real one said, "I don't want anything sordid."

And I said, "Neither do I," although I would have slept with him on a bench in the waiting-room or in the backseat of a car.

And he said, "Oh, Christ, I'll miss you so."

And I said, "Well, you know that all you have to do is to write me and I'll come."

And it was the real Richard who said, "There is no nice way of saying this," and the unreal Richard who said in the pub, "Fuck off."

Mrs. Blood

So I was really down, you know, because I had wanted that part and I knew I was better than Rosemary but she looked it and I didn't. (I knew the way you know something for sure, know it so hard it makes you bitter and makes your heart thump, even when what you know for sure is wrong.) And then she phoned from this party and said, "Why don't you come over," and I could tell from her voice she was already pretty drunk and maybe feeling bad about the play, so first I wanted to say "You're drunk" the way Mama used to say over the phone, "Stop that phony accent," and make me feel bad because I knew it was phony but had been enjoying it. Then I wanted to say I wouldn't come so that she would feel bad about my being all alone. But I really wanted to go because at that time I loved parties and besides, as I said before, I was feeling down about losing out on this part which I was sure I should have got. So all I said was, "All right," and Rosemary said Colin and Suzanne would walk over and meet me as I wasn't quite sure just where the party was.

I met them at the corner of High Street and we walked back together, and in a way I felt even lower because they were married and together and Colin was teasing her about being bald because she'd just been in the hospital to have a d.&c. But he did it gently and because he loved her and because he hardly was aware of me at all. He and Suzanne were maybe five to ten years older than the others and had a slightly different status. But they were gentle people and I really wanted to stop them and tell them how lonely I was and about Richard because nobody knew about it then.

And the party was well under way when we got there. Everybody drinking or jiving and Rosemary sort of leaning on her boyfriend and looking very beautiful and very drunk and waving at me from the corner. You know how you usually feel this party will be different and maybe I'll meet the real one this time? Well, I hadn't felt that since I slept with Richard and I guess what I was really thinking was, "Please God don't let him be here," even though I knew he must be and that was, after all, the real reason I had come. And soon I saw Jack, also drunk, and one of Jack's girls and also Fiona so I decided to go into another room quick. And in that room was a man I'd met at the beginning of the term, so after a while I took him home with me. And the next day Rosemary said, "You'd better pull yourself together because you're getting quite a reputation for being fast." And I started to cry, but I still couldn't tell her about Richard, because in spite of the drinking she was a nice girl and wouldn't understand why I had ever slept with him in the first place. So I said I'm sorry and I'm not mad at you or anything but I'm still feeling low about that play.

Mrs. Blood

When Nicholas was born we sat outside the hospital and smoked cigarettes and I said, "It looks like a bloody factory."

And he said, "It will be all right," so finally in we went and I was really proud of myself because I was so much in control. And Jason kissed me good-bye and I waved very cheerfully and was not at all afraid. And he was born quickly so that Jason had hardly got home and into bed, and when he came back I was sitting up eating tea and toast and the sun was streaming in the windows. It was so different, you see, and I hadn't really been afraid at all, even though up on the delivery floor I could hear a woman screaming. The intern was a Negro and his name was Mr. Brown which both of us decided was pretty funny and I told him how every time somebody stopped me with Mary and said what is your little girl's name, I always wanted to say "Little Girl"

77

and watch their face, and how sometimes I made up a crazy world where all the fathers and mothers were called "Father" and "Mother" and the dogs were called "Dog" and the babies "Baby." But I'd had a shot of Demerol so of course I was a bit high. Anyway he laughed and said maybe that's what had happened to him and all the Browns in Trinidad were called Brown because somebody decided to call them after their color.

And Jason had brought me some zinnias from a flower stand and I don't know why that worried me but it did, because they were already going brown and some of them had ants in them. And I knew I wasn't supposed to like all the phony pretty-pretty bouquets the other women had but somehow I wished he'd taken a little more time over the flowers and then I felt bad for thinking that and smiled at him and said, "Have you seen your son?"

Mrs. Blood

So there we all were in the car and just giggling and talking by then, but maybe it gave off a whiff of sin or something, because suddenly Daddy was there at the top of the steps with a shotgun and was calling down to us, "Now you both get in here right now," his voice sort of snarling but not at us as I well knew but at Mama, who had cussed him into this ridiculous position. Because of the nightlight above the door I could see him really well, standing so forlornly with the gun and in one of the plaid mackinaws he wore when we were there at the camp. He wore them from the time we left home, however hot it might be, and when he was finally forced to strip down a little, maybe by the time we got to Rome or Sherburne, he kept the mackinaw there on the seat between him and Mama and wherever we stopped for gas or to pee or let the dog out he said, "Ayeh, we're just on our way to my father-in-law's place up past Excelsior." (He didn't dare say "our place" in front of Mama, but I heard him say it more than once when she wasn't with him.) Then would ensue long conversations with the gas station attendant or the hot dog man or whomever about the weather and the good fishing he'd had that year down in Pennsylvania and we'd all sit baking in the car, the dog with her ham-colored tongue completely unrolled, and panting, until Mama finally said, "Warren, War-ren." And he'd look around with a guilty smile on his round, almost little-boy face and say, well, the missus was callin' him, so s'long for now. And that was another thing, the way he put on this real upstate twang and began using words like "missus" and "real nice" and "swell" and even "ain't." I guess because he wanted to identify with the people he harangued or maybe because that was his ludicrously mistaken idea of noblesse oblige. And Mama would say, "What d'you want to tell all our business for to every Tom, Dick and Harry you bump into?" And when we stopped for lunch in Utica she'd often disassociate herself from us by having a sandwich and a dixie cup of sherbet instead of a double hamburger or a "Texas Hot."

But when I saw him up there waving that shotgun around (and he was terrified of guns) and calling down to our little group in the car, I only felt rage at her for making him do this thing and humiliation that he was weak and bullied and wished he'd been a cop or truck driver right then instead of a socials teacher. But I came right away and told Trigger and the others to just shut up and don't they dare laugh at my father, and Jane came too though she was furious with him as well as Mama, I could tell. (And with me because of what had happened on the beach.)

So we went up the stairs and pushed past him but remembering not to bang the screen door so Grandpa wouldn't wake up. I wanted to say I was sorry but it just was so out of character that I couldn't say it because this new pity was something I didn't want to admit, not even to myself, and something I didn't yet (or maybe ever) know how to cope with. And we went past Mama's door (she was sleeping in the hired man's room for some reason or other that night) and she said, "You two get in here," and questioned us pretty thoroughly and said we were nothing but tramps to go away from the dance with riffraff like that and apparently she'd been all the way up the road to the Pinny's and that's how she'd discovered we'd come home with Trigger and his friend because most people recognized him as the lifeguard at the public campsite. And we both said "sorry" a thousand times and I practiced over and over in my head all the forms of the verb *connaître* until finally she said we could go, only not so politely as that of course, and I wanted to scream at her, "Did you know I came within an inch of getting fucked tonight?" Only what was the use?

And I could hear the old icebox door open and close softly so I knew Daddy was prowling around looking for something to eat, which is what he usually did when there had been a scene. And as soon as we got in bed Jane started on me.

Mrs. Thing

If there were more pain this might be easier. "Is there any pain?" asks Dr. Biswas every morning in his soft but rather high voice. His voice is somehow a combination of the "liquids and nasals" we learned about at school and very different from the loud voice of the officious Dr. Shankar which has very little "sing" about it or the voice of Frances Hare which is so "veddy, veddy" proper. "Is there any pain?" But aside from the occasional twinge there is no pain, just a dull ooze of fear which begins in the morning when I wake up and remember where I am, and why, and spreads through my arms and legs until it finally stops somewhere just behind my tongue.

We discuss his French classes and I recite for him, *"J'entre dans la salle de classe,"* all the way through, to demonstrate the kind of nonsense we went through.

He contradicts me. "But why is this nonsense? You have learned French by following certain rigid patterns. As for myself I think the old methods had a great deal to recommend them. They gave confidence, I grant you of a mechanical kind, just when you needed it. I find it very difficult to appreciate a French newspaper article or a poem when I am still struggling and having so much difficulty with the grammar and vocabulary."

"Oh, yes. But our little memory lessons didn't help us much when we left their safe and familiar progression. What good is it to have a beautiful accent or a perfect command of an extremely limited vocabulary?"

"It is something. And it gives us the confidence we need to move on to the next step."

"Hmmm. I do not believe you can learn to swim on dry land." And that switches us to the University pool, where he has been swimming on the weekend and where he saw Jason and the children.

"They are very beautiful and very good. You should feel proud of the way they behave when their Mama is not around."

And the weak tears fill my eyes. "Ask me again if I have any pain!"

"What! You have pain? Where?" He is immediately concerned.

"In my heart."

He smiles shyly. "Ah yes. But you have a good mind. You know it is better for you here, and perhaps, if the good prognosis continues, you can go home soon."

"Do you really think so?"

"Why not? Once the bleeding stops . . ."

"But it hasn't stopped. It never stops."

"You must remain calm and quiet. Would you like some more pills, a little bit stronger maybe?"

"No."

And then it is time for him to go and I weep quickly behind the plastic screens before Esther and Alexandria can come to pull them back. And the pain of my self-pity is a terrible thing about which Dr. Biswas, intellectual, mystical, Indian, male, will never understand. He is right. We must stick to the patterns. Big girls don't cry. Madame must not cry in the presence of the natives. I put on my lipstick like an old-fashioned district commissioner dressing carefully for dinner in the jungle.

Mrs. Blood

I am an old log thrown up by the sea, and the past clings to me like barnacles. There are no victims. Life cannot rape. There are no bad experiences. Say your beads and be silent. And call out to Jason who has no ears, "This is my body," and fling back the sheets and cry out to him who has no eyes, "And this is my blood." And take his head between your hands and force it down, crying, "Drink this, eat this in remembrance of me," and afterwards cry, "Bow down," and cut off his head with the beautiful silver blade of the fury and pain you have been hiding underneath the white vestments in which you clothe yourself and behind the white altar upon which you sleep.

And cry out to Jason who has no hands, "Touch me, there and

81

there and there, and don't stop, no don't stop." And show him
the shadow of the great bird who hovers above the altar and
describe to him the whine of the unseen instruments. And the
veil of the temple shall open and he shall see what I see and be
consumed on my broken altar.

The wafers are crumbling and the wine is old. A dog stands
drinking the water from the fount. I did not wish to be a god and
I swear to you I shall not come again.

And Daddy said to someone he thought was Mama, just before
he died, "Please."

Mrs. Thing

Today they have given me a pillow. Dr. Biswas says he doesn't
think it will hurt if I sit up a little bit. I tell him not only my
soul but my flesh is eternally grateful, for my elbows are red and
raw despite constant applications of Vaseline and Nivea. He suggested gentian violet and I told him why I couldn't possibly
use that. He is amazed that I have worked in such a place.

"Is this because you consider me such a lily or because it is
déclassé?"

"No, no, not at all. But somehow it does not fit with the impression I had formed of you."

"Too sensitive."

"Yes, that may be it." He tips his head slightly to one side when
he is embarrassed. He is so thin and brown that if I were a giant
I would ask my mother if I could eat him with my fingers.

"Don't you think that at seventeen one has extra layers of
spiritual skin that allow one to do just about anything without
being upset by it?"

"Not in every case. As for me, at seventeen I was filled with
horror by the conditions in my country, and at night I used to
weep because of it."

"Then you are a poet. There was nothing poetic about me
then. And I wanted the money. Also I saw very little connection
between me and those people—maybe no connection at all. You
identified with what you saw and maybe it was easier because
poverty and disease are 'acceptable' in a way that madness is not."

"Yes. Madness is the sign of a weak soul. Tuberculosis enters from without."

"They were much more humane about madness in the old days when they maintained that the victim was possessed by devils—something, as you put it 'from without.' "

"But now we know more and we do not laugh or torture those who are mad."

"Don't we? We tell them it's all in the mind, heal thyself, things like that. Or we shock them awake with electricity or insulin or snip little telephone lines in the brain."

He shrugs. "These things help."

"Maybe. Drugs to quiet them, shocks to wake them up. Do you think they can ever go back? In the past, and here still probably at least in places, exorcism allowed the victim to retain his dignity as an individual."

"But quite often the magic or exorcism fails."

"A good failure. The juju has lost to malevolent spirits, not to paranoid schizophrenia or whatever. And sometimes the madman is treated as a prophet or a god."

"You don't believe in progress?"

"I believe in pity."

"You are the poet."

We smile at each other as worthy antagonists. He likes to visit me, and although his casual attitude toward birth and death is something I can never hope to attain, or maybe don't want to, we understand at least a part of one another. Lying here, my brain grows musty from disuse and I am obsessed by the least twinge or rumble of my traitor body. The pills help, but not too much, as when the body is exhausted at night and the mind refuses to shut down. Dr. Biswas and I, both being foreigners, both "educated," both parents (and I think both lonely), enjoy our daily ritual of talk, where we at least hone the intellect, if nothing more, and realize that there are minds as well as bodies in the world. Sometime I think I will ask him whether it was the wailing of women that made him weep at seventeen and decided him for gynecology. Or he is simply obsessed with specialization? One suspects Dr. Shankar's motives for becoming a gynecologist. His is not a gruff exterior hiding a heart of gold. He likes power;

his boots tell me that about him, as well as his voice. But Dr. Biswas is young and delicate and intellectual. Why not some specialty in which blood and Vaseline and female orifices are not involved? Pathological medicine—aesthetic masterworks of disease and all aberration sliced thin and seen through glass. It is a strange profession. I must ask him about his mother.

Meanwhile I will enjoy my pillow and my elevated position. He says maybe two pillows next week if I am good. Suddenly I feel that things may work out after all. The child rides quiet and I can smell the frangipani trees down below us through the open window.

Dr. Biswas waves as he comes back through the ward. "You look happier already."

"I am."

"Good. But no dancing." He glides out on his little pointed shoes. What is his wife like, I wonder. What do they talk about at home?

Mrs. Blood

One only tries to get to Zed if one believes that Zed is there. Mrs. Ramsay was wrong to admire her husband for such a ridiculous attempt. One should stick to the square one lands on and wait for someobdy else to throw the dice.

In a church in Sevilla we stood at the back and listened to a Mass being sung before a flock of old women and little boys, all dressed in black. What were they doing, the women; what was he saying, the priest? In the darkness and the smoke of incense they didn't see us and we stood there fascinated and frightened, as though we had stumbled into the very anteroom of hell. Why all in black? Why old women and only boys? Young boys, too, with new haircuts so that the backs of their necks showed pale and vulnerable above the tan. Black is for death and Mass is for rebirth. But why? What horrible tradition was being reenacted here in this church which was not in any of the guidebooks and which we found while looking for a cafe?

It was very cold inside the church and candles burned before the little side altars and tiny chapels. There were plastic arms and legs and photographs like all the others. Rosemary whispered, "I have to sneeze."

84

"Go out then." But as she tiptoed back to reach the leather-curtained door the priest stopped singing and pointed at her.

And the flock of old women rose up shrieking. Clutching the little boys, they rushed at us, and we fled the church, the street, the neighborhood. But later on, back at the pension, nobody could tell us what we had seen. And now I want to know. What was the next step? What were they going to do with the little boys? Why had their hair been cut? Did we save them?

And in the park, sitting on the tiles which told of Don Quixote, Rosemary said, "I guess we weren't supposed to be there."

"I guess not."

"But why didn't they shut the door?"

"They didn't expect us."

And in the catacombs the young priest blew his candle out and laughed.

Moral: If you wish to move to another square wait till somebody throws the dice, count accurately (avoiding hotels and *GO TO JAIL*) and carry your own candle. Added caution: Proceed slowly when approaching Zed. There are no guardrails or warning signs. You will recognize it only by the rocks and the sound of water down below.

Mrs. Thing

Jason's visits are becoming impossible. I resent his muffled excitement. It reminds me of children who have been told to keep quiet because Grandma is ill. He tries not to talk about his work but it obviously interests him.

They went to the bush to get berries for dyes and to gather samples of earth. The students are wary of him—they do not wish to tramp around in the heat; why should he? He finds this amusing. He has been to a village outside the town and shows me sketches of the children there. One child hid in the back of the car and had to be returned, unrepentant, to the howling mother who thought he had been stolen. It is all so new and exciting—he is strong and healthy and in love with new experience. I have nothing to offer him in exchange. I resent this terribly, as though he were trying to describe, casually, some girl with whom he is already having an affair. He tells about the shortages and the plumber who never comes, the nest of cockroaches he found in the underwear drawer. But it is obvious these things do not faze him. He tells me about dinner at X's or Sunday curry at the Club and I know he has gone there and had a good time, knowing with a clear conscience that I am in "good hands" and that Joseph and Nicholas and Mary adore one another and are over in Joseph's quarters eating oranges or just sitting in the shade. I should thank Fate which put off this confinement until there was a Joseph to take my place and wonder how Jason would feel if this had happened back in Canada. But the bad me resents the ease of his adjustment—I am the only one who has to suffer. Nicholas and Mary are well and love the school. He is proud of them and their response to Africa and to a new domestic situation. They are invited everywhere. Mary M. has been kindness itself—we must do something for her when I get out. He had never realized how kind virtual strangers could be. Pa has sent me some cologne. Here are some letters.

And the unreal talk goes on. He reads the mail to me and becomes restless. Will Elizabeth never ring the bell? He is like a relative visiting a prisoner locked up for some crime in which the visitor was vaguely implicated.

I tell him I can't eat the food (a slight exaggeration), can't sleep (a lie).

"Have you told Dr. Biswas? He seems a very nice man indeed. We saw him at the pool on Sunday."

"I've told him. He says he'll give me some more pills, but I don't want that. I want to go home."

And always the weak, resentful tears and Jason's helpless, worried shrug.

"You just hang on. I'll come tomorrow." (Thank God, the bell.) "Is there anything you want?"

"I want all this to be a dream."

He kisses me. "I know. It's rotten luck. But do what they say and maybe you'll soon be home."

"Maybe."

He goes out quickly.

Mrs. Blood

"And the craziest thing happened in Florence," Rosemary said, laughing just to think of it.

"In this pension," I interrupted, "called the *Casa Contenta*."

Rosemary gave me a look. "You tell it."

"No. I'm sorry, Rosemary, you tell it."

"Well, we'd had a terrible time finding a place but finally we rounded a corner and there we were in a very quiet side street and there was this pension right in front of us, so we just walked in and asked if they had a room and they did."

"We were so hot and tired we didn't even ask to see it or what the price was or anything," I said.

Rosemary looked at me, thought about frowning, didn't, nodded in agreement and went on.

"The funny thing was, it was a beautiful room, twin beds with real mattresses, and very cool because the windows were covered with those wood shutters, you know, the ones that are slatted and let in the air but not the light."

"But it had one curious thing."

"One curious thing. The ceiling was covered with nudes—well, not exactly covered, you know, but along each corner was a really sexy painting of a nude and each with different colored hair—blonde, brunette, redhead and black-haired."

"How funny!" they all said, practically in unison.

"Yes. We never did find out why. Anyway, the price was very reasonable, only 720 lire each, so we were really delighted. And no other Americans around.

"We were so happy we sent the boy out for gin and orange juice and ice and invited him to have a drink with us."

"It was a brothel!" said one of them who thought she was very clever.

"It was *not*. Just a little pension on a side street. Why it was so cheap I don't know. But things are cheap all over there if you know where to look."

"Get to the good part," I said.

"All right. Well, we went out for supper and walked along the Arno and did all the usual things, only we were very tired because the train had been so hot and because we'd had no siesta. So we went back early and smart-pants here said why didn't I open the shutters as it was so terribly hot and we'd have a breeze all night. So I did, just before getting into bed, and then we both went sound asleep without even talking."

"So?"

"So wait a minute." She turned to me, laughing. "You tell the rest. It was your fault. Oh God, it was funny," she said.

"O.K. Well, I woke up first, feeling really delicious, you know, because it was the first decent mattress I'd slept on in a long time, and I lay there face down, enjoying the bed and the quiet and the smell of coffee somewhere in the house. And then," I paused for emphasis, "then I got the peculiar feeling that somebody was looking at me. I thought maybe Rosemary was awake so I rolled over toward her bed—she was sleeping by the windows—and I couldn't believe what I saw!"

"What?"

"Well, those shutters I'd told her to open the night before were actually doors which led right out on to this little alley, and there, sitting very quietly, were about six workmen all staring at Rosemary, who was sound asleep on her stomach, stark naked, with the covers kicked off!"

"What did you do?"

"Well, I screamed 'Rosemary!' but I didn't really know what to do because I was naked too, under the sheet, and I couldn't very well rush up and slam the windows shut that way!"

"So what did you do?"

"I shouted at them, 'Avanti, avanti!' only of course I really meant to shout 'Via, via' or whatever 'go away' is—I forget now."

"Perdeti," she said.

"Oh, yes, how could I forget that? You really need to know that, of course, in Italy."

"And?"

"And they laughed and applauded and were all for stepping over the sill when Rosemary started screaming and they ran away."

"We nearly died."

"I kept thinking we'd be recognized by one of them and it really made me nervous. And you know Rosemary's hair!"

"Were you?"

"No."

And the clever one said, as we left the restaurant, "Are you sure you didn't mean to shout 'Avanti' all the time?"

"Ha, ha. It's funny now, but it wasn't very funny then, I can tell you."

"Did you move?"

"Are you kidding? We just got a padlock from the boy." And we could feel their admiring glances warm against our backs as we went off down the street to class.

Mrs. Blood

He is corked up in there like a pear in brandy. Only the wine is red, not white, and there is a leak. I can feel him in there bobbing against the sides of his prison.

My Caliban; my dear. We have a secret pact to destroy each other when the right time comes. He will peck his way out, crowing thrice, and will straddle my broken shell, proclaiming to the multitude that that which was love is death and that which was life is love. And no one will assay to touch me because of the shards which gleam greenly against the white altar and the wine shall run over and down and expire in a hiss when the sun sticks his finger in the window. Drops of red pain, rivers of pain and the earth outside rusty with dried blood. This is my body.

But he shall die too, for they will push him back, crying, "Not yet, not yet. The rains are still upon us, and the vultures watch carefully from the roofs of the houses of the people."

And one of my shards will pierce him through; and bird and shell, bottle and wine will lie together on the broken altar of the past.

And the voices will mutter, "We knew it, we told him," while the careful vultures will smile hungrily in at the window and beat down the bars with their wings.

Mrs. Thing

Today, while Jason and I were talking, I could suddenly feel the blood gush out, and without thinking I thrust my hand beneath the sheet. It came out covered in bright new blood and the room tilted. Jason seemed very far away and I called out to him, reached out my bloody hand. Then I fainted. When I woke up just now Elizabeth was sitting by my bed.

"What happened?"

"It was nothing. A little flow of blood. You became alarmed."

"Why is there more blood? Why this little flow? What is happening in there?"

"I am not sure. The doctor is coming soon."

"Where is my husband?"

"He is downstairs. He will come back soon."

"Am I dying now?"

"Tsk. It is nothing: a little flow of blood. You will not die."
Dr. Biswas hurries in and pulls on his rubber glove.

"Please, what is the matter? What is happening?"

"It's all right. Just a little more blood than usual. What a pity.
I thought it was easing off." And his finger gently probes. It comes
out with a nasty, sucking sound and the glove is covered in blood.

"What is it?"

"It is all right. The cervix is not dilated. A small piece of the
placenta seems to have pulled away. Lie very still."

"I'm frightened, doctor!"

"The nurse will give you an injection."

"It is very hot in here. I can't breathe."

"Lie still. You will be all right."

And Elizabeth gives me a quick jab of something new, something which makes of this new development a fact so minor that
I am easily able to soar above it. The noise of the fan ceases to
terrify me and becomes a homely purr. Alexandria gently washes
my bloody hand and Jason is allowed to come back. What a kind
man he is. I love him after all. I smile at him.

"It's nothing," I say. "Just a little bit of blood. The baby's
all right. I'm all right. Don't worry."

And the love I feel laps me gently as I plunge into sleep.

Mrs. Blood

We were sitting in that pub off Notting Hill Gate, and Richard
had brought along Jack and the girl Jack was living with and a
man called Geoffrey whom I liked immediately except that he
wore dark glasses the whole time—green-tinted ones, rather old-
fashioned looking, which cast a greenish glow across his cheeks. Did
Richard assume I already knew him or did he just not care? He,
Geoffrey, sat quietly drinking half-and-half and looking at me—
or so I thought, because of course I couldn't tell what with the

dark glasses and all. He said he was a writer. I said of what, and
Jack said, "Of graffiti," and he laughed in that silent gasping way
he had. Jack's fingernails were cracked and dirty and I could feel
my legs tense and wondered why I hadn't noticed his hands before. But he seemed to admire Geoffrey, in spite of the remark,
and to consider him one of them.

Geoffrey said quietly, "What do you do?"

And Jack said, "I could tell you a few things she can do," and
the new girl, who was very dark and had a definite mustache,
laughed hugely, showing really horrible blackened teeth. She
was Estonian or Polish or something and her teeth were really
bad. She didn't shave her legs either and the crisp black hairs
curled thickly beneath her stockings.

"I don't think that's very funny."

"Don't you? Why not leave, then?"

"Richard . . ."

"What?"

"Can't you make Jack shut up?"

"Why? Is he offending you?"

"You know he is."

"I don't know anything."

"I can give her ten orgasms in one night," Jack said.

Richard laughed, "Well done, noble thane."

The Estonian girl looked puzzled, and Jack put his hand on
her lap and opened it wide, then shut it with a snap ten times and
pointed at me and then at her crotch.

"Shut up!"

"Why? You are extraordinary. Aren't you proud of being so
extraordinary?"

"It's not true." I looked at Richard, who was leaning back
against the wall and rolling a cigarette. He smiled.

"Not true with me, certainly. But I'm not Jack."

Geoffrey gestured softly at Jack and Richard. "Why upset the
girl? Your conversation is disgusting."

"Sorry, darling," said Richard, lighting his cigarette. "Why
don't you take her home? It might be interesting."

"Don't be ridiculous!" He finished his drink and stood up.

"Will you walk me home?" I said. Hadn't he been soft and
gentle?

91

"Sorry," he said, "it's against my religion."

The three others laughed gaily, already high on the possibilities of the evening ahead.

"Sweetheart," said Richard, "Geoffrey is gay, aren't you, Geoff? He'd rather walk a dog home than a girl."

"You really are disgusting," he said and walked away.

Jack finished off his drink. "Shall we go and apologize to him?"

Richard shrugged. "He doesn't care." And he ordered three half-pints for himself and Jack and the girl, smiling at me and saying, "I'm sorry you're just leaving."

And I stood outside wondering how people managed to keep on living.

Mrs. Thing

Is it possible for someone with a toothache or a headache to be in love? Love is something, maybe, exclusively for the healthy. I don't mean the love of the poets; solitary, anguished, unrequited. But genuinely joyful love—a radiation towards "the other," a concern, sexual excitement. My discovery that I do not love Jason may therefore be false gold.

I do not love him now because I am ill and frightened. I will love him again when the crack is sealed, the ache is removed, the consuming self-obsession disappears. But on the ship Jason wanted to make love and I responded. Was it to reassure myself that the crisis was indeed over? And last week, thinking of something long ago, quietly, touching myself, swollen, pursed lips and the heaviness at the base of the spine. And my hand stained with dried blood. Yet I still think I'm right. If there is no pain, no fear, then it is possible to reach out towards someone else, to dare. The pain and fear shrivel and pickle us like alum. We do not wish to love or be loved. We wish to be alone to observe our traitor body or our traitor mind. Thus Nicholas kicks the rock he stumbles over and I pick a fight with Jason because I want to hate him, fighting pain with greater pain. I want to tell him I have been unfaithful to him, where and when and maybe even why. Yet I cannot. I am a victim of my sense of sin. It is not consideration for Jason that stops me but fear of the gods. I cried out to him that night "I'm being punished because I didn't love my father." And he said, "Nonsense," but I could tell that he was frightened. What if I am being punished because I was unfaithful? What would he say to that?

I keep my secrets hidden, like grenades, beneath the pillow.

Mrs. Blood

These things I know to be true:
1. Fragile or perishable articles are not subject to indemnity against damage.
2. *Le numéro de l'appartement complete l'adresse. Toujours l'indiquer est une pratique à encourager.*
3. The streetlamp outside our house appeared like a wilted chive or onion in the heat of the summer night.
4. This receipt must be presented if order is to be picked up at store.
5. There are no victims.
6. No enclosure is permitted. *Ne rien insérer.*
7. Jason said, "Girls shouldn't wear nightgowns like that if they really want to get some sleep."
8. This building is guarded by patrol dog.
9. A charge will be made for all canceled appointments unless 24 hours' notice is given.
10. "There is also inside toilets."
11. Jason never loved me.
12. Proust had it easy with his tea and bun.

Mrs. Thing

> **Scorpio** (Oct. 23–Nov. 24): Not a very conclusive day. You tend to get tired easily. Try to see the positive angle of things—in fact, you are on the right road and have nothing to fear.

And at the Odeon they are showing, 6:15 P.M., "Tigress of the Seven Seas."

How many Scorpios have opened their papers and read the horoscope and pondered. Another inconclusive day. The humidity is tiring; there is nothing to fear. Perhaps a trip to the cinema because of the tiredness. Who chooses these films of which I have never heard? And the property of Mr. S. E. Aryeetey (2nd Defendant Judgment Debtor) known described as House No. G1098/2 situate at Harrley Junction will be sold by public auction on 14th October, 1964, at 3 P.M. Sale ordered by the Deputy Sheriff. Mr. Aryeetey has a week in which to ponder his horoscope (which is situated just below and to the right of *Auction Sales* and the publicization of his shame) and wonder where he took the first false step.

In the next column over, an Englishwoman seeks work, mornings only, November–end of year. What sort of Englishwoman; why? What does she do in the afternoons? Is it all right now for Englishwomen to advertise for work? Perhaps she came out to marry someone and changed her mind. Or her husband died out here (though that is not so likely).

I read my newspaper like a menu, avidly selecting the items which give me the most food for thought.

There is a memorial statement to a chief who "passed away to Higher Service Above" a year ago:

> The Blow was total
> The Wound unbearable
> The Loss irreparable

"God shall wipe away all tears." And he stares at me, weighted with gold crown, gold rings and bracelets, stern, upright, an "affectionate memory."

Dr. Biswas has told me it was the custom of every chief to have a "soul" or young boy who accompanied the chief everywhere and who died when he died. This was considered a great honor.

"Does it still happen?"

"I am not sure. I know very little about the customs now."

Yet the drums beat in the villages all night, recording births and marriages and deaths, and I have seen for myself the juju stall in the market crammed with claws and powders and obscene wrinkled things.

Did Nii Kpakpo Oti II have a "soul" of his own? Did that "soul" die with him, and if so, how did the honored mother feel then? Ritual murder is not murder; it is ritual. "God shall wipe away all tears."

And the tears of Mr. S. E. Aryeetey? And the Englishwoman ("secretarial work—anything")? And my tears? "Try to see the positive angle of things." Like the relatives of Nii Kpakpo Oti

94

11. And the positive angle of the ceremonial adze as it swings down, singing, toward your neck?

Mrs. Thing

Every Sunday an old woman they call Auntie Mary comes to preach and sing at us. She goes to all the wards, male and female, and sings her hymns and praises God. The women in the ward make fun of her (or most of them do), but she just ignores them or sings even louder in her high, thin, very nasal voice. She is a member of one of the smaller evangelical sects, mystic-evangelical I guess, and Esther told me Auntie Mary is supposed to have been coming here for years and that she lives in a shack behind the old market. I do not recognize the hymns she sings and wonder if they are original with her, or original-African, at any rate.

She wears a very faded European housedress and ankle socks and black "court pumps" as I guess they would be called. Her hair is the color of Brillo, and also the texture, and her body is thin and ropey. What has she found that keeps her going? For she must be very old, nearly one hundred perhaps. What is her Jesus to her and how does she see him when she closes her eyes and begins to sing? Sometimes, as though it were a wire, her thin voice pulls the other women in in spite of themselves, and they call out "A-men" or "Praise the Lord" in English. Why in English? Surely this can't be the result of missionary zeal. Or maybe it can.

Frances Hare told me about an American she met last week who has been sent out here as a missionary by some very peculiar group in California. He drives a bright blue '65 Cadillac and rents a big house on City Road. On Sundays he dresses in a white suit and preaches in a tent just outside the City. All of his "children" who have been saved are required to wear white as well. It is almost too much like Elmer Gantry! Frances says he is "extremely rough-spoken" but has "five charming children. Dear Trevor has asked to have them *all* to tea!" and a wife with a club foot, "poor soul. And Southern, I think, by her accent." The really funny thing is that he told Frances that when his tour is up next year he intends to come back privately as a used-clothes salesman!

How he squares this with the little bitty children dressed in white I cannot see. I would like to meet him, maybe just to dispel the suspicion that it's Burt Lancaster on location and this missionary is an unpaid actor in some new Lancaster carnival. Would his Jesus recognize Auntie Mary's Jesus on the street or in the boardroom? I have a feeling the thing *she* sees when she closes her eyes and begins to sing, pulling us in after her through the power of her conviction, is some sort of beautiful bird, not a man at all, and her voice strains up to meet it.

We have other religious visitors as well. An enormous African White Father, very striking, who appears now and then and talks to the few patients who are Catholic. He looks as though he lives very well indeed—his skin is shining and seems full to bursting.

I did not know there were black White Fathers. I thought they were only missionaries. There were two on the boat but they only wore their "uniforms" the last night out—Father Doyle and Father something else. I had seen them at the swimming pool and in the bar—particularly in the bar—and they seemed to have many friends of both sexes. Then the last night out there was a fancy-dress and I looked up from my dinner (Jason and I hate fancy dress, Jason particularly, and we were eating quickly to get up and out of our cardboard and crepe-paper hats and the general air of phoney gaiety. And yet we were gay because we were really there. Why do the hats bother us so? We are too self-conscious), and there, framed in the doorway, were the two men I had seen, usually in swimming trunks, leaning against the bar or stretched out in deck chairs. They were dressed in long white cotton robes.

"I don't believe it," I said to Jason.

"What?"

"Look. There. Those two playboys have come dressed as White Fathers. Somehow I don't think that's very funny."

Jason looked up as the two men headed for their table, a table which included many bottles of wine or ale each meal and a great deal of laughter.

A woman at the next table leaned over toward me. "My dear," she said, "they *are* White Fathers."

Mrs. Blood

The woman is the Venus flytrap, tinted a mordant pink, mouth open wide to catch the unsuspecting guest.

But who is to blame? She did not ask him to be enamored of her scent. And this land too is female and open and deadly. There is always the warm sticky smell of charcoal on the air, like dried blood, and the flowers wait with swollen lips for you to stumble against them in the dark. And the unrepentant hyrax calls from the top of the tallest tree while the snakes wait quietly below and the flatulent frogs punctuate the darknesses with their belches. The people burn in the daytime and lie like half-dead embers in the night. The drums beat against the walls of darkness with their bandaged fists and the vultures look sideways at one another and put their greedy heads beneath their wings.

The smell of the female flows across the land and the insects whine with excitement. "Take this in remembrance." "Drink this." And the warm lips close around them and they die.

Mrs. Thing

I think I know now what it must be like to be blind. Lying here, my vision limited pretty much to a 180-degree arc with myself at the center and the window and the corridor at the two extremes. I am losing interest in looking at the same old things (except the newspaper which I devour) and find myself listening instead. And smelling. Morning is Dettol and Mansion Polish, the feel of the thermometer cold against the back of my tongue, the squeaky feel of cornstarch, Elizabeth's steady but slightly heavy footsteps, children crying somewhere, lorries outside and the smell of diesel fuel, the difference when the fans are switched on, Mrs. Owusu's perfumed sweat, the smell of flowers as the sun begins to cook them. Afternoon: the heat hovering like wings, the fu-fu pounders, the smell of a cigarette in the corridor (Mrs. Owusu), my own stink as the freshness of the morning is canceled, sweat and blood, sometimes the smell of rain, Jason's footsteps, groundnut stew, fish, ether if someone is brought back from an operation. Evening: charcoal, rotting vegetation, oranges, Esther's footsteps as distinct from Alexandria's, the musty smell of mosquito nets, the moldy paperback detective books I read, laughter outside, monkeys, the hyrax, my wilted nightgown. Thus I grope my way from day to night. And I try to imagine the sounds of a day with Nicholas and Mary and Jason, here in the house on the compound. But they are

97

in a different house now and I cannot place them. Where is the children's room? What color are the cushions on the chair where Jason sits? What did they have for dinner? What is Jason reading, thinking, drinking, saying? They are on a strange road and I stand at the corner unable to cross. They no longer exist except as photos in an album, like our past life. Now they have an album of their own, and I too have my own unutterable souvenirs.

Mrs. Blood

Bird on Safe—Cash Missing

A strange bird believed to be a dove was found resting on a safe of the office of the District Commissioner in Agapo—Axim.

A spokesman for the office said the amount of money missing was quite large and was only discovered to be gone when the safe was opened.

A police spokesman who described the discovery as strange said investigations were being conducted.

The bird died soon after its discovery.

And when they open me up the dove on my forehead will shriek and whistle thrice and my empty belly will be borne on a purple cushion above the heads of the crowd.

The birds beneath the crust will sing-

The people weep-

The dove is dead.

The prosecution said on September 25, border guards on duty near the Pioneer Cement Company on the frontier found 52 people with loads of cocoa attempting to cross into Togo.

Heels

They took to their heels but the guards succeeded in arresting 15 of them and recovered 52 loads of cocoa they were then carrying.

Glad they are Back

Although belated I take this opportunity of welcoming the police patrol cars back on the roads.

We all missed these cars terribly during the many months that they remained dormant.

Fortunately the unannounced disappearance of these cars
caused no panic in our society, nor did the lawbreakers take
advantage of it to increase their nefarious activities.
Help the Police to Help You!

Scorpio (Oct. 23–Nov. 21): Make appointments for the early
morning when you will find the right people to help you.
Keep calm and beware of jealousy.

"Listen," he said. "I love her dearly, but when my crazy wife
ordered *les alouettes* in the restaurant and they came with their
little heads on, in a nest of *pommes frites,* the little heads sort of
dangling over the side—well, I wondered what kind of a chick I'd
got mixed up with anyway!"

And the pied pipers underneath the crust began to sing.

Can you tell real Stork from butter?

Mrs. Thing

The mattresses here are covered in heavy-duty plastic. On top of
that goes the first sheet, then a mackintosh sheet across, and then a
draw sheet. By noon it is like sleeping on sand with a sunburn.
Esther and Alexandria virtually smother my back in cornstarch
when they bathe me, but it doesn't do much good. Even with the
pills I find it difficult to rest and am terrified of getting bedsores.
The two girls are very proud of my delicate skin, and my bath has
become a great ritual to them, much as one might look forward,
I guess, to dusting a rare figure of ivory or alabaster. My left side
belongs to Esther, my right to Alexandria, and they move slowly
down me, running their fingers over my pale shoulders, my arms,
my legs, and exclaiming to Elizabeth, who is busy writing up the
order book or making swabs. The other women in the ward join
in and there is much good-natured banter at my expense. My skin
gives me a kind of Gulliver-quality, for them, along with my virtually horizontal state.

"What did she say?"

"She said you are unbaked bread." Laughter.

"What are they saying?"

"Tsk. They are saying . . . well . . . they are asking what color is
your pubic hair."

But I do not mind, now; it is a break in the loneliness, and their
laughter is not unkind. I tell them the story of the Princess and the

Pea, which they repeat, with great glee, in the vernacular. I also tell them it is not a good thing to have such skin and I secretly believe they agree with me, although they always argue very politely on the other side.

But then the head nurse returns from one of her many visits God-knows-where and we all keep very still and Esther and Alexandria move quickly off to someone else. We are like schoolgirls caught talking after lights.

I do not understand the basis of Mrs. Owusu's dislike; but as she dislikes everyone it may have little to do with my being European. Elizabeth is the only person she is really afraid of and that may be because Elizabeth is quiet and efficient and gives an impression of incorruptibility. Esther and Alexandria say "Sister is very bad woman," but this is all so general it's hard to tell *why* she is very bad (very disagreeable certainly) and they just giggle if I ask. She is certainly unattractive physically, short and squat and with the kind of frog face we often associate, back home, with the face of the older Negro. Maybe her ugliness has made her cross, but the wig and the magenta lipstick she wears on her days off may indicate that she does not see herself as ugly at all.

When she looks at me, or examines my body, I am suddenly afraid. I do not trust her and I feel that she would quite calmly ignore or disobey a doctor's orders (particularly the orders of poor little Dr. Biswas) if she didn't like them.

I am sure she beats her servants.

Mrs. Blood

Every Saturday he brought me a brown paper bag full of eggs and bacon and tomatoes. And we would have a huge breakfast, Jason cooking, and fried bread and coffee to complete it. Once I said to him, "I love you because of your Saturday breakfasts."

Then we would wash up and catch the bus into town, usually to go to the Bull Ring and wander through the markets. I liked the auctioneers and Jason liked watching the people. Or we would sit in the park in front of the Cathedral counting pigeons and waiting for the Woodman to open. Or eat cockles and winkles at the fish market, standing up and being super-lavish with the vinegar.

Once I bought a pair of stockings for a shilling and only one of them had a foot; and once Jason bought me a huge bunch of artificial flowers complete with artificial ladybug. And sometimes we would wander down to Lewis' food floor and eat as many free samples as we could find and see a movie and maybe eat some curry at a cheap place we knew about and then go back to my place and make love.

And it was very good that time, and very gentle. But I used to wish his name were Richard too, so that if I called out in my sleep I wouldn't hurt him. But that passed too and Richard dropped back with all the other names, like when you're going through a phone book concentrating and "Jason" became the only name worth looking up.

All that's changed now, they tell me. The Bull Ring is torn down and there are new roads and overpasses, and when Jason went in with Pa that time he couldn't find the Woodman.

"Even the street was gone," he said, and we looked at each other, appalled and maybe a little frightened.

Mrs. Thing

Why do they give me all these potatoes? Six potatoes and a tough turkey leg and greens and gravy. I have never eaten six potatoes in my life. The whole plate nauseates me and I push it aside and think of omelettes and fresh green salad or cold chicken and a single roll. Asparagus.

The staff nurse comes. "Please. You must eat. This is European food. Why don't you like the food?"

"It is good food for someone who has been working hard. A big man, maybe. A child. I can't eat all that."

"You must think about the child."

"I'm sorry. I do nothing all day. I'm not hungry." (I find I reply to her in short clipped sentences, the way she talks to me.)

"What do you want then?"

"Well"—I must be careful, diplomatic—"I know you say I can't try your food . . ."

She gives a cackle of laughter. "Hee! It is too much pepper. Not good for you at all. Your stomach must be quiet."

"Well, could I have some rice maybe, or a boiled egg and some bread and butter?"

101

"You would like a boiled egg?"

"Yes."

"You have eggs for breakfast." (Fried, cold, but edible. One is hungrier then and the heat has not begun.)

"I don't mind."

"All right." She goes off muttering to herself and says something in dialect to Esther and Alexandria which makes them giggle. I wonder if they are laughing at me.

And today I receive for lunch five potatoes and a slab of meatloaf, greens and gravy, two eggs and a bowl of plain white rice. And the little slip of paper in the gravy reads as before, "Full European."

Mrs. Blood

Grandpa had a big silk parachute someone had given him. It had a huge red circle on it, and when I asked why, he said, "Because the man who owned the parachute believed he was descended from the sun." And I looked up "descended" (because he would never tell us the meanings, you know) and saw the man come slowly down out of the sun under his big white parachute.

"Is the man dead now?"

"I expect so. Dead as a doornail."

And when the war in the Pacific was over we didn't even know it, at first, because Grandpa's camp was so isolated, you know, but we saw all those fireworks going off at the other end of the lake and Grandpa said to run up to Pinny's and see if they know what the devil's going on. So Jane and I ran like crazy and Mr. Pinny met us at the door all smiles and said, "Tell your grandad the war is over," and we went tearing back yelling and screaming because our side had won.

Grandpa said, "Well, this calls for a celebration," and told Jane to get the pope's telephone number (that's what he called Vat 69 only I didn't get it then) from the gun closet and gave her the key. Grandpa never took a drink or smoked or anything like that or gave anyone the key, even Daddy, so I could feel how important the end of the war must be.

And we all had one drink—even Jane and I had a little one—and

102

Grandpa went over to where the parachute was and looked at it and said that was the end of that then.

And Daddy got very sentimental because he didn't drink either and because he had been too old to fight in this one, and stood on the porch and blew taps on the old bugle and it would've been absolutely perfect if we'd had any leftover fireworks; but they did let us stay up and watch all the ones going off at the other end of the lake.

And I asked my grandpa, "Do you think they still believe they're descended from the sun?" And he gave a funny laugh and said he doubted they thought about it very much just yet.

Mrs. Thing

Today I was taken to the lab for a blood test. Why, suddenly, it was not enough for them to come to me I do not know, and at first I was very frightened—anything frightens me now—thinking perhaps they were going to do something other than a simple blood test. Something complicated and theatrical which could not, even with the plastic screens, take place on an open ward. It turned out the lab assistant was off work and so the man who regularly comes to siphon off my blood was unable to leave the lab. It felt very strange to be sitting at right angles again as Alexandria wheeled me across our gleaming floor and along the corridors. A young American was playing guitar for the group of children who play by the bend in the corridor. He was very startled to see me go by and I thought for the first time of those two Englishmen I saw on M-3 and wondered if they'd gone home yet. I realized, too, that our ward was relatively quiet compared to the rest of the hospital. The noise from the courtyard seemed a stadium roar and the voices of passing people were very loud. Also we seemed to be zooming along at a really terrific speed, but Alexandria just giggled and said I had been lying still too long.

The test took no time at all, but I had to sit and wait for Alexandria, who'd gone off to the pharmacy and was to pick me up on her return.

The lab was very small and rather helter-skelter, like a high school chemistry lab, and the paint here, as in the gynie clinic, was flaking away from the concrete walls. A nurse from another ward came in with a little basket of tubes full of blood and set it down on the counter near me. I felt it threatened me, somehow, and I wished Alexandria would hurry up.

What really surprised me was that I was glad to return to bed. This minuscule trip had exhausted and confused me. I just wanted to lie still and tread water. Any sudden demands and I might drown.

Mrs. Blood

"Hello, Mother. Listen. Rosemary wants me to spend another night here, is that O.K.? I'll take the first train tomorrow. . . . "What?" "Oh, I'll be careful. . . . "Yeah." "Yes, Mother. *Yes,* Mother. No. No, I won't forget. Yes. O.K. Yes. . . . O.K. Good-bye."

And then we went down to the B.O.A.C. office to see if he could get on a flight the next day and went back to Rosemary's to leave a note and pick up my suitcase.

"What now?"

"I don't know. The important thing was to keep you here another night."

"Are you hungry?"

"Very."

So we went to a hotel near Times Square and Richard said, "I wish you didn't look so young." And that worried me because I could hardly show any identification, could I? So I put on my dark glasses and let him do the registering.

And then we lay naked on our stomachs, ten floors up, and watched the Miss America finals on the television and tried to guess who'd win. Then Richard discovered he didn't have another condom.

"I hate those things. It's like making love with mittens on."

"Better than making something else."

"Go and get some, then."

"It seems such a lot of effort to put all those bloody clothes on again."

"I'm not going to get them."

"Oh, Christ." Then he looked at my tin of talcum powder and smiled. "I've got it."

104

"Got what?"

"The answer. I think. Wait a minute." He got up and took the powder and went into the bathroom and closed the door. I could hear water running in the basin and Richard laughing to himself. The man on the News said the temperature in greater Manhattan was 87 degrees. The traffic down below rushed on as though unaware of the dangers of hurrying in such heat. I wondered if Rosemary got my note and what Mama was doing just now. Maybe they were all sitting on the front porch waiting for a thunderstorm. Or maybe Daddy had gone for ice cream.

I wished I could just go forward with Richard forever.

"Richard!"

"Shan't be long."

"What are you doing?"

"Proving that necessity is the mother of invention." He came out smiling like a Cheshire cat.

"What are you up to?"

He showed me and we began to laugh.

"You're horrible."

"No. Just inventive. It should be all dry now. Doesn't it smell nice?"

"Get that away from me."

"Just think of it as a hand-me-down."

"You're disgusting."

"Do you really think so?"

"No. . . . Come here."

"Come where?"

"Here."

"All right. Here I come."

"Richard."

Mrs. Thing

There is a man who comes to suck my blood. He is very cheerful, and with all the other little tubes lined up in a wire mesh basket, which he sets cheerfully on my end table, he reminds me of nothing so much as the friendly neighborhood milkman. He jabs very quickly, but the needles are dull and I wince, which upsets him. "Please. I am very sorry."

105

Then he bends over my arm like a cavalier and begins. Afterwards the little dot of cotton and my arm gently folded back against the wound; a tiny label on my little tube, and off he goes. And sometimes I see him not as perverse milkman but as keeper of a strange greenhouse where exotic blood-colored plants stretch forward eagerly their parched drinking tubes. Or of an aviary where sunbirds hover and drink, for the tubes themselves are like the ones we used to fill with sugar-water for the hummingbirds.

I could never pick my blood from all the others, like the woman on the I.T.V. who couldn't tell real Stork from butter. "Death be not proud . . ." and blood be all alike, or I should say, be strong or weak, which is why Grace Abounding jabs me with her tin jackhammer once a day. Once the blood-collector showed me a little chart with colored circles, rather like a color chart from the paint store. Only all the circles were varying shades of red. Underneath there were percentages, and this is what we all are measured against. Imagine him sitting at his laboratory table playing his macabre game, fitting us all into his patterns, which are only correct to the nearest ten percentile.

Apparently the blood of the people does not clot very well; it is too "thin," whatever that means. Jason says that when the grass-cutters nick themselves with one of their machetes they bleed terribly, but he has seen Joseph cut himself preparing supper and simply go out and wrap "a certain leaf" around the place and the bleeding stops. I would like to find that leaf and wrap it tightly between my legs. What would Joseph think if I sent for some?

It is strange how much knowledge there is in the bush. The people wrap their meat in papaw leaves because they make it tender. And the departed Mrs. Maté told me, "Don't eat papaw now." Do they use it for abortion? I ask Dr. Biswas.

"They believe it can cause abortion. It is the same in my country."

"Is this true?"

He gives a delicate shrug. "It is quite possible. There is something in the juice which breaks down muscle fiber."

"Ugh."

"They are doing research now on many of these things. And," he adds, "what do you think meat tenderizer is made from? Have you ever looked?"

"No."

106

"Look next time."

"Tell me."

"Papaya. The same as papaw."

Mrs. Blood

Listen! The children are playing in the corridors and on the stairways:

> I am Zacharias
> I am Number One
> Number One stole the meat from the cookin' pot.
> Who, me?
> Yes, you
> Couldn't be!
> Then who?
> Number Two stole the meat from the cookin' pot.
>
> I am Zacharias
> I am Number Two

They must have seen a taxi or an ambulance drive up before the open courtyard down below. I hear them laughing, shouting. What Nicholas and Mary shout on the schoolbus, coming home:

> Monkey!
>   Banana!
>   Cocoyam!
>   Driver!
>
> Monkey!
>   Banana!
>   Cocoyam!
>   Driver!

Lie still and listen. There are children out there laughing in the corridors of pain.

Mrs. Thing

Do we lie horizontally for birth and copulation and death because then we are in closest harmony with the sky-roof above us and the earth-floor below? But who are "we"? The civilized, those most truly aware of and most truly out of touch with nature. The primitive woman squats down in the field in the same position she

107

uses to evacuate her bowels. Probably she is mounted from behind or standing up at least. She lies down just to die.

How strange we Europeans are, with everything going on beneath clean sheets. Why do Jason and I always turn the lights off when we make love? Why did we rarely—even before the children —make love in the daylight? Why have we never been able to make it standing up?

We women are the only females virtually always in heat, whose sexual apparatus faces out, not down. Was our pubic hair to protect us from thorns and underbrush and crawling insects? How strange that it should remain all these long years.

The old myths about the enormous size of the Negro's penis have been dissipated, but it is interesting that they ever got started; for this is a white man's myth—savagery, lust, enormous prowess and enormous appetite. "Like animals." Our lust has been intellectualized into love between the sheets, maybe once or twice a week and not at all if she doesn't feel like it. Nothing forced. All gentle. Yet often this is sham. Gentleness masks indifference, "love" masks the absence of desire.

Jason and I lusted after one another, briefly and beautifully, because we met in a winter when we both were lonely. Why couldn't we leave it at that? Why did I insist it was love? Why did I want a definitive scalp for my belt? Why is he not just a memory, like all the rest? Now we are linked together like some grotesque infant with two of everything except some vital piece—backbone perhaps. Our history prevents us from ever drawing apart: Mary, Nicholas, the past as "we," not he and I.

To shake hands and walk away swiftly in opposite directions— that would be the fine thing to do.

But that would leave Nicholas and Mary weeping, like the woodcutter's children, alone in the forest and prey for any witches who happened upon them weeping there.

Wedlocked to one another; and no keys.

People traveling in the same railway carriage rarely exchange addresses. Lovers should be like that.

Mrs. Blood

. . . IN 3 MONTHS
The official said that a total amount of 10,070 cedis 23
pesewas was collected on the old road as against 6,154 cedis

90 pesewas on the motorway in September. The corresponding figures for August were 27,595 cedis 89 pesewas on the old road and 8,663 cedis 70 pesewas on the motorway.

In October the old road yielded 25,585 cedis 72 pesewas and the motorway 8,665 cedis 25 pesewas, the official said.

He remarked that the ultramodern motorway, despite its fabulous cost and advantages over the old road, has proved less popular to the motoring public.

SLEEPING SICKNESS

Delegates from Liberia, Sierra Leone and Guinea have begun a conference in Monrovia, Liberia, to seek more effective ways to fight sleeping sickness.

The conference had originally planned to open last July.

Mr. Fagg asserted that Africans were influenced by the language of the country which colonized them. For example, the French-speaking African was rhetorical while the English-speaking African was pragmatic in expressing views on a problem.

BLACK LEGS

These reports indicate that the corporation harbours a number of black legs who do not like the people's enjoyment of real freedom and are, therefore, exerting themselves in every conceivable way to sabotage our revolution.

Since early this year, the reports allege, there has been a systematic suppression of programmes reflecting the spirit and aspirations of the great revolution. There has also been unnecessary reassignment of duties to and deployment of the senior staff to minor stations where their services will be least needed. . . .

We hold the view that the corporation needs a general cleanup which should be undertaken immediately and must be meticulously executed. We call on the government to act without delay.

FOR SALE

STEREO Bush gramophone with extension loudspeaker— C192.00 .10 Golf clubs and bag C 60.00. Tissot Watch—C 108.00. Liberman and Gortz binoculars C 48.00. Phone C. Newman, Nede 65699 Monday, October 20.

Wanted?

Selling or Buying?

Changing Your Name?

A

Daily News

SMALL AD—can help you.

Mrs. Thing

Today I stood up and walked over to the window for a minute. My feet seem terribly far away and most unreliable in relation to the heaviness which seems to envelop the rest of me. I remember Alice's debate about how she would send Christmas presents to her feet.

I wobbled dreadfully, but Esther was on one side and Alexandria on the other in case I fell.

I looked down from the window for the first time. How harsh the sunlight is, and the grass (because the rainy season has not yet ended) is a beautiful but almost vulgar green. The outside world seems very frightening somehow—the color and light are very demanding compared to the pale hospital greens and creams.

Alexandria says, "Soon you will be going home," and I can feel the fear-sweat pour down my back.

"I think I need a chair."

All sympathy, they rush to get a pillow and a chair while I cling to the windowsill and the room spins like the roundabouts we used to play on in the park.

Dr. Biswas came while I was sitting up. "Ah, but this is very good. I see you have taken my advice. How do you feel?" (He is not the beaming sort, but I could see how pleased he was.)

"Very weak. Dizzy. I nearly fainted by the window."

"But of course! You cannot lose a lot of blood and not use your muscles for many weeks and feel otherwise. That is to be expected. But is there any bleeding?"

"Not yet."

"Not yet! You are becoming very negative. What is the matter?"

"Nothing. I just don't believe it."

"You have become too introspective."

"Perhaps. Perhaps I have simply accepted the whole thing."

"What? That there will be more bleeding? Certainly that is possible. I told you the odds when you came here. You knew that long ago."

And the hateful tears begin. Esther and Alexandria are worried. Why am I crying? Dr. Biswas is obviously exasperated.

"But what is the matter?"

"Nothing. I don't know."

"I think," he gives me a traitor's smile, "it is time for you to go home."

"Home?"

"Yes. Tomorrow afternoon. That will give us twenty-four hours to observe you since your little walk. Then if all is well you can go home. Of course you must return if there is any change. Also I will give you some tablets, to be safely locked away, you understand; then, in an emergency, you will have something at hand for the pain. If you do not use them you must return them all to me; they are very dangerous."

"What are they? I don't like pills."

"You don't like pain, do you?"

"Would there be much pain?"

He shrugs. He has been operating and is not so attractive with the little green cap hiding his hair. "We call it a 'little labor.' It is not like the real thing, of course."

"Wouldn't you come out?"

"If I could, of course. But one cannot always time these things."

"I don't think I want to risk it."

"You are risking nothing. What will happen, will happen. It will probably do you much good. You must stay in bed at first, of course."

He looks at me intently from behind his heavy glasses. I see only an alien face—the face of the professional.

"I will come tomorrow morning and see you and sign the papers."

Esther and Alexandria help me back to my new-made bed. It is all so familiar now. I do not wish to pull up anchor, but just to drift quietly on the predictable waves of Senior Officials F-3. Nicholas will crawl all over me; Mary will ask too many questions; Jason will be busy with his work. And I will have to be nice to all those ladies.

And if I lose the baby? Screaming in an upstairs room, windows wide open against the heat, the compound listening and Jason losing face forever.

And if I stay? The contempt of Dr. Biswas (who is not stupid); the increasing disinclination to look out of the window at all; the hurt on Jason's face; the ladies amusement at my "peculiar" attitude (for everything is known, eventually).

111

I am a flower bent crooked by the wind. How is it possible to stand straight?

And my horoscope this morning:

Questions that have recently become a bit upsetting can now be settled to your satisfaction, and in the afternoon you will feel much happier. Chance of stimulating acquaintances.

But there are always the pills. If they work. Or the possibility that nothing at all will happen.

I must obey; but this time I will count the dead men and obey the warnings. And I will wear dark glasses against the sun.

Mrs. Blood

A precious mother is
Jane.
A voice we loved is stilled.
A place is vacant in our home which
never can be filled.
We cannot forget a dear
Mother like you.
Your kindness, love, advice, we
still long for:
The wound is still fresh in us.
May the Lord preserve you till
we meet.
REST IN PEACE

. . . .

RINGWAY HOTEL
Tonight
proudly presents
A New Programme
entitled
"The Mid-Month Blues"
featuring
RAMBLERS BAND
vs.
BLACK SANTIAGOS
from 9 P.M. to 4 A.M.

. . . .

112

Our usual Free
Saturday Afternoon
music for dancing and
listening pleasure comes
on today.

Gate Fee—FREE
Good Service, Drinkables.

. . . .

Award for finder of a State Insurance key holder containing
2 door keys and 1 safe key. 1 portmanteau key and a knife
left on back seat of a taxi in Nede. Should send it to nearest
Police Station or telephone 66943 Nede.

. . . .

DEVELOPING/PRINTING. THE DEO GRATIAS STUDIO.
High and Cathedral Streets junction. Nede.
Telephone 61321.

. . . .

You must get your day better organized so as to have time
to attend to your health.

. . . .

PEACE

He was for peace; he fought for it; and he actually achieved
it before he died.

. . . .

OPERA: 7:00 p.m. Jis Desh Men Ganga Behti Hail "A"
(*Indian film*).

I heard him talking to Mum the other day: he said he enjoys
banking with Barclays 'cos they offer such fine service.

He talked about all sorts of things they do. I can't remember
all of them 'cept travelers' checks which we got when we went
abroad.

> They can pick the *quality* drink even when blindfolded
> Reine
> Marie   A compliment of Fine Taste!

"Adam and Eve and Hitme were on a raft. Adam and Eve fell off.
Who was left?"

"Hitme."

"Ha. Ha."

113

PART TWO

"Is hell then, such a place to be dreaded? Thus, even admitting of an after-life in the bottomless pit, which I do not, hell would only be the paradise of those whom nature has created fit for it. Do animals repine for not having been created men? No. I think not. Why should we, then, make ourselves unhappy for not having been born angels."

OSCAR WILDE. *Teleny*

•

Mrs. Thing

I couldn't remember where we lived. The whole thing was a disaster. But to begin at the new beginning. Jason had said he would come at two o'clock. I was up and sitting on a chair at ten, when Dr. Shankar stomped by in his boots.

"What? Going home?"

"Yes."

"I wouldn't let you go if you were my patient. Still, good luck."

So that when Dr. Biswas arrived I was already shaken.

"Are you sure it's all right for me to go?"

He shrugged. "It will not make any difference one way or the other, I've already told you that. You have the pills?"

"Alexandria has gone down to the pharmacy to get them."

"Good. Remember to keep them out of the reach of your children. And if you do not use them you must return them to me. They are very dangerous." Then he smiled and shook my hand and told me to come to the clinic in two weeks. And went away.

Elizabeth and Grace Abounding stripped my bed and remade it and I sat on my hard metal chair feeling lost and redundant. At lunchtime I ate my lunch sitting up against the clean bed, my tray spread on newspapers to keep the bedspread clean. And I was lost and alone and remembered once waiting for my mother at some friend's house. My mother was late, and the other girl's mother was obviously impatient for me to be gone. Finally she said, "I'm sure you don't mind if Mary goes ahead and has her bath and supper," and I followed them upstairs and watched miserably from a chair that had been brought in from the bedroom while Mary had a bubble bath and then got into a quilted

117

bathrobe which was exactly like the one I wanted for Christmas—white, with little flowers on it—and then we went downstairs while she had her supper and I sat on another alien chair and was ignored completely. The mother's lips told me my mother was wrong to leave me so late and I felt ashamed and wistful; but even then (I must have been six, or seven at the most, for I remember running my tongue back and forth against the empty spaces where my teeth were out) I felt the other mother's attitude was cruel.

Mary had lamb chops and peas and mashed potatoes and a milk jelly molded like a rabbit for desert.

"I'd gladly feed you," Mary's mother said, "only I assume your mother will want you to eat at home."

And when my mother finally arrived and was apologizing and talking hurriedly to Mary's mother, I was so furious with her for humiliating me so that I burst into tears and rushed out of the door without even saying thank you.

Now I felt an even more irrational anger at Jason, who should have canceled his classes and come to get me early, not left me sitting here on this metal chair, making my back ache and leaving me exposed to the curious glances of all who came into the ward. Anger at Elizabeth and Alexandria and Grace as well, who went on with their routine—like Mary's mother—and didn't stop to talk.

Finally Staff Nurse came in and asked what time my husband was coming.

"Two o'clock."

"We have a patient for that bed. You will have to sit elsewhere. There is a chair on this side." She gestured toward the partition.

I had not walked farther than to the window and back. It seemed sadistic. Suddenly I'd had enough.

"I'll leave now."

"Par-don?"

"I said I'll leave now; I won't wait for my husband." My weak, little-girl's voice humiliated me still more. Did they really expect me to race around the ward, keeping out of their way like some lost puppy or lost child? And there were other beds in the ward. Why must it be my bed that was needed? If I had been Dr. Shankar's patient Staff Nurse would not have moved me. ("If you had been Dr. Shankar's patient," said my nasty inside self, "you would not be sitting here at all.")

"Tsk. Do you not wish to wait?"

"No. Can I get a taxi?"

"I don't think I can let you go alone. Dr. Biswas said explicitly your husband was to come for you. You are very weak."

"Let me call Dr. Biswas."

"Tsk. He is gone home until three o'clock."

"Let me call him at his home."

She shrugged. "If you wish. But I will call." (She is very possessive about "her" telephone. But I was glad, for my legs had begun to shake and I wasn't sure I'd make it to the desk. From where I sat I willed him to be at home and to say that I could leave this place. I felt now that I could hardly bear to stay another minute.) Her voice was contemptuous as she described the reason for her call. But he said yes, and on the strength of that—his obvious understanding of my position—I was self-possessed enough to walk firm-legged from the wheelchair to the waiting taxi. Elizabeth had wheeled me down.

"Good-bye for now. The next time I see you it'll be to get rid of this lump." She laughed.

"I hope so. Good-bye."

And then I was sitting back against the cushions and moving out away from the hospital. As on the day I came there were people everywhere—men, women, children, milling about like crowds of extras for some tropical extravaganza. And the vultures still wheeled above or waited silently on the rooftops.

I turned my face toward the road into town and gave the driver our new address.

Only of course I had the directions wrong and once we got to the compound I couldn't find the road. I explained to the driver that we had moved since I went into the hospital. He gave me a strange look, then shrugged and went back to the gate to ask directions. I am sure we passed some of the ladies who had come to visit me. What did they think when they saw me in a taxi? They must have known that Jason was supposed to pick me up. And what if the security officer should spread the story of how I didn't know my own way home? He and the driver were laughing and chatting in the vernacular, the driver blowing smoke rings with a professional air and twice pointing in my direction.

They were at lunch and Joseph was the only one who answered the honking of the horn. "Eh! Madame."

And then they were all there and Jason was helping me into the

house and Mary and Nicholas were shouting out their accumu-
lated news and there was a good smell of Joseph's bread and
roasted groundnuts and all I could think of to say was, "Thank
God it doesn't smell of Dettol."

Mrs. Blood

"You must arrange for a taxi," she said, "and get yourself there
in plenty of time. Of course if Father is home he won't mind taking you, but you don't want to count on that."

She went on polishing the silver for a while, then glanced at me.

"You really have to rub hard on that big plate."

I rubbed harder; the smell of the Brasso and the Silvo made my
head ache. And after lunch I went for a long walk and thought
about the taxi.

And on Boxing Day Jason had to work, so I went out to a
friend's with them for dinner and the woman said, "I *do* like your
dress."

And she said, immediately chiming in, "Yes, isn't it nice? Sweetly
pretty, I call it. Not like the awful old thing I wore when I carried
Jason. Same old wraparound thing day in, day out. I burned it the
day I came back from the convalescent home."

"I can just see you doing that!" the other one said, laughing.

"Rotten old thing it was," she said. "I hated it."

"This was a present," I said.

"What?" They all turned and looked at me.

"I said this was a present."

"Yes, and very nice too. It suits you."

And when we got into the car Father said, "Bloody awful trifle."

And she said, "Then what did you praise it for?"

"Oh, to make her feel good, you know, but it was nothing like
your trifles, dear."

And she said, "Well I just don't understand why you do these
things. Anyone would think it was the world's most magnificent
trifle to hear you talk."

"Well, it was bloody awful."

"I just don't understand you."

I took a lot of walks that winter, while Mary grew like spring-
time underneath my frozen heart.

Mrs. Thing

I lie in bed and listen to the morning sounds: Joseph calling to the next-door steward as he leaves his quarters. No. First the sound of Mr. Acquah's radio which he has left on all night in order to be awakened by the news. Da da de dum de dadda de dum. Good morning. This is the Overseas Service of the BBC. The announcer's adenoidal voice lifts and sinks as though he were, in fact, bobbing along on the ocean and giving the news, in heroic British fashion, as he fights the giant waves. Half past five. Jason says he is used to it now and can sleep through. But I am awake and tiptoe to the bathroom, sliding carefully from the bed to see if there is any blood on the sheets. None. I pat my belly as though to tamp the baby down and crawl back into bed. Now Joseph calling, *"Wo ho te sen, Wo ho te sen"* and laughing at something the other man has said. The key in the kitchen door and then the sound of Joseph chopping pineapple and oranges and grapefruit for our salad. The voices of nurse girls hurrying toward their charges. A lorry starts up across the compound and other radios have joined Mr. Acquah's.

The home news, in English, comes on at six o'clock, and at 6:15 there is what the papers call "patriotic music"—mostly marches.

Why should patriotism carry connotations of aggressiveness and marching feet? But it does, and that is why the "Star-Spangled Banner" is such a failure. It is impossible to march to it or even to sing it loud and quick.

The bottom louvers on our bedroom windows are painted national-police-blue and the sunlight against this reminds me of seeing once, or maybe only reading about it, yellow creamery butter in a blue bowl. At this hour the sun can still be contemplated with pleasure.

Jason turns over; his classes begin at 7:30. He always comes awake quickly, ready to meet whatever the day may bring.

"Hi."

"Hello. How are you this morning?"

"Fine. No complaints."

"Have you been awake long?"

"Since the BBC came on."

"Anything interesting?"

"Arsenal beat Blackpool, 3–Nil."

"Very interesting." He smiles because I can joke and have no complaints and he can leave the house with relative peace of mind.

Mary takes Nicholas down the hall to the toilet, and suddenly I am sad because they didn't come running in and obviously Jason has told them not to bother Mummy. Joseph comes up the stairs in his worn-out weekday sandals. Slap, Slap. Slap.

"Cock. Cock. Cock." He always knocks and says it at the same time.

"It's all right, Joseph," Jason calls. "We're up."

Joseph brings in my breakfast on a tray and Jason goes to dress the children. They come in and stand at the foot of the bed.

Mary has one very thick braid and one thin; Nikky has a button missing from his shirt; and I feel once again the maudlin tears— "poor little things"—behind my eyelids. Sometimes I think Jason does it (unconsciously, of course) on purpose. But that's not fair; he just never notices such things.

"Nikky's got a button off. Can you bring me my sewing kit?"

"Don't bother about it. It doesn't matter."

And Joseph calls up, "Master. Breakfast ready."

"It matters to me," I say.

"Please, Mummy, breakfast is ready." (Mary)

"O.K. O.K. But maybe after breakfast Joseph can bring Nikky back up and get him another shirt."

"I'll tell him."

Only of course Jason doesn't and I have to call down after Mary's gone on her bus and Jason has left in the car.

Nikky fidgets—he wants to go back to the kitchen where Joseph is letting him help with the bread. His bus doesn't come until half past eight. I smooth his hair and he shakes his head crossly from side to side in order to rough it up again. Am I like Frances Hare? Is there any difference between dear Trevor and dear Nicholas except a year of age? Jason has always said I fuss too much.

And yet, if they go with buttons missing and braids undone the ladies will discuss it over coffee. "Poor things. They *seem* very happy, of course, but you can see they need a mother's touch."

Or will it be the other.

"Isn't Jason just too marvelous? Mary always comes to school

122

with her hair done, and Nicholas, bless his heart, never loses any of his buttons."

"I wouldn't be surprised if Jason doesn't sew them on."

"He certainly is coping beautifully." But which way do I want it? What do I want? I resent all those who have not my cross to bear. Resent Jason particularly—his health, his happiness, his ability to be "one of them" so easily.

My morning euphoria has worn off and I push away my tray, toast and marmalade untouched, like some neurotic semi-invalid in the best ladies' magazine story tradition. All I need is the bed-jacket and a couple of bottles of medicine on the end table.

"Joseph!" But of course he is out by the road, with Nicholas, waiting for the bus.

Mrs. Blood

"Who's that playing the piano?" I asked.

And she said, "That's the poor little thing next door."

"Why is she a poor little thing?" I asked, thinking maybe it was because she couldn't afford piano lessons.

"Mongoloid," she said, "poor little creature."

I turned another page of the photo album. "August," it said, "1939, with Derek and Jessica in Devon." Short curled hair and polka-dotted dresses. Prewar smiles. And all over Europe there must have been summer snapshots analogous to this one.

"How old is she?" I asked.

"Five," she said. "She's a dear little girl, really. Perfectly beautiful blonde hair. You'll probably see her before you go—she often plays in the garden. Her parents try to treat her as much like a normal child as possible."

But after tea, when I was picking some raspberries at the bottom of the garden and heard the thud of a ball and a rather guttural cry, I closed my eyes and looked the other way.

"The one blessing is," she said as we poured hot paraffin over the rows of ruby jars, "that they rarely live past the age of twenty."

I heard the piano several times after that and imagined the huge soft head bent intently over the keyboard.

. . . .

123

"When I had you," Mama said, "they put a bit of gauze over my eyes. I think they did it always, then. Just to make sure everything was all right, you know, before they let the mother see her baby."

"Oh my God!"

She was offended. "Frankly I think it was a good idea."

You would.

Mrs. Thing

This afternoon we went to a children's party. All the parents were invited as well—"Dear Mary and Nicholas, Saturday 4–6, bring Mummy and Daddy"—and this seemed very strange to me. I wanted to stay home; I have become almost neurotic about not exerting myself more than absolutely necessary, and too many people know my history. Mary M. told me it doesn't hurt to be too careful. "After I had my second miscarriage Roger wouldn't even let me go to the toilet when I was carrying Gillian." And if she, rugged, capable, cope-able, who could drive to the doctor's with her child's bitten-off tongue on the seat beside her, feels that way then somehow it must be the right way to feel. Jason, too, is very nervous. I can see him watching me. I think he would have preferred it if I'd stayed in hospital. Little Mrs. Hare sent around a mackintosh sheet last night, "just in case," and Jason was both frightened and horribly embarrassed. Now if I'd only broken my leg or been bitten by a snake! It was his oversolicitude, plus Mary's pleading, that finally decided me to go.

And it really was an impressive party. The Birds have a large, sprawling house off the compound, and Mollie Bird, who had come to see me once in hospital, has some sort of home economics degree.

The children sat on low cushions on the veranda and gawked at a long cake made like a train—the sort of thing one sometimes sees in magazines but knows better than to try. There were four or five different kinds of cookies and Fanta or Sprite as well as sandwiches. Beer or tea and sandwiches for all the "mummies and daddies." It was the best children's party I have ever seen. "Of course," said Mollie, in answer to someone's praise, "I've got Emmanuel to help me." But even with an Emmanuel (or my beloved

124

Joseph) to fetch more cushions and an Emmanuel's son to mop up spilled drinks and show the children where the toilet is, I could never stay calm with such a crowd.

And Mollie is pregnant as well; and a newcomer, like me. Already she seems to know half the compound and stopped to tell me I *must* come to the Thursday coffee morning—"I'll take you next week." The women in smart summer dresses which many had "run up" themselves, the men in bush shorts talking departmental politics; the children in hair ribbons and cool dresses or clean shorts: all kept animated and amused by Mollie's organization.

"How do you *ever* do it!" called out one woman as Mollie bustled past with an empty plate. "The shortages!"

"Oh, I brought things out, you know. And my mother sends me things."

The woman looked at her friend and you could see them giving Mollie an A+ for planning. "One of us."

What did we bring? Six pastel nighties for me, half a trunk of books, summer clothes for all of us (*one* pair of sandals each!) and sheets, bedding and dishes. The women laugh at Frances Hare, who brought a silver tea service and thirty yards of the best nylon marquisette for curtains as well as an attitude which can only be described as "old-colonial"; but they, farsighted and practical, brought the really "necessary" things for social survival here:

Christmas presents and Christmas crackers, dried fruits for cakes, tins of yeast for bread, birthday presents and birthday favors in enormous quantities, not to mention at least a year's supply of contraceptives and several pairs of shoes for all the family. I have listened to their talk; I know. I am not a practical person but why did Jason not consider these things? "The woman's role."

I was a romantic and Jason has never believed in buying more than you absolutely need. This was a very *English* children's party, in spite of the open veranda and Emmanuel and his son and the fans sluggishly churning the hot and scented air. Perhaps, then, Jason would see it as all wrong—a transference of the old environment rather than an assimilation of the new.

Why not fresh fruit salad and some local sweets? But I know the answer to that one. We all have fresh fruit salad every day and the local sweets are hideous imitations of European candies: over-sweet and violent in color.

Jason, on the way home: "What an incredible party!"

Nicholas: "I want a cake like that for my birthday, Mummy."

And Mrs. Hare, to me, just before she left: "Dear Trevor has had *such* a good time this afternoon! I think we must have a little party for *him* very soon. Would you like that, my darling?" And dear Trevor scuffed his shoes against the cement floor ("Don't do that, pet") and said nothing.

Then they went off, Hugh smiling back at the people he'd been talking to and giving a little cynical shrug. How strange they are, Frances and Hugh, and the child like a shock absorber between them. Each despises the other, and they don't pretend otherwise, as many couples do. Sabina Sutcliffe told me that when she and Roland met them at the airport Frances' first words were, "Well, we're *determined* to make a go of it."

Of what? Their marriage, Africa or dear Trevor? And why did *we* come?

Mrs. Thing

As we moved toward Banff the little Scottish lady kept saying, "Which one is Mt. Eisenhower?" and I wondered if there were many mountains named for women.

"Can you think of any mountains named for women?"

And he said, "Not right off. But lots of lakes."

"Do you think that's symbolic?"

"What?" He was studying the guide.

"That lakes are named for ladies and mountains are named for men."

He shrugged. "More famous men than famous ladies."

"There," he said to the old lady across the aisle. "It's the one coming up now, on your left."

"Did you know 'Alp' means 'nightmare'?" I said.

"Whatever made you think of that?" he said, and then, "Mary, tie Nikky's shoelace, can you?"

And then silence while the mountains drew us in.

And at Banff he took the children off to stretch their legs. I gazed at them wistfully through the glass window of our compartment. "How do you feel?" he asked, when they got back on.

126

"Hungry."

"Come on, then," he said to the children, "let's drag the old bat to the dining car."

"I want ice cream," Mary said.

"Me too."

"You look a picture," said the old lady, passing us on her way out. "Such nice wee kiddies."

"Thank you," we said and smiled at her over our ice creams.

But why did I think of Alp? Another sign. The nightmare was a woman. Mountains are named for men. There are no mountains in this country and just one lake. Jason has been down to it. "You'd never make it," he said firmly when I asked if I could go.

Mrs. Blood

How long does it take for the blood in a dead man's veins to dry? Full fathoms five thy father lies. And if drowned, or buried at sea, how long then? Does it all dry up like unused ink in inkwells or does it lie in the lakes and tributaries of the body like stagnant water?

"All I know is," she said, "I hope they slash my wrists before they put me in the coffin."

Strange that your fingernails should grow—as though to help you claw your way out.

Why do we bury them lying down? They do not sleep.

And the rains here are enormous, devastating. How far down must they dig in order to feel secure?

I do not wish to be washed up and floated down to the town.

"Well, I don't care how it comes so long as it's quick," she said.

Then, "What are you laughing at?"

Mrs. Blood

"Listen," he said. "Harry says you weren't invited to the party."

"I was so. Ruth-Ann asked me."

"But it's Harry's party, really; it's at his house."

"It's Ruth-Ann's party too—she said so. Harry and Sheldon and Carla and Ruth-Ann. That's what she said."

"I dunno. Harry says you weren't invited."

"Do you want to go with me or not?"

His dark, worried face met hers.

("But isn't he Jewish?" Mama asked.

"So what?" But she could see her Mama thinking—poor little thing—and her eyes behind the glasses were going all red and watery.)

"No," he said. "Harry says you weren't invited."

And at 12 years old she wrote in her diary, "I want to die."

Mrs. Thing

Mrs. Kodzo, who lives next door, beats her servants. The first time I woke up in terror.

"Jason!"

"Wha?"

"Jason. Wake up!" And he sat up and listened with me to the sound of the nurse girl weeping and the thud of a body being flung against the wall. "Auntie! Auntie!"

"She's being beaten up!"

"I know. It's happened before."

"Can't we do something?"

"What? It's not our business."

"She'll kill her."

"No, she won't."

And for what seemed like hours we sat there uneasily while the girl screamed, "Auntie! Auntie!" and her body hit the wall. The drums from the villages near the compound were celebrating or mourning birth, death, what? And I felt alien and afraid and remembered how we had both misconstrued the sign outside the petrol station:

REX. 8:30 TONIGHT.
PAY UP OR DIE.

The next morning I heard the nurse girl laughing and giggling as she waited for the nursery school bus with one of Mrs. Kodzo's many children.

When Joseph comes up to take my tray I ask him about it.

"Good morning, Madame. How is your body?"

"Fine. Joseph, you know Evelyn?"

"Sa. Yes, Madame."

"She was beaten up last night."

Joseph smiles, almost with relish it seems to me. "Yes, Madame."

"Do you know why?"

"Somethin' to do with Mr. Kodzo, I think, Madame."

"I see."

He picks up the tray. "That girl." He shakes his head. "She's no good, no good at all."

"But it is not good to beat other people up."

"No, Madame."

I hear him talking to himself as he goes back downstairs. "No good—at all." And laughing.

Mrs. Blood

"Is that the one you want, love? Mother and I thought perhaps a more portable model."

"No. If it's all right with you I'd really like that one."

"Right you are, then; I'll see about it in the morning. Half a minute while I get my pencil. Ah. Here we are. What d'you think, Mother?"

"Very nice, dear. It's a very pretty pram."

"Well, we said we'd do it and you ought to have a good pram to start out with. I'll get them to deliver it next week."

"Oh, Fath!" she said, putting down her needle "*No,* dear. You can't do that!"

"Why not? We could keep it in the passage."

"Oh, it's not *that,* dear. It's . . . well . . . nobody has expensive things like prams delivered until the baby's born. Nobody. You mustn't do it, Father dear." She picked up her work.

"What? Why? Oh. I see." He stood there, awkward, the catalogue in his hand.

"Well, I'll order it, shall I? It's all right to do that, isn't it?"

"Perfectly all right, lovie. I should if I were you. If you have to go into town tomorrow it would be a good time to see to it."

He nodded, relieved. "Well, there you are, love," he said. "It's all settled, then."

And Jason, back late, eating his warmed-up supper in the sitting room. Listening at the bedroom door.

"I don't know, dear. She said she was tired. I expect she's fast asleep by now."

Rest of the World News:

BABY HAD FOUR ARMS

Vera D, born two years ago with four arms and four legs, is reported to have become a sociable gay and quite normal baby after work by a Soviet surgeon, according to Tass.

"My little patient is quite all right and feels fine," Tass quoted the surgeon, Professor Yuri Gelevich, as saying in the North Caucasus town of Stravropol.

As well as four arms and four legs, Vera was born with two bowels, two pelvises and five kidneys and a second, smaller trunk without head or heart.

She was operated on in Stravropol last May. According to the surgeon she is now quite a normal girl and has only a scar left to mark her former deformity.

Mrs. Blood

Somebody had brought a bottle of champagne and somebody else had given us a bunch of flowers and both our folks had sent telegrams, so we felt terribly grown-up and chic and drank far too much of course (because we'd bought a bottle of champagne as well, just in case) and thought it was terribly funny when the cork popped out and hit one of the boys right in the eye. And Stanford (Rosemary's boyfriend) almost didn't get off the boat at all and had to run like crazy because they'd already started to pull the gangplank up. And he said to me, "Take care of Rosemary, won't you?" which really burned me up, because (a) I knew Rosemary wouldn't take orders from me, and (b) I was rather sweet on him myself.

And really we were rather glad when they'd all gone, even Stanford, and the ship began to move. We stood on the deck and waved in a superior manner and as soon as we thought it decently possible we turned away from those tiny waving figures and went down below to sort out where everything was and to see if there were any interesting people on board.

And the ship got caught in the tail end of Hurricane Judith but we never missed a meal.

You can take anything when you're young.

The night it struck we went back to the cabin after a party, and Rosemary's trunk had fallen down; and her coat, which had been shut in by mistake, had all the bottom part ripped off. The dresser was a shambles. But we just laughed and laughed because it was a real adventure, and besides, you can take anything when you're young.

Mrs. Thing

Every morning Jason went in to the College on the train and every evening he came back at eight. I would hear the whistle and sometimes I would go down to the station to meet him. But it was a bad road to cross in the dark and I was afraid of getting knocked down. I kept forgetting and looked the wrong way and cars would suddenly spring up at me like animals.

The twelve hours in between were a deep pit into which I threw whatever I could find: reading, walking, sleeping. I learned to really sleep that winter. But the alternatives were too oppressive. I had no energy, no joy, no ambition. It was as though, when he left the house, he took the real me with him and I was just a stand-in, waiting in another person's part.

Usually she only lit the fire in the breakfast room and I would huddle there, waiting until I could decently go upstairs and take a nap. (She had all the housework done by "elevenses.")

I was very cold that winter and finally got terrible chilblains from sitting too close to the fire.

We left Jason's plate of dinner warming for him in a saucepan, the heat turned low.

I felt as though I were simply bobbing in the water, keeping my head up, waiting to be rescued.

And that was the first winter of my discontent.

Mrs. Blood

"When I was young and full of ragery." Buxom Alison, middle-aged and still obsessed with her *belle chose*. But no mention of any children in spite of all those husbands.

When I was young and full of ragery, I borrowed a shilling from my love just so I could wonder at the beauty of his skin while he was sleeping.

When I was young and full of ragery Jason and I were having lunch in his parents' garden. There was something beautiful, with bread and red currants. "Summer pudding," he said it was. And hungry, we ate all the cold meat and all the bread and butter and every bit of summer pudding and then lay together on the well-kept lawn oblivious to the back-bedroom windows of the other houses along the row.

And when his parents returned I cried, "I did enjoy the lunch!" And Jason had a sudden fit of coughing.

· · · ·

"Bloody awful trifle," he said, backing cautiously down the drive.

And she said, "May you be forgiven!"

· · · ·

And Richard jammed the compartment door shut and stood against it, oblivious to the irate looks of people getting on. And then he fixed his coat against the glass and said, "I've never made love between Oxford and Watford Junction."

And I said, "What if somebody comes?"

And he laughed and said, "What if?"

When I was young and full of ragery.

· · · ·

"Avez-vous du pain?"

Mrs. Thing

Two days after I got home with Mary I dreamed that I knocked over the pram or let it go, while I was out walking; and the baby's head came off and rolled out into the road, where it was crushed by an oncoming car. I was very frightened about that dream and woke Jason up and told him.

"It was just a dream," he said; "go back to sleep." In a minute or two he was breathing heavily again.

But I sat awake, hugging my knees and willing myself not to get up and check the baby, who was sleeping in the next room.

It was no good, and finally I tiptoed out into the cold hall and

132

down to Mary's room, where of course she was sound asleep in her carry-cot on Jason's old bed.

But she heard me and poked her head in. "Is anything the matter dear?"

And then he, too, yawning and crumpled in his striped pajamas, "What's the matter, Love?"

And I said, "Nothing. I just felt like checking on the baby."

And he said, "Is something the matter with her, then? What's the matter with her?"

And I said, "Nothing. I'm going back to bed now."

And she gave me a strange look and later I heard her say, "Well, I'm wide awake now. Make us a cup of tea, Father, there's a darling."

And Jason slept on. Innocent. Untroubled. After a while I stopped telling him about my dreams.

Mrs. Blood

I am covered with memories like barnacles. Weighed down, encrusted with them so that only the vague outline of my original shape remains.

Going through the culvert, Papa would honk his horn loudly and the sound would bounce back at us, and Papa for once would drive like hell.

Sometimes we would go and see Aunt Deveena, who wasn't really an aunt at all but grandfather's second cousin and very old and who lived in a rickety frame house with her niece and her niece's husband who wore real farmer's overalls and never said much.

We would drink raspberry vinegar and scuff our shoes against the porch railing until Mama had finished talking to the old lady and Papa had had a smoke or maybe a few buttermilk cookies, which he loved.

But mostly we would go straight to the cemetery and play in the tall grass or try to make out all the old names and dates while Papa dug the geraniums into the ground beneath my grandma's stone. And Mama would complain that Alfred was supposed to cut the grass more often and father really ought to get after him.

There were four little stone lambs near grandma's grave and

some near other graves. They were the graves of babies who had died.

But, you know, it wasn't a sad place there. I liked the tiny village and the tall sweet grass and the smell of geraniums on my fingers.

We made daisy chains for the lambs and played in the tall grass until Mama said it was time to go.

The old lady had an ear trumpet—black, with silver-gilt decorations on it.

"Hello!" we would shout. "Hello, Aunt Deveena!"

And she would smile and nod, rocking back and forth in the cool, slightly musty parlor.

Then we could go outside and have our raspberry vinegar and maybe some buttermilk cookies from a jar shaped like a little pig.

"She sure appreciates your stoppin' by," the niece would say as we got back in the car and turned around toward home.

Mrs. Thing

Sometimes I would let a mosquito settle on my arm and watch it suck and grow heavy with my blood. Only to kill it at the last minute. But we knew, of course, the mosquitoes carried no sickness there. Here we cower under nets or screens and take our Sunday-Sunday medicine. Only a madman would offer his flesh to a mosquito here.

The ants bite and puff adders hang from trees and spit your eyes out like snuffing candles. The landscape drips with poison. You can take the skin right off your lips with just one chili pepper.

Don't touch the dogs—they may be rabid—and never let a child run barefoot through the grass.

Always roll up the windows of your car and put Dettol on even the smallest cut.

"And Dr. Ansah said, 'Oh, ho! You've got tropical ping-pong.' And Roland said, 'Why do you call it that?' And he said, 'Well it is passed back and forth, you know, from the man to the woman and so on and so on and so on.' And Roland said, 'How do I get rid of it?' And Dr. Ansah said, 'You use this ointment and I'll give you a prescription for a certain powder.' And Roland said, 'Is that all?' And Dr. Ansah said, doing something with the papers

on his desk, 'Not quite. There are some pills you both must take
and there must be no drinking and no sexual intercourse during
the treatment.' And Roland said, 'I'd rather have the itch.' "

"He didn't!"

"Yes, he did."

"What did Dr. Ansah say?"

"I think he was rather shocked, you know. I told Roland he was
naughty."

"Jean Harmon has it," Sabina added. "She says it's horrible."

"Ugh. It's amazing what you can get out here, isn't it?"

"Roger has dengue."

"Does he?"

"Yes, he does. Mary told me at the post this morning."

"Would anybody like more coffee?"

"Both the Ames children have malaria."

"Aren't they Christian Scientists or something like that?"

Mrs. Blood

> **grāve**[1], *n.* Excavation to receive corpse, mound or monu-
> ment over it (secret as the ~), OE *graef* (*grafan*
> GRAVE[2])
> **grāve**[2], *v.t.* (p.p. ~n, ~d, as stated), carve, sculpture, en-
> grave; (fig.) fix indelibly (on, in mind, etc.; ~n, ~d).
> [com-Teut; OE *grafan*, *cf.* Du. *graven*, C. *graben*, deg.
> cogn. w. groove]
> **grāve**[3], *a. & n.* 1. Important, weighty, needing serious
> thought, (of faults, difficulties, responsibilities, symp-
> toms) formidable, threatening, serious, dignified, solemn,
> slow-moving, not gay; sombre, plain, not showy, hence
> ~ly (-vl-), *adv.*
> 3. *n.* ~ accent. [F, f.L *gravis*, heavy, serious.]
> **grāve**[4], *v.t.* Clean (ship's bottom) by burning off accretions
> and tarring while aground or in graving-dock. perh. f. OF
> *grave* = *grève*, shore
> **grāvid,** *a.* (literary). Pregnant. f.L *gravidus* (GRAVE[3])
> Thou shalt not make to thyself any graven image . . .
> "You are very ill," he said gravely. "You are gravely ill."
> And the grave will decay you
> And turn you to dust
> Not one man in fifty
> A poor girl can trust.
> **grieve**[1], *v.t. & i.* Give deep sorrow to; feel grief (*at, for,*
> *about, over*). [f.F *grever* f.L *gravare* (*gravis, heavy*)]

"Avez-vous du pain?"

Mrs. Blood

People's voices are like doors. Elizabeth's—heavy, carved, ebony maybe, swinging slowly inward. Dr. Biswas—tinkling and full of motion—the bead curtains in Mediterranean bars.

Mary M.—good English oak, solid, dependable, attractive too.

Mary and Nicholas—stretched muslin or canvas, temporary and full of sunlight.

Jason—a vault. You have to know the combination. Frightening if you can't remember. (Reassuring if you can.)

Dr. Shankar—heavy, and often slammed. The door to something official.

Frances Hare—very ornamental, full of scrolls and arabesques. Suspect somehow, and possibly a false front.

Me? Bamboo or paper stretched on balsa wood. Fragile, impractical, easily broken.

And the doors swing out (come in) or back (stay out) and it is difficult to move along the corridors, the door-filled corridors, and remember what to say and how much pressure to apply.

And there are doors that open for you once but not again.

Richard: "There is no nice way of saying this." And the door closed gently in my face.

Later, knocking, a voice said from the distance, through a door above a jeweler's shop on Goodge Street, "Go away."

Mrs. Blood

O merciful God, giver of life and health, bless, we pray thee, thy servant N. and those who administer to *him* of thy healing gifts, that *he* may be restored to health of body and of mind, through Jesus Christ our Lord. *Amen.*

In my father's house there are many mansions: if it were not so, I would have told you.

I heard a voice from heaven, saying unto me, Write.

From henceforth blessed are the dead who die in the Lord: even so saith the Spirit; for they rest from their labors.

O spare me a little, that I may recover my strength, before I go hence, and be no more seen.

As occasion demands, the Minister shall address the sick person on the meaning and use of the time of sickness, and the opportunity it affords for spiritual profit.

Minister.	O Lord, save this woman thy servant
Answer.	Who putteth her trust in thee.
Minister.	Be thou to her a strong tower
Answer.	From the face of her enemy.
Minister.	Lord, hear our prayer.
Answer.	And let our cry come unto thee.

"What's *that?*" I said.

"Tsk," said the night nurse, letting down the nets. "A certain animal. He lives in the bush."

"It sounds like a baby crying."

"Tsk," she said. "It is only this animal."

"I don't like it."

She smiled and moved to the next bed.

And I dreamed I had left my baby at the top of a coconut palm and he wept against the darkness and cried out to me.

When I awoke it was dawn.

Mrs. Thing

I suppose I should be grateful that this happened here. Joseph makes the breakfast, Joseph makes the lunch and dinner, Joseph makes the beds and washes clothes (bent over the bathtub, a bar of Sunlight in his hand, rhythmically scrubbing, kneading the clothes almost the way he kneads the bread). He takes Nicholas to the bus and fetches Nikky and Mary off the bus at lunchtime. I don't have to lift a finger if I don't want to. Breakfast in bed, and then the cheerful sound of someone else putting my house in order. At ten o'clock he makes me coffee and brings it up. If Jason is having coffee at the club, Joseph leans on his broom and talks to me—usually about the news of the world (his last employers gave him a beautiful transistor radio), sometimes about his attempts to find a new wife.

"Hey, Madame, how is your body?" But he knows, of course, that all is well because he does the sheets.

Sometimes I think what chaos there would be at home—and what expense. Jason doing as much of the housework as he could; Nikky hanging around my bed, even if we could find a baby-sitter; Mary starting school—lunches to be fixed, teachers to see, the whole complex superstructure of our lives eventually toppling around our ears. Debt, unhappiness, bitterness. What is it Pa has said to Jason and me on various occasions? "You don't know how lucky you are."

I get up for lunch and then talk to Jason and read the mail while the children nap. Afterwards he takes them to the pool and I sit, feet up, on the veranda, and close my eyes and will everything to be all right.

All that long trip—the great train ride, then the visit, then the boat, then the visit, then the boat and then the bumpy ride up from the coast. What if? "You don't know how lucky you are." Once Jason mentioned this himself, "I guess if something had to go wrong . . ."

But if we had not come at all?

And Mollie Bird, healthy and bovine, comes to see me. "Did *you* have yellow fever shots?"

And I discover pregnant women don't have yellow fever shots. "I didn't know then."

"I expect everything will be all right. You look much better." I try to be polite—she's very kind—but her activity makes me guilty and annoyed, too, because I don't want to make any extra effort to be more than the steady cage for my fragile bird. I sit very still, until the sweat running down my legs turns to blood in my imagination and I have to go and look. It is impossible to relax.

She wants me to go to her coffee morning tomorrow. It's at her house.

"Go on," says Jason; "maybe it will do you good."

"I don't have any energy to be polite."

"I'm sure they'll understand that."

"I'm afraid."

He gives me one of his politely incredulous looks. "Did the doctor say you couldn't go out? I thought *he* thought you'd be better out of the sickroom atmosphere. You've got to relax and just take what comes."

138

"I'm not afraid of *that,*" I mutter defensively.

"What, then?"

"I don't know." But I do know. Ladies' groups. Being judged. The contrast between myself and Mollie. My obvious frailty.

("My dear, why would a woman like *that* even *want* to come out here?"

"I feel sorry for her."

"I don't. She'd do herself a lot more good if she'd get out a bit and stop sitting at home and thinking about it. You can cause these things to happen, you know."

"Jason certainly copes magnificently!"

"Doesn't he? And Nathan says he's awfully good with the students."

"It must be hard on him."

"It must.")

"Afraid of what, then?"

"Nothing. I don't know. Perhaps you're right."

And Jason gives me his "good girl" look and says he'll come and get me at the break tomorrow and pick me up after classes.

The order of our life here has deceived him. I resent the pride which forces me to accept his offer.

So now I sit on the veranda and close my eyes, listening to the steady thump of the fu-fu pounders (Joseph and the others preparing their evening meal) and feel vicariously the merciless sun which beats down like the fu-fu pounders, forcing the landscape to submit to its demands.

Already the hibiscus flowers in the sitting room are dying. They have opened too early and too wide and all their energy has been sucked out by the sun. Blood red, they float limply in the tepid water and wait for night.

A platoon of soldier ants is crossing the garden. I get up and with my foot I push a stone in the middle of the line. There is a moment's confusion and then they re-form and become two lines moving purposefully around the rock.

Nothing will stop them. Whatever drives them is bigger than my stone. The veranda floor is concrete and Mary has been drawing pictures on it with her chalks.

"You don't know how lucky you are."

Mrs. Thing

At Freetown we took a bus tour of the city. There was an enormous silk-cotton tree on the way up the hill to the Parliament building.

And at the museum we looked at masks and faded photographs of important events in the city's history. I couldn't concentrate because the heat and the noises and the smells were so new and so exciting. It was impossible to particularize in any way. What was important was not the fertility dolls or stylized masks arranged so carefully in their glass cases, but me, being there in Freetown with Jason, and breathing African air. I felt as though I were a diver about to begin a slow descent in search of treasure. I took deep breaths and was impatient to submerge.

The museum and its artifacts were not the treasure I was looking for. I wanted to walk in the crowd and feel the pressure of living Africa.

Children followed us out—there were about twenty of us, some Nigerians and Ghanaians who had been in Britain and were returning home—demanding pennies.

"Hey, you give me penny?"

"Hey, are you from Chicago, Illinois?"

"Hey, I will show you this fine, fine city. Come with me." Laughing, cheeky. It was too good-naturedly aggressive to be called begging.

Then to the arts and crafts exhibit which was terrible. Realism at its worst and with no feeling.

"Coffee-bar art," one of the women said, looking at a large painting of an African girl smilingly holding out bananas. Jason was upset by the exhibition. I could feel him thinking, "This is what we have done," and wondering if *that* was what he was supposed to teach his students.

At the Parliament building we peered in at the legislative chamber (vacant then) and smiled at the five seats, separated, for the opposition, and the top sheets of the official stationery in the library were tan with dust and disuse. These things did not really interest me.

But on the way back (we were very late and the driver drove like hell—Jason and I were worried because Mary and Nicholas

140

had stayed on the boat with friends) it began to rain, and some of the Africans, sitting by the broken windows, calmly raised their umbrellas and continued talking.

For the great, beneficent silk-cotton tree and the umbrellas inside the bus the trip was worth it.

"Happy?" Jason asked.

"I can't wait to get there," I said.

And Mr. and Mrs. Mackie, who had been out in Lagos for years, said, "Once you've had a taste of Africa, you know, it's always in your blood."

That night, while Mary and Nicholas slept in their flannel pajamas in the air-conditioned cabin, Jason and I walked the steamy decks and talked about the future.

Mrs. Blood

The skins of the fathers shall be visited upon the children.

Cast your dead upon the waters.

"I don't know," she said miserably. "I don't think there's anything I can do about it. I don't mind belonging to the club and all that but I can't dance with them." Only the way she pronounced it, she said "ah doan know" and "ah doan mind." And I thought enviously that surely that must be the prettiest accent in the world.

She was pretty, too, "real pretty."

Rosemary said, "I ought to hate her, but really I feel sorry for her—it's not her fault."

"She shouldn't join the club at all, then. It's too obvious."

And the woman came red-faced and furious out of the room and told me, "You can go in and get felt up by that black man if you like, love, but I'm going to have a proper English doctor or I'm not comin' back at all. I think it's disgusting. I do really."

And when it was my turn I went in and quickly got up on the table. But I couldn't look him in the eye because I'd heard the shouting before the other woman came out and I knew if I looked at him I'd cry.

And I wanted to say to him, "Once I put an extra shilling in the gas—and I was poor—just to lie beside a man like you and marvel at his skin while he was sleeping."

He had large hands, and he hurt me, but I couldn't say anything about that either. Perhaps his hands were rougher, too, because they remembered what the woman had said.

"I think it's disgusting, I do really." And she stomped off to the administration office.

Mrs. Blood

They used to show movies in the dining room, because it was such a small boat, you know, and not one of your fancy Cunard ships. Really ancient movies—"Trilby," "Lifeboat,"—I can't remember the others.

The chief dining-room steward ran the projector and we all crowded in, even the passengers from the first class, because they were bored and would rather sit through the thing again than talk to one another.

Then after the sandwiches and coffee were passed around we'd sneak off to the crew's quarters for a while. Or sometimes up on deck, just smoking and talking and looking off into the darkness. Happy. Young. Adventurous.

And once behind the lifeboats, saying to the Irish boy Mattie, "I'm not that kind of girl," and wishing I didn't have to say it.

In a way it was easier once we hit the hurricane because we were only allowed on the deck in daytime and then only if we held onto the ropes.

The chief steward said that women leave their morals at the bottom of the gangplank, but he was talking to the doctor, at the bar, and the remark was addressed to everybody in general. Actually, he liked us very much because we treated him as something more than servant and teased him about his liver.

Once he showed us some awful pictures of an appendicitis operation they'd had to do on top of two of the dining tables pushed together. And some other pictures of a sailor being buried at sea. Just his coffin, covered in the Union Jack, about to be pushed over the side. That was on the Mediterranean run, he said. He was always trying to scare us.

And Rosemary, trying to get comfortable one night, said, "I wonder what it's like to make love in one of these goddamn bunks. I'm not sure I'd want to spend my honeymoon on a ship."

"I think they usually go away a few days first."

"Imagine if *he* got seasick. I think that might be worse."

"My cousin got her period the morning of her wedding."

"God. How awful."

"She cried and cried and wanted to call the whole thing off, but the doctor gave her something to stop it."

"What?"

"I don't know." We lay there, contemplating the wonders of modern science. The little ship rocked heavily from side to side. I wondered if Rosemary had ever gone all the way. "Rosemary?" But she was asleep. Probably not. She didn't have to.

Mrs. Blood

And the next day the director yelling at her—you could hear him all down the corridor—"You're not insane, you're just promiscuous!"

But she wouldn't have anything to do with the baby, you know, so she must have been crazy, mustn't she?

"My dear little buttercup," said Mrs. Karensky, over the cottage pudding, "she's crazy like a fox."

Mrs. Blood

Grandpa kept Sears Roebuck catalogues in the outhouse and we liked to read them together, giggling over the ladies in their corsets and the peculiar long underwear for men. Sanitary napkins in bulk, douche bags, curious attachments for people who wet the bed.

The outhouse smelled bad and bugs banged against the little half-moon window Grandpa had added as a joke.

Nobody ever ordered anything from Sears that we could remember. Yet each summer there was a new catalogue and we would fight over who'd get first dibs to look at it.

Only Grandpa had always attached the catalogue to the wall with heavy cord so of course you had to read it in the outhouse. I still can't put a catalogue in the sitting room.

And on the outside, because it was the war, you know, he had nailed up a sign he got from some gas station in town.

IS THIS TRIP NECESSARY?

Mrs. Thing

I went to Mollie's coffee morning. There were maybe ten of us. Sabina Sutcliffe I knew, and Mollie of course, and most of the others I had seen at Mollie's children's party.

The food was beautiful: various sandwiches and some real Stilton cheese with biscuits and a "gateau cake" as the English call them. Again I heard the exclamations, "I don't know *how* you do it," "My dear Mollie, you are incredible!" and so on. Which she is, of course. Because most people give up trying to create elaborate baked goods—there are too many shortages.

The women talked about stewards, and the University school which is considered rather déclassé and most seem to send their children to Hillside school which is private and has "very high standards, my dear." Also, one assumes, fewer Africans and fewer African teachers. (I later find out none.) I was surprised to hear that Mary M. (who was not there, but of course she teaches at the nursery school. Would *she* go to coffee mornings anyway?) sends her children to Hillside. Jason says it's because of the Eleven Plus exams back in England, but I'm not so sure. The women, except for Mollie, who seems to cook the way she does for pure pleasure and is "social" but not a snob, seem dreadful snobs. It even seemed to me they patronize Mollie because she is rather casual about housework and does crazy things like hitchhiking to the coast because she felt like it.

Someone said someone had told her there wasn't going to be any flour in two weeks' time. This was discussed fervently. Who had said so? Oh. Well, she should know. Those U.N. people have special supplies, but they know more about the regular stock than most people. Oh dear, we'd all have to rush into town and buy up flour. (Which should, if the rumor spreads quickly, produce the predicted shortage in two weeks' time!)

Someone was going that very afternoon. Oh, what a bind—I promised to help out at the library. Do you think? I'll do my best. That's awfully good of you. And so on.

Mollie's little boy, long-haired and grubby, ran in and out, chased by Emmanuel's son. (Another strike against Mollie, I think, but I'm not sure why.) Should she have a nurse girl? When she goes out of the room I see Sabina and a noisy woman from

Cheltenham exchange glances and gaze in the direction of the veranda. I'm beginning to like Mollie more and more.

Mollie's little girl is out riding her bicycle up and down the road in front of the bungalow. Occasionally she comes in and stares at us with her round, rather calculating eyes. Later I heard her ask one of the women if she could go and play at her house.

"No."

"Why not?"

"Not today."

"When?"

"We'll see."

The women are very polite to me, very solicitous. Would I like a cushion, a sandwich, another cup of coffee? But I can find little to say to them and begin to feel hot and rather faint. (This always happens when I'm afraid.)

Why shouldn't I enjoy that sort of thing? The fan purring comfortably overhead, the chatter of friendly women, the smell of good coffee and a pleasant, leisured morning with no guilt attached, for wasn't Joseph at home doing the nasty, menial things we hated to do in our own countries? Cleaning toilets, dusting, washing clothes. And weren't Mary and Nicholas happily in school? Hadn't I always said to Jason, laughing, that my ideal was to lie around and eat chocolates and read love magazines? Haven't I been a champion of "gracious living" even on very little money? Surely here was "God's plenty" as far as any frustrated housewife was concerned.

But all I wanted to do was go home. I was not only bored but afraid. Afraid of what? I can cook. I am educated. I have what one of the dear ladies called my "storybook children." My husband is already liked—and not just liked, admired.

But I would not dash into town, even if well, to buy up flour. I would not volunteer at the library or take a carload of children to the pool. I cannot "run up" dresses unless I have a pattern or cook without a recipe. I am not, really, very self-reliant or very sociable. I feel like the Eastern bride who is taken out West to live alongside her hardy rancher husband.

That is what I fear. Right now, under cover of my "delicate condition" (which has already branded me as not quite *comme il faut*), I do not have to compete with these capable ladies. They

145

know there is nothing they can't do and are therefore relaxed about letting someone else do it for them.

Jason's mother would love it out here.

The sun filtered through the louvered shutters of Mollie's bungalow and outside grapefruits and oranges ripened on the trees. Our men were out there, across the compound, building new Africa in the minds of young men and a few young women. Jason was out there, trying to reawaken their interest in their aesthetic birthright. Mary was in Class One, laughing, learning new rhymes, drinking new wine in old bottles:

> Elephant Elephant
> Where Have You Been?
> I've been to the river to wash
> myself clean.

Nikky is holding hands with Negroes without even thinking about it—color-blind, happy. The farmer in the dell.

Joseph is back home chopping fruit and maybe just pulling the bread out of the oven.

Would you like another sandwich, a cake, another cup of coffee?

Fool! Isn't this what you wanted? Yet I shiver and wish for half past twelve to come and Jason to ride up in his white *Cortina* and rescue me.

The cheese stands alone.

Mrs. Blood

I am like an old man set down at a feast for which he has no appetite.

Mrs. Blood

There was no one in the flat and the electric company had cut off the lights. "I've got a candle somewhere," he said, and I stood by the door, in the darkness, waiting. "Here we are," he said, and his face and one hand flared up cruel against the dark.

"I'll light the fire. Have you got a shilling?"

"Yes."

"Give it here."

And we drank tomato soup from soup tins he had washed and saved. "It's cheaper than buying dishes." He had maybe a hundred soup tins stacked neatly in the corner.

In the morning I heard a peculiar, once-familiar sound. A creaking noise, like ropes against a float or the sound of stiff leather. And the voice of a woman calling to her neighbor across the way. A voice falling into a well.

"Richard!"

"Hrrh?"

"Wake up. Oh, please wake up."

"Hrrh." Sitting up, so thin, wrapped tight in his gown like a shroud. John Donne.

"It's snowing." I got up and went to the window. "It's been snowing all night. Let's go out for breakfast."

We dressed quickly in the freezing room and ran outside.

When Macgregor's opened we drank hot chocolate and ate a dozen cinnamon doughnuts between us. And walking away, Richard said, with his ironic smile, "That's the first time I ever left lipstick on a coffee mug."

Mrs. Blood

Melville knew that white is sometimes sinister. "You're as white as a sheet." Fear. The white curtain which hides the unknown. Lucifer, brightest of God's angels before he fell. Part of the fear of hospitals comes surely from all this deceptive whiteness.

Gordon Pym's white curtain behind which lurks the thing that may destroy us.

White shrouds for the dead. Donne in his winding sheet. No man is an island.

And in the Japanese garden, the dirty white bellies of the oriental fish.

"They look like bloody bandages."

"What do you know about bloody bandages?"

But then, he wanted to be a poet. Made love like a poet too, standing up against a tree with my skirts kilted around my waist like a young girl wading.

147

We had a music teacher in the sixth grade who made us learn all the old chestnuts: "Barcarole," "The Daring Young Man on the Flying Trapeze," "Old Black Joe" (only someone had written in my book "Young Yellow John" in pencil). One day a girl that nobody liked went up from the back of the room and whispered importantly in Mrs. Nemser's ear. Suddenly we were all told to stand and face the door and were marched out to an unfamiliar tune, Mrs. Nemser pushing the loud pedal for all it was worth and calling, "Quickly now Row One, and then Row Two," and then de-dum-de-de-de-dum, de-de-dum. "Return to your classroom, please." And the girl we didn't like whispered importantly that she had found a dirty Kotex underneath her chair. We thought she was disgusting.

Mrs. Blood

I don't ever remember seeing a pregnant woman when I was a child. Nor asking a question about sex. Where were all the pregnant women? Where were all the little friends with baby brothers or baby sisters? Did the women, then, stay indoors, behind drawn blinds? Did my infant eyes simply accept protruding abdomens as part of the general view (just as I cannot remember what our milkman looked like, although I remember the iceman's truck and the bill collector's shoulders as we watched him go away from underneath the upstairs window shade)?

Once we were walking back across Front Street Bridge and Mama looked down in the brown paper bag she was carrying and said, "Now isn't that the limit. I wanted paper napkins."

But when we said, "What's the matter?" she said never mind.

Papa slept in the back bedroom, a room full of the matchbooks which he collected and pennies which he let collect in drawers. It smelled of tobacco, and the bed was old and looked uncomfortable.

Mama slept in one of the bedrooms at the front and she had twin beds but nobody ever slept with her.

And this was because Papa had asthma and sometimes had to get up and walk around at night.

Or so they said.

Mrs. Blood

We learned to make love noiselessly and almost without motion, like mutes or ships moving carefully through mine-filled waters.

But sometimes the bed would creak and the voice of Jason's mother would call to us from the other room, "Is that you, dear? Is everything all right, dear?"

"Halt. Who goes there?"

And then of course it was no good.

Mrs. Thing

Jason's favorite trader came this afternoon while I was sitting on the veranda. He is not a typical "Hausa Man"; not a typical trader anyway. Very tall, in a spotless white robe, beautifully decorated, and with the little embroidered moslem cap on his head. A tall, thin, ancient man with a white beard and cool, slightly contemptuous eyes. In the fairy tales or myths he might be the disguised god or the Wise Old Man.

He comes from Mali, he said, and I spoke my shy French to him which seemed to please him very much.

He had three bearers who came with him. They carried the bundles, of course, not he, and the last, a very young man (perhaps his son), carried an old tin cabin trunk on his head. This turned out to contain his very best things, all of which had small white price tags tied on them. Again this is not usual.

Jason says you do not bargain with this man—you merely accept or reject his prices.

The bearers squatted on their heels in the corner and smoked cigarettes. The old man began arranging his things.

"Madame has been very sick."

"Yes."

"It is all right now?"

"I don't know. I hope so."

He nodded. Philosophical. One doubts if words like "hope" or "fear" have any meaning for him.

"Madame would like to buy?"

"I have no money. Your things are very beautiful."

He does not argue like the other traders—"Ho, Madame is very rich!" looking at our house, the radio, the car, Joseph in the kitchen. "We will take a check. Madame has any dollars?" This man accepts my statement. We wait in silence.

Jason and the children arrive just before the rain. Joseph turns the outside light on and Jason, squatting too, sits outside, running his hands over ivory and old brass, picking up the masks very tenderly. One feels the old man approves of him. He unwraps an ivory carving from a piece of rag. "You like this?" It is a lion, beautifully carved, mouth open, legs braced against attack. Jason takes a deep breath and picks it up, then passes it to me.

A lion to fit in the palm of my hand. I can feel its strength. The old man watches me. "How much?"

"Five pounds, Madame."

Jason, "Would you like it?"

"It's too much."

"Not for that kind of carving."

"I don't know. It seems extravagant." I hand it back and shake my head. "No."

Jason gives me a peculiar look. I can still feel the lion's strength, warm, against my fingers.

I take the children in to hear a story. I want to punish Jason, but why? I am cross with the old man for tempting me. *"Au revoir, Monsieur."*

"Madame."

I close the veranda door against the mosquitoes and leave Jason outside squatting, holding the ivory lion in his hands.

Mrs. Blood

When we got to Quebec City I said I wanted to go up to the Plains of Abraham. Jason carried Mary up the hill and I took the empty carry-cot. I couldn't get the feel of history so I took off my shoes and stockings and walked expectantly across the grass. But all I could think of was what a nice day it was and how strange to be in Canada again. I remembered Richard's drunken postcard written somewhere between London and Montreal and

150

how we had laughed so hard in a strip joint that the manager had told us we would have to leave.

Later we wandered through the old city and had lunch. Everyone was very friendly and commented upon Mary, asleep at our feet, *"C'est votre premier tresor?"*

And back on the ship Jason said, "What are you thinking about?"

So I said, "Do you realize we'll be in Montreal in the morning?"

Mrs. Blood

The first stirrings of lust came while I was reading *The Chinese Room*. Before that there must have been such feelings but I don't remember them. (Although I was aware of lust, for very young I turned down a page corner in a book called *God's Little Acre* to show it later to my friend.) But reading "The Chinese Room" I could feel myself expand, and then a terrible desire to bear down, to come open and receive inside. But what? Who? Where was he? (The feeling known again when the child began to come, but never quite like that with Jason, never so violent or so heavy. And I remember I had on a plaid dress a downstate aunt had given me and that downstairs Mama was cooking something with onions for dinner.)

I was twelve years old and knew then Mama had been right when she said I was a lazy, spiteful girl and also musn't be so bold. She'd seen me talking to the paper boy, oh yes.

Next day I gave back the book to the girl who'd lent it me. And she said, "How'd you like the place where she jumps up on him?"

And I said, "I thought it was disgusting."

Mrs. Thing

I am a man set down at a feast for which I have no appetite. The smell from the frangipani tree is sickening and the sunbirds hurt my eyes.

Joseph brought my coffee, and bringing, spilled some in the saucer.

"It doesn't matter."

"Sure, Madame?"

"Sure." My cup runneth over . . .

. . .

I could feel the warm strength of the carver entering my fingers, warm blood dropping slowly in my icy veins, and I resented the man who had such power, such excess strength to give away.

"Do you like it?" Jason said.

And I said, "It's too much," and went inside to read the children's story.

"Once upon a time . . ."

Mrs. Thing

Jason sees me vegetating, feet up, and is content. Twice he has come home and taken me off for coffee at the club. The coffee is bad—one must use sugar in order to drink it at all—and there are very few wives present at that time in the morning. Hugh Hare was there once—he interests me more than the other men. Older, with a thin, cynical face and usually kidding someone. How old? Forty? Fifty? He does the Art history and uses something he calls an epidiascope.

"When you're all better come and see my epidiascope." I see genuine concern in his eyes and a desire to make me smile. He leers at me. "Come up and see my epidiascope."

How did he and Frances ever get together? Perhaps she was his nurse during the war—he is old enough, I'm sure.

Jason says he drinks a lot and the marriage doesn't seem to be a happy one.

We have had an invitation to dear Trevor's party. (I knew it.)

Next to the club is the bookstore and we went in there, where I breathed in the heady and familiar smell of dust and new bindings. I bought Mary and Nicholas a new box of colored chalks and then Jason took me home and went back to work.

What does he think about? Am I a "duty" to be performed? Something called "keeping her spirits up!" or "just checking to make sure?"

Last night I woke up and wanted him and was ashamed. Why

152

haven't we got between us the kind of honesty that admits of such a confession?

I lay in the dark and listened to the drums and wanted him so badly my legs ached with the effort to stay still. Why couldn't I wake him up and tell him that?

We might have laughed about it.

Mrs. Thing

One of the senior lecturers died today. I've never met him, but Jason told me after dinner. Someone in architecture—from Poland, I think, or maybe Russia. His car hit a concrete abutment. They said he got out of the car and had been sitting on the wall—they could tell by the bloodstains—but he was dead when a lorry driver found him.

What did he think about, sitting on the wall with his broken head?

Did he know he was dying?

Did he care?

Surely it is better to be killed instantly than to get out and walk around and maybe think you're safe. Because of the bad roads and the shortages of cars and car parts there are many sudden disasters here.

But poor Mr. Repski had to wait—how long?—on the lonely road, in the heat, maybe the flies already attracted to the blood, maybe even a vulture circling overhead. Dazed? Frightened? What? Did he call for help and no one heard him? Did he die bravely, bloody head held high and gazing at the sun?

Will they bury him here or send him home to Russia? If he knew he was dying, did he wish he were at home, under a cooler, more sympathetic sky?

"He was very tall," Jason said, "and almost bald. An older man. You may have seen him."

"No," I said, "never."

But I see him now.

Mrs. Blood

And she dropped one of the bunnies on its head. The next day it lay trembling uncontrollably in the corner of the garage until her mama said she'd better bring the poor little thing inside. But she found she couldn't touch it and ran away down the street.

That night she stood in the corner of the spare room, crying while the driven, demented creature ran round and round in ever-diminishing circles, as though searching desperately for something it had lost. Then it shuddered twice and died.

She knew it was her fault and stared with horror at the white thing on the faded linoleum.

Her mama picked the creature up.

"What are you going to do with it?"

"Put it in the garbage, dear. It's just a dead thing now."

"I want to bury it in the garden."

"That's not healthy; some dog will dig it up. Or it might have some disease. No. Absolutely not."

"Please!"

She buried it down below the apple tree, right at the edge of the garden. In a shoe box. She knew she'd have to say a prayer because God made it, so she said Now I Lay Me and then sang the Doxology because the prayer didn't seem enough.

But what her mama didn't know was that she'd dropped the bunny on purpose, to see if it would fall on its feet, like a cat. Mama just thought it was an accident, and all she ever said was, "I don't know what your grandfather was thinking of. You can't raise rabbits in the city."

Mrs. Blood

Once, waiting outside the old Capitol Theatre, in the crowd of screaming kids who got out of school to see "The King of Kings" I saw a girl without a nose. Just a line of bone and darkness.

And once I was crossing the street and a car turned the corner —a car driven by a man who's head was completely covered in new white bandages. Just cut-out places for his eyes and nose and mouth, like some hockey player.

And yet another time I took a good look at the pencil-seller who sat by the Court Street Bridge. He had leather pads on his knees and wore dark glasses but I don't think he was blind.

154

Yet I took no notice of the warnings and went on roller-skating in the spring.

"Be careful!" Mama always called out from the front-porch swing. "Be careful."

Mrs. Thing

Or was it simply the burden of my lust for Richard which I carried with me for a long, long time and finally set down with relief on Jason as a hobo might set down a bundle which has suddenly become too burdensome to bear?

On Saturday mornings he would bring me a brown paper bag of bacon, eggs, tomatoes and a loaf of bread. And cook my breakfast for me.

Fattening me up.

Mrs. Blood

"Space your calls instead of making several without a break.
"Talk only as long as necessary on each call.
"When you finish talking replace the handset properly.
"Make certain that the line is clear before you dial.
"Ask your youngsters to be considerate too."
"Christ!"
"But the actual process is much easier," I said. "In England I always forget to press Button 'A.' "

. . .

Pat-a-cake, pat-a-cake
Baker's Man
Bake me a cake as fast as you can
Pat it and prick it and mark it with 'B.'

. . .

"Richard," I said, "come away from the telephone book."

Mrs. Blood

Richard said, "You don't look half bad in the morning."
And I used to be afraid to open my eyes, sometimes, in case it

155

was all smashed and I would find myself lying in a field of pump-kins and tired white mice.

On the train from New York we played "hangman." And just outside of Scranton he said, "Oh, Christ, I want you," so we left the train and went to a hotel and phoned to say we'd be a little late.

And the name of that hotel was the Crest Motel and Restaurant with these "All Star" Features for your comfort:
* Imperial Grill
* Complete Banquet and Meeting Facilities
* Heated Swimming Pool
* Expresso Coffee Bar
* Television
* Optional Kitchens
* Completely Fireproof
Yeah.

Mrs. Blood

Give us this day our barely dead.

. . .

Some of the holes were so deep you could see cartilage, trans-lucent as saltwater taffy, lying just above the bones. Nurse Prim-rose did the actual digging, Mrs. Karensky carried the cologne, and I brought swabs and gentian violet and an emesis basin for the waste.

At each bed we would stop and check the hips and back for beginning sores.

And it was just something we did, you know—part of the day's work.

Old Annie Fannie would sit up in bed rolling shit between her hands and waiting for us. "Here I am. Here. Here. Come here."

The smells were the sores, and the Old Spice Cologne we used on the Kleenex with which we covered our noses, and urine, and drying feces.

For we did the bedsores, you see, before we changed the linen, flinging the heavy canvas sacks down the great chute to the base-ment where fifty female trusties put them in the big machines and washed them clean again.

And they weren't really women to me, you know, just screaming, kicking monstrosities or parodies of human beings. Sometimes you wondered how they got that way, but usually you just went about your business and when the shift was over you just locked the horror in and went on home.

Only I took a bath and washed my hair every night that summer because I had trouble locking in the smells.

Mrs. Thing

Strange how once I thought myself so in love with Jason that I couldn't sit next to him without wanting to touch him or be touched. Now I think we are like Siamese twins, irrevocably joined to one another in a back-to-back position. Not looking at one another, *unable* to, lying wide-eyed in the darkness and wondering how it happened.

We know too much about each other's weaknesses; the landscape is too familiar.

I used to carry his love inside me like a growing child. Now there is only a guilty emptiness as though I had committed some shameful, illegal act.

Now he moves out, heavily because I am joined to him, waiting for the miracle that will cleave us, not together, but apart.

Mrs. Blood

> Cleave ¹, to split. (E) Strong verb.
> Cleave ², to stick. (E) Weak verb.
> Cling (E.) ME *clingen*, to become stiff, be matted together. AS *clingan* (*pt. t.* clang, p.p. *clingen*), to dry up, shrivel up.

> I lie
> You lie
> > Come love lie
> > beside me lie
> Your lies
> > Beside me
> Let us sing
> > together
> > > Cling
> > > > together
> > > Clang and clungen
> > shall be ours.

How many lies, then,
have we laid together,
Made together?
Come.

Mrs. Thing

No one ever talks about all the lizards in West Africa. Palm trees, snakes, heat, drums, even the fans (think of Graham Greene). Maybe I'm only aware of them because I have to sit still so much. They are everywhere in the garden and even sometimes in the house. They climb up the netting and hang there, so that if you are inside they look like tiny humanoid corpses, their bellies are so pale, or manikins. The males have dull orange throats and seem to pose, sometimes, head up, as though they know they are more attractive than the females.

They have wise, cynical eyes and although I am not afraid of them the way women are sometimes afraid of mice or snakes, I sometimes feel threatened by the way they look at me or hang against the windows with their pale, corpselike bellies pressed against the nets.

The whole landscape is busy. Soldier ants, lizards, sunbirds, once in a while a jungle parrot so violently colored it looks like a child's toy from Hong Kong or the five and dime. Snakes (only we don't usually see them), flying insects. As though the sun had spawned, through a kind of spontaneous combustion, a whole world which goes on parallel to ours, a kind of "double now." Termites too, eating away at the parquet floors, and cockroaches mating in the upstairs bureau drawers.

A biologist here told Jason that if all traces of human life were wiped from the earth, the routes of the ants would be clearly visible. Everywhere. If I am feeling gloomy I think of Miss Havisham's parlor where she kept the dreadful wedding cake.

But usually it does not bother me. It is all part of the other we came to seek. Nikky and I saw a rhinoceros beetle yesterday in the driveway. I had never seen one before except in the *National Geographic*.

"Hey," I said, "d'you know that beetle can peel a banana with his nose?"

Nikky was delighted and ran to Joseph to get a big banana.

But the creature, who belongs in Lewis Carroll, scorned our offer and just went clicking on up the drive until he disappeared into the bush. Nikky wanted to keep him in a jar, but just now I can't bear to capture anything, having so recently gained freedom myself, and so I wouldn't let him.

Joseph saved the day. "Hey, Nicholas" (Nee-ko-laas), "come help with chop." And Nikky runs away to the kitchen, where he sits on the big wooden table and eats groundnuts while Joseph cooks the dinner.

Each day now I can feel myself relax a little more, like some tight-curled paper flower opening slowly in the clear water of Joseph's benevolence and the delight at being home again. Last night I could even look at Jason with some kind of objectivity— not just as the terrible man who had brought me here to be ill, but as my love and friend who has had to suffer quietly and alone with no nurse to hold his hand or show him albums.

It's been hard for him, and somehow I must remember that he too, like Mary and Nicholas, needs reassurance.

Bitterness flowed out of me and disappeared, and I could feel the warmth I have toward him filling up inside again. Like Tank *A* and Tank *B* in our high school algebra.

I went over and touched his face with my hand and told him it was all going to be all right. Then, because I couldn't bear to watch his face, I told him about the book I was reading and suggested a game of Boston Whist.

So that last night I felt for the first time as though I belonged in Jason's house and hadn't stumbled into a stranger's place by mistake.

Mrs. Blood

At the *boucherie chevaline* the horsemeat was a brilliant red, uncanny and slightly sinister. "What d'you suppose it tastes like?" I said.

"Shall I buy you some?"

"No, thanks." But while we stood outside the window many people came and went, buying the rich red meat for dinner.

"I wonder," he said, "if they feed them specially, or if it's just any old horse."

"Why is it so red?"

He shrugged. "I don't know. Shall I go in and ask."

"No." I pulled at his arm. "Come away."

"You don't want to look anymore."

"No. It makes me feel sick."

"You're too squeamish."

"Please come away."

This is my body, which was given for you.

. . .

"And one of the most amazing things," she said, "was the way the driver said '*Allons, allons,*' and the horse knew what he was talking about. For a minute I thought to myself, 'What a clever horse to understand French,' when I have such difficulty with it."

"Jesus," he whispered. Then politely, "I know exactly what you mean."

Mrs. Thing

Our cat is gone. Joseph says, "Somebody have kitty for chop," and laughs in what I can only describe as an un-Josephly way. "Somebody get she for chop," and he laughs again.

"Don't," I say and shake my head toward Mary and Nicholas, who have been playing with Lego on the floor and are listening, wide-eyed.

"Maybe she go for bush," he says with a wicked smile. "Maybe no chop. Maybe she go for bush." Joseph did not like the kitten, who was always jumping onto the kitchen table and getting into things.

He would put down the food each evening and "tk-a-tk-a-tk-a" very quickly, then catch the little cat and throw her outside. I have heard him mutter he would "make she for chop," and I wonder suddenly if perhaps he has eaten her himself. But no, he is too loyal to the children. Occasionally, though, one senses behind the mission-school Joseph another Joseph who is much less altruistic and more "primitive," if one can use that word objectively.

He is very superstitious, for one thing, and often goes to the market for fantastic remedies from the juju stall. I think he knows what the dark side of life is all about, and violence appeals to him. He tells me tales of fights he has seen or heard about. ("That man he was no good at all.") And if he had the chance I suspect he would join the militia here just to carry a gun.

All this I only suspect, of course. To me he is always polite and deferential and concerned. But I have heard him singing on Sunday nights, in his quarters, maybe after a bout with too much palm wine, and the song has sent a shiver over me.

Just as I shivered when he laughed and said, "Somebody get she for chop."

How Jason would smile if I said to him, "Look, dear, I don't like the way Joseph says 'chop.'"

But he likes saying it—"chop"—and the word becomes alive and as sharp as the knife he hones every night on the same back stoop where he fed the cat.

Later Mary asks if people really eat cats, and I say, "Yes, I guess so. But who would want to eat a kitten? There's nothing to it." This seems to satisfy her.

"In France," Jason tells her, "there are many butcher shops where they sell horsemeat for people to eat."

"And in the south," I add, "people eat rattlesnake sometimes. They say it tastes like chicken."

"That's not the same thing as eating cats," she says. "You can't keep a rattlesnake for a pet."

"I can," says Nikky. "I can keep a snake."

"Not a rattlesnake, stupid."

"Yes."

"No."

And we smile because a crisis has been averted.

Why do we object, though, to the idea of eating cats, or even horses? Is it because we have "domesticated" their flesh? Just as we would never eat our friends or any other human being. Should I have said to Mary that there are still a few places where people eat one another? And why?

If I ate a bit of Jason, believing it would make me strong, would it in fact do so?

And what if I ate a bit of Joseph?

161

Peace grows inside me like a pearl. Tonight the rains came down hard after supper. Then the lights went out. Mary, who is terrified of fire, insisted she didn't want a candle and would go upstairs in the dark. Then Nikky, of course, said he didn't want a candle either and Joseph stood there, a candle in each hand, puzzled and maybe a little amused at their fear. I wonder if he was afraid when he first saw electric lights?

Jason said it was nonsense and they'd go upstairs now—he'd go with them—by candlelight, and get undressed and into bed. He took one of the candles from Joseph and told them to come on. Mary's shadow cringed against the wall, and Shadow-Jason, huge and black, pursued her.

"Jason!" I said, feeling her fear almost as though it were a scent.

"Be still."

Shadow-Jason took Shadow-Mary by the hand, and Shadow-Joseph followed with Shadow-Nicholas.

Because of the rain on the roof I couldn't hear what was happening upstairs but I could feel Mary crying, shrinking back from these strange men who floated in and out of the darkness as huge hands and faces. I hated Jason because he did not understand and again felt powerless against his unimaginative strength.

After a while, my head full of rain noise and the awareness of Mary, upstairs, crying, I couldn't stand it any longer and went to the foot of the stairs. "Jason!" Nothing replied but the impatient drumming on the roof. "Jason!"

And then down the stairs came Mary in her nightgown holding a lighted candle, then Jason, then Nicholas and Joseph. Mary's eyes were full of the candlelight and she walked slowly and carefully down to meet me. "See. I'm not afraid of it. Touch it, Mummy. See."

And Nikky, "Mummy. Touch it."

And I knew the fear I smelled was my own as well as Mary's and that Jason was right—you must walk straight up to fear and take it by the hand.

So we sat, Jason having taken the children back upstairs and tucked them in, and the rain drummed on the roof, beating at it, asking to be let in.

But the house stood against it as Jason had stood against the fear and had made Mary stand against the fear as well. And I know he too could feel Mary's terror but ignored it, knowing she must come to terms with it. And so we sat, by candlelight, listening to the rain and floating securely in our little ark, listening to the waters rise.

Shall I tell Jason that sometimes I am afraid of this violent rain? Would he take me outside and put it in my hand?

"Jason . . ." But he had fallen asleep. I sat there, peace growing inside me like a pearl. The child kicked reassuringly against my abdomen. "Not yet," I whispered calmly. "Not yet."

Mrs. Thing

There are only two seasons here, wet and dry. The rainy season, the dry season. It is strange to think that now, when the rains are beginning to ease off and the lush green of our garden will shortly, so I'm told, pale into a dry and brittle brown, back home the wind carries the first hint of the approaching cold and children are getting ready for Halloween. I wonder if we are psychologically in tune with the physical environment in which we grew and therefore if it is dangerous to be transported far beyond the sea. In Vancouver I sometimes feel a strange emptiness when it doesn't snow at Christmas and I don't think it has much to do with Christmas card scenes or nostalgia. After all, my Christmases were not that happy, even in retrospect. It is rather as though my body is prepared for a blow that never comes, and I am left tense and unfulfilled.

All the horizontal things—sledding, making angels in the snow —and the great contrast in temperature between the outside world, which I stamped from my heavy boots as I entered the house, and the hot air from the house, blowing upon me like warm breath as I opened the door: I miss these. My *body* misses them.

And now I find that, without an autumn, again I feel a sense of loss and incompletion.

It is more violent to move from the very wet to the very dry. Having only two seasons, somehow they will both seem excessive. Our paperbacks are already going moldy, and when I went to put on my runners the other day—they have been sitting in the cupboard since I went into hospital—they were covered on the inside with a fine silver-green fur. It gave me a horrible shock— like imagining what it would feel like to drink out of the famous fur-lined teacup.

Joseph says we must put light bulbs in the cupboards to keep them dry. The whole house has a slightly damp and unused smell, except for the kitchen, where presumably the heat from the cooker keeps the damp away.

The mattresses, too, smell musty. Perhaps Jason and Joseph together could lift them out in the sunshine some day soon.

Joseph says when the dry season comes, and the harmattan, we will long for the rain again.

A dry wind, "so dry she make it very difficult to spit, Madame."

Sabina said that last year a beautiful Bambara carving they had bought split right in half.

I hate the heat. It is the one thing I really hate about this place. But with the rains to depend upon I find it bearable. And when the rains stop? Will I too crack like the Sutcliffes' Bambara?

Now, as the day goes on, one can still feel the rain behind the heat, count on it, wait for it. It's almost sexual. But later?

"So dry she make it very difficult to spit, Madame." No wonder the Muslims hold the feast of Ramadan then. To be told not to spit when you cannot spit is no great hardship.

And now, back home, mothers are beginning to take out last year's mittens and last year's caps and the magazines are full of recipes for Christmas cakes.

The thermometer just inside the door reads 83 degrees and this afternoon Jason is taking the children to the pool. Joseph has been baking bread and roasting groundnuts all morning. If I went down into the kitchen to begin a Christmas cake it would be like descending into hell.

Even the baby seems to feel the heat today and gives only a desultory kick or two to reassure me he is still all right. How hot is it in there, I wonder, and does it ever change?

164

Last year Mary and Nicholas had to wear heavy cardigans underneath their costumes, and I, waiting at the bottom of the steps, shivered under the fierce October moon.

Mrs. Blood

And why did it occur to you to dress them as Alice and the White Rabbit for the fancy dress parade? Why that?
All the children won, of course. "They always do," said the woman who had asked if I played Duplicate.
Every day the purser went down and moved the plastic ship a little nearer to our destination.
Nikky won the "under threes" in the orange race and afterwards we discovered they had slit his orange and stuck it on to the spoon.
"They probably all were," Jason said reassuringly and took Nikky off to spend his five shilling certificate at the shop.
And wasn't it all such fun and didn't we all have such jolly times?
But tell me: Why did it occur to you to dress them as Alice and the White Rabbit? Why?

Mrs. Blood

After Richard left me it was as if the whole of London had vanished in the fog and I was alone on a never-ending beach. No matter how far I walked there was just me and my solitary footprints and nobody else at all.
Sometimes the unreal me was followed by soft, slightly perfumed Indians who walked along beside me and suggested unspeakable things we might be doing. They wore pastel turbans— pale pink, lemon, pale green—as though the tops of their heads were exotic flowers, and they smelled of patchouli and spice. And sometimes I would run down into the tube stations to get rid of them.
But the real me walked alone along a sunless beach, and even the sea was hidden by the mists which walked around me, stalking me, waiting for me to slip or stumble.
What was I looking for?

Richard, of course. I knew when the fog cleared he would be there ahead of me, waiting, repentant, eager to embrace.

And the man in the raspberry-soda turban said, "Would you care to partake of a cup of tea?"

And the policeman said, "A nice girl like you should be fast asleep in bed." But I showed him my Alien Certificate and he let me go.

Who is Richard? There are flowers. Only flowers. And there are no victims.

Mrs. Thing

Jason sought me as a new child seeks its mother's breast—blindly, desperately, sure I had the answer to his pain. There was no "technique," no sophistication. He rooted in me, helpless, needing comfort. It was not gentle and yet it was innocent—so unlike Richard who I always suspected was somewhere detached, observing us, observing me particularly from one hard little corner of his brain.

With Jason I felt each time that I had done something for him. I was never overwhelmed and utterly abandoned, lost, as I was with Richard. Richard was gentler in his touch, yes, as a virtuoso's hands are gentler upon the piano keys. Sure. Professional. Delicate.

Rather like the touch of Dr. Biswas, only without the general sympathy which made him weep, at seventeen, for the women of his race.

How important hands are—for eating, for dressing, for speaking even (the old joke about how to describe a spiral with your hands behind your back), for making love. Imagine being armless, gripping only with thighs and feet. Not to be able to caress the back of your lover's neck or touch his eyelids or grasp his hair. Just smooth, from the waist up to the shoulder and over into the neck. Fish.

Richard's hands were long and delicate, and even when he lived in that filthy flat on Duke Street, always clean. Jason's hands around his coffee mug in the El Sombrero: ingrained with paint and grime, nails uncut, the surfaces roughened and pitted

166

from the concrete he'd been working with. Square hands with short, thick workman's fingers.

His clothes too—the clothes of a laborer and plaster in his hair and on his glasses. I had not thought of the artist in these terms at all and now saw him, after the introductions, as perhaps a poor boy, maybe from Gosta Green or even worse, on scholarship at the art school.

Later I found out that the trousers he had on that day were an old pair of his grandfather's and that he was utterly indifferent to what he wore or how he looked. But I still could not disassociate his person from the slums of Birmingham and the first time I was taken to his parents' place for Sunday dinner—taken by a very correct young man who delighted in clothes, and, at the time, in me—I couldn't believe it as we turned into the fashionable suburban road with its rows of sedate houses, manicured lawns and gleaming cars.

"Are you sure it's Jason we're going to see? Jason?"

He laughed and swung the car into an immaculate pebble drive. "There he is."

And Jason in front of the house, on the stoop, in an unfamiliar dark green suit, a tie, polished Sunday shoes: "I'm so glad you could come."

Yet it still seemed unreal, as though he had been posed in front of that house, the way one poses in front of a "scene" at the seaside photographers', the way I was to pose later for him in front of the Chateau Frontenac.

Then I saw his hands, and smiled, and knew it was all right.

"Hello," he said shyly. "I'm so glad you could come."

Later, after dinner, the three of us walked over the country lanes to the home of the elegant young man.

We found a dying robin on the way and picked it up and took it with us. "Mother would love to have a go at that," he said.

He lived in a tiny, crazy cottage, and "Mother" turned out to be delightful, untidy, surrounded by cats and a smelly old dog and a huge and lusty unkempt garden. Everywhere there were half-eaten dishes of table scraps.

Action. Reaction.

Which way will Nicholas and Mary go?

That was a happy afternoon.

167

Mrs. Blood

They come out, if properly, head first and downwards, diving into life through the blazing red-ring of their mother's agony, as though through a hoop of fire. They are held up and admired and patted on the back as though they, and not the broken, spent thing lying on the table, were the heroes.

And once you have caught them, held them up and slapped them into breathing
                    You cannot throw them back.

Earlier, when just a cipher —under seven inches like a trout— perhaps they could be thrown back; only thrown back not to thrive and grow but to become no-thing, an excrescence.

Dive for life they do, as you or I, braver or younger or in another clime, might dive for pearls. And opening their eyes for the first time under air, as we might under water, they blink and begin to wail.

And the bloody thing in the bed or on the table smiles and forgets the horror and the outrage and holds out her arms to receive her violator, her hero, her fish, saying, "This is my body which was given for thee. Feed on me in thy heart by faith and thanksgiving."

Mrs. Blood

The night I had Mary, Jason was at the Bridge Club playing Duplicate.

"Stay with me, Jason."

"The nurse says I have to go now."

The warning bell as ringing. *Pring a pring a pringgg.* A small hand bell kept on Sister's desk in the foyer.

"Stay with me, Jason."

"The nurse says I have to go now." Desperate to get away, like the Japanese fishermen who will frantically cut their lines rather than touch the dreaded wolffish.

"Stay with me, Jason."

"Now you be a good girl and I'll see you in the morning."

Out in the corridor I could hear them talking, telling him it would be hours yet, with the pain licking at my back, my sides, my insides and knowing it would be soon.

Consumed with pain. Consummated. That was at eight and the child was born at ten. Rip. Rip. And then rest in peace.

And then the nurses saying, "Did you know that little Mrs. McNeil had a lovely baby daughter?"

And I, "Fuck your little Mrs. McNeil."

But afterwards all forgiven. Jason, my love, see what we have molded out of ourselves? How could he have known?

And the Head Sister smiling and saying, "My, you're a fast one, aren't you?"

And I said, "Look at my legs. My legs are shaking. Why won't my legs stop shaking?"

And she, "Oh, that's just a little reaction. A nice cup of tea and maybe a sleeping pill and you'll be yourself again."

But I hid the sleeping pill under my pillow and lay awake, slack-bellied and proud, and thought of my daughter sleeping just above me like a guardian angel. How could I ever be afraid of anything again?

Mrs. Thing

Today we went to dear Trevor's birthday party. Like the Birds, the Hares live off the compound, quite near our first house—the very first—in a rather elegant, semidetached affair with a huge rectangular "lounge" as all the English say, and a semicircular veranda large enough for Trevor to ride his tricycle on. As at Mollie's, the parents were invited as well as the children, and there were masses of food, all carefully protected under muslin food covers, peculiar contraptions that reminded me of tiny greenhouses, so that I almost expected the sandwiches and jellies to grow before my eyes. There were even pale pink rabbits made out of blancmange, which for some reason didn't appeal much to the children and lay gently melting in their dishes as the afternoon wore on.

Frances looked even tinier and more fragile than ever. She must've worked very hard on all the food, and yet the party never got off the ground. Partly because of Trevor, who obviously didn't give a damn whether he had a party or not (and that in itself says something about what a sad little child he is) and who played by himself, in the corner, most of the afternoon. But also because of the tension in Frances, her terrible desire (because she is Indian? Unhappy?) to have everything absolutely perfect. I kept thinking of those first words, "We're determined to make a go of it." Also Hugh, who was already slightly drunk and made it clear that he disassociated himself from the whole fiasco.

He and most of the "Daddies," to use Frances' word, stood in the far corner near the refrigerator—near the beer, in other words—and talked department politics. The "Mummies" talked their usual steward-babies-shortages trilogy. Frances said she "simply *refused* to skimp. I told Hugh, if we have to do without butter, you can do without your precious beer." The women exchanged amused glaces. Apparently Frances and whatever steward happens to be working for her that week are a familiar sight in the Kingsway and the U.T.C. Somehow she always manages to get butter or dried fruit or imported chocolate—whatever happens to be scarce. She speaks very loudly and firmly, calls for the manager, tells him about dear Trevor, and eventually places the brown paper parcel of whatever it is she wants in the big shopping basket which the reluctant steward has been holding patiently all that time.

Joseph says, "Mrs. Hare she very bad woman, Madame,"— this because of the way she treats her stewards, I guess. But I don't think she's bad. In fact, her enormous (surface) self-possession, her absolute certainty that she is superior to "these people," is almost enviable. Sometimes I think she sees herself as Trevor's real (physical) mother—Trevor so blonde, so fair of skin ("My dear, he mustn't even stick his nose outside until half-past four"), so obviously Anglo-Saxon. Perhaps that is why she takes him everywhere with her and not, as she says, because "There is no one suitable to leave the poor child with."

All the "right" children were there, the department children and the coffee-morning children as well as three young Lebanese, two boys and a girl, who belonged to the "charming" family up the road and who stood patiently, without speaking, near their nurse girl.

I thought of the boy I had seen at the hospital. The older boy was about the same age, wore the same immaculate khaki shorts, white shirt and gold wristwatch. They look, somehow, like rich pastry and sugared sweets, olives and olive oil. Plump, light-brown, eyes like dates. The girl was about ten—much too old for Trevor's party, one would think—and already a small dark mustache was forming over her upper lip. Beautifully dressed in white linen, with gold necklace and gold earrings. She spoke to no one, not even to her little brothers, and ate only one sandwich.

"Isn't she quite adorable?" said Frances, linking her arm through the bangled arm of the child. "Someone's going to be a terribly attractive young lady, isn't she?"

But the girl just gave an almost professional little smile and said nothing.

No games were played, although I could see the prizes, beautifully wrapped, in a basket on the sideboard.

"Play with the others," I said to Mary and Nicholas; but they, naturally shy, seemed to have caught the general icy infection and stood quietly by my chair, going up to the table to choose some food when goaded by Frances, then returning to eat by me. It was the same with the others. Dear Trevor and the fans were the only really mobile things in the house. Trevor rode round and round the veranda; the fans rode, slower, round and round in their appointed order.

Then suddenly Hugh was sitting next to one of the "Mummies"—the one with the frizzy hair and loud over-the-garden-fence voice—and must've stretched his legs out just as Trevor had finally decided to get off his tricycle and join the party. Trevor fell over Hugh's legs and bumped his head, quite hard, on the terrazzo floor.

"Did you *see* that!" cried Frances in her high little well-bred voice. "He *deliberately* tripped the poor lad. Come here, darling, come to Mummy."

But Trevor, howling, had buried his face in his father's lap and refused to budge. And in Hugh's eyes I saw real love for the child, and pain too, and began to like him.

"Did you see?" asked Frances, rather frantically. "*Deliberately* tripped him. Come to Mummy, Trevor. Come and let Mummy kiss it better."

Everyone began to gather up their children and murmur thanks. It would have been impossible to stay. Even Frances did not urge it. "Oh, must you go? Good-bye then." But said absently, as she sat bolt upright in her chair and stared across at the still-unmoving figures of her husband and her son.

"There were favors," Mary said as we drove back down the Hare's road toward the junction. "I saw one wrapped up with my name on it. We didn't get our favors."

"Never mind. Mrs. Hare forgot. I expect you'll get them some other time."

"Could we go back and get them now?"

"No. "

"Why not?"

"Because."

But I was half-tempted to ask Jason to turn around and go back just to see if everything was all right. The stillness, the way Frances looked at Hugh, the thin neck of the silently weeping child: it frightened me.

But we could hardly say (as we would have to, now that Mary had mentioned it) that we had come back for the favors.

Who was Trevor's real mother? Where is she now? And would she care what was happening to her son? Pulled tight, his soul stretched between the two enemies he loved.

And the rest of us, deserting him, slinking off like cowards.

Mary and Nicholas were very quiet in the back seat of the car and we finished the ride home in an uneasy silence.

Mrs. Blood

And when there is a black mamba down there in the bush they tell us to keep the children in.

Black Mamba, Black Samba, Black Jamba, why do you threaten my child? You may have my green umbrella, you may have my crimson shoes with crimson linings, you may have my green youth and my crimson soul and all the flapjacks your little forked tongue can eat.

Black Mumbo, Black Jumbo, leave my child alone.

They have sent the beaters out to find you. Soon they will return triumphant with your limp body slung upon a stick. They

172

will find you out no matter where you turn in your frantic turnings.

But meanwhile we must do what we can to keep the children in.

Mrs. Thing

Jason has had some adzes made from an old lorry spring. He is on the veranda now, attacking a piece of mahogany.

"What's it going to be?"

"Oh, I don't know yet. I'm just fooling around."

He stands with legs astride, virtually barefoot, for the local thongs he wears are no protection, and every time the adze comes down I flinch, expecting him to cut off a toe. Mary and Nicholas are sitting on the railing, watching, and even Joseph, tea towel slung over his shoulder, has come out of the kitchen to have a look. Some small children appear in the field beyond the house. They see Jason— or Jason's arms and the adze—and stop giggling and whispering to one another. Is it so strange, then, to see a white man doing this? Obviously Joseph thinks so, for he chuckles to himself and shakes his head as he retreats to the kitchen. In a minute I can hear him talking to one of his friends at the back door.

Poor Joseph! He would be happier, I think, with an engineer or perhaps a scientist. Jason is constantly shattering his stereotype of the white man. "Master" doesn't care what he wears, never shouts at his steward, helps to carry the groceries from the car himself, economizes on beer and booze in general.

"In Gold Coast time," says Joseph, looking at the table set for a curry dinner with the Sutcliffes, "in Gold Coast time we have twenty-one side dishes minimal. Min-i-mal, Madame." And he is sure the evening is doomed to failure!

We have no tablecloth to fit such a long table and the scratches on the table bother him. He wishes we would buy him a white mess jacket like the other stewards. He is one of the highest paid stewards on the compound and yet we tell him we have very little money (which is true).

I think he would be happier if we beat him.

173

"Hey, Joseph," I call.

"Madame?"

"Maybe master make sculpture of you from that wood, hey?" He stands in the doorway to the kitchen and grins with delight.

"Yes, Madame."

"You like that, Joseph?"

"Yes, Madame."

"Great big sculpture to put in front of the bank maybe?"

"Yes, Madame."

I raise my arm in the usual gesture of the status of the President. "Like this."

He goes back, laughing, shaking his head.

I sit in the easy chair and listen to my men: Joseph the African frying onions in the kitchen, Jason the European wielding the "primitive" adze. Both are happy—at least I think so—and the steady *thud-thud* of Jason's adze is like the beat of the great heart of Africa which produced our Joseph (corrupted, although he does not know it) who has come in from the heart of darkness and is frying onions in a clean well-lighted place. After which, dinner over, he will return to his quarters and fill his noble lungs with the smoke of Tusker for Men while he reads the daily paper and ponder—what? Jason's "peculiar" desire to work with adzes, the latest plane crash, his horoscope, internal politics or the twenty-one side dishes, minimal, back in Gold Coast time when things were simpler for everbody, black and white alike.

Sometimes I would like to pass my hand across his cheek and say that it will all come out all right. But that might be the crowning blow which would shatter his psyche forever. When I think of Joseph and maybe all the others his age who grew up before Independence—particularly those who were stewards and houseboys and proud of it—I remember the bit from Arnold about wandering "between two worlds, one dead, the other powerless to be born."

Mrs. Blood

Dividend Forecast

Another week with 10 draws on the National pools coupon include two from the cup tie and three from the Scottish second division.

174

These scattered draws on the long list of the coupon means fairly good eight and seven treble chance pools pay out this week.

There were seven home teams and one postponed match. Claim by telegram for possible 24 points on eight and 21 points on seven treble chance pools.

4 always good. 3 draws: fair. 8 results: poor. 12 home teams failing to win: bumper.

Change of Names

I, George Tetley Odonkor, State Sugar Product Corporation, wish to be known and called Rynors Mensah Odonkor. Former documents still valid.

Amusements

Ramblers for Swedru 29th terrible.

F. Micah's shaking Anim-Apon 6/10/65.

OKuKuseKu shaking Akwabaa 25th.

OKuKuseKu shaking capital scene 29th Superlative.

Lido tonite presents real Monday sensational jamboree with Super Avengers' Band playing top hits for 1964. It's really swinging. Fans nevers miss.

Going to England?

The problem of your

DOG or CAT

is solved at Hazel House

Quarantine Kennels

Elsted, Midhurst, Sussex.

MARRIAGES, BIRTHS, DEATHS. In Memoriam. Thanks for Sympathy. Wanted to Let or Amusements, Clubs, Hotels, etc. Is 6d. for five words or part thereof for each insertion.

THE STATE FISHING CORPORATION

Says . . .
Good fresh fish gives you

* good eating
* good health
* good value

Start

eating

more

FISH......

Today!

175

STATE FISHING CORPORATION
Branches throughout the Country.

Ne rien insérer.

Mrs. Thing

It is impossible for me to see other people as separate from myself. Jason is my husband, Mary my daughter, Nicholas my son. I can only imagine what they are thinking by imagining what I would think if I were in Jason's position—which is quite different from imagining what I would think if I were Jason! Thus when I was in hospital, ashamed and defensive because of my physical weakness, I saw Jason as ashamed and embarrassed too. I wonder now if that is really so. Is not my unconscious anger with myself really responsible for all my fury at Jason? Simply because he is not and never will be me, because he looks at life from a different—and maybe clearer—window. He is only angry and embarrassed when I give up. It's strange, but sitting here on the veranda, eyes closed against the glare, I have been thinking not only about Jason, whom I have continually wronged (mentally when not actually verbally accusing him of things) but about my father and how much like him I am. I remember once, coming back from our big trek to New York I think, and going up Jacob's Ladder. We had an old car and my father became afraid, really afraid as we climbed higher and higher. He was swearing and Mama was her usual contemptuous self—"Don't make such a fuss; just get on with it"—and yet turning on us when we made some sarcastic remark from the back.

Finally he said he couldn't go on. "Jesus, I can't get up that hill in this old car." Pulling off the road, wiping his forehead. I felt contempt for anyone afraid of hills (for it was the height that really scared him, not the possibility of brake failure). I also felt frightened because adults shouldn't give up and pull off on the side of the road. I felt cheated, utterly humiliated. So *this* was my father, this green-faced, sweating, cursing little man who had taken us partway up a long, long hill and, so far as I could see, was prepared to leave us there.

He didn't in the end, although maybe, for him and all of us, it would've been better if he had. Mama's tongue whipped him forward and upward until the long hill was negotiated and we were inching down the other side.

That's what Jason really gets embarrassed about—when my fear threatens to completely shatter me, as when I cried out to him in the hospital that I was being punished for something and that I would surely die. He doesn't understand that kind of fear because he has never allowed it to take hold of him.

It isn't enough to finish the race any old how. One has commitments to the others to whom one has joined oneself. My father left me a legacy of fear which is like a sinister version of the goose that laid the golden egg. The more I make use of it, the more I have to use.

He used to grab my arm suddenly, when we were crossing the street. Now I grab Mary and Nicholas, passing on the clutch of fear like a secret handshake. I must learn to keep my hands at my sides, to smother my cries as one would smother the small but sinister beginnings of a forest fire. I find I want Jason to respect me, to be proud of me, whatever happens.

And then I wonder why I say "whatever happens" and feel the clammy fingers of my father's ghostly clutch circle my arm once more.

Poor man! He inched through life the way he inched our old Buick down the hill that day.

Hence, horrible shadow, poor little Papa, hence. I will not return the pressure of your trembling hand. I shall move out from the shade of this veranda and stand bareheaded in the sun until I feel the hot breath of Africa upon my cheek and let him kiss away the damp salutation of your lips.

I want to learn to take chances and hang upside down in the frangipani tree and look at the bloody mouths of the hibiscus without flinching. After the baby comes I must learn to run again.

Mrs. Blood

Sometimes I wake up frightened in the middle of my mind.

Mrs. Blood

Bloody Mary.
Bloody awful.

"Bloody thing," he said, and sucked hard at his finger.

"They're bad this year," I said.

"Today," he said, "we will discuss the symbolic significance of the bloody and bawd of Christ, that is to say bloody Mary, who propelled Him, shrieking, into the musty straw and thought all over that which had just begun."

And someone at the back of the class held up a hastily printed sign: Sir! YOUR FLY IS OPEN.

> O Paradise, O Paradise
> The World is growing old;
> Who would not be at rest and free
> Where love is never cold?

Mrs. Thing

Events are blurred, as though the hot breath of Africa had already blown upon the mirror of my mind.

Did I have Sole Ambassadeur the night we left or did I suddenly hesitate, remembering that other time and trying to force myself to eat in front of Jason's parents?

Jason had steak, and so did Helen and Jonathan. I remember that because the platters came with little aluminum steers stuck into the meat. "Rare," "Medium Rare," and another "Rare." It made me feel slightly sick when Jonathan pulled his out and the prongs were dripping with blood.

But did I have the Sole or was it the sweet and sour spareribs? I should have kept a diary, like that poor old man on the boat. "Friday, August 1st, Father [that would be Jason] had a rare steak and baked potato with sour cream and a salad with Thousand Island dressing. Mother—Sole Ambassadeur and a bottle of Nuits St. Georges. Weather clear. Helen and Jonathan along as well."

They sent us a photograph taken by a street photographer. Jason's tie is crooked, as usual, and he looks so young! My pain has run over his face like waves over smooth sand, leaving him corrugated, marked, perhaps for all time.

I look—how do I look? Slightly drunk, happy, about to take a bon voyage. A stranger. A face in a blurred mirror.

I must write and thank them.

Mrs. Blood

He was limping when he came up the walk. "What's the matter with your foot?" I said.

"I stepped on a piece of glass this afternoon," he said.

Later on he took off his moccasin and it was soaked in blood. "You ought to have stitches," I said.

"Naw," he said. "It'll heal up by morning."

I can't even remember his name but I remember the look of his moccasin.

I only went out with him once. That foot didn't stop him from trying something. And afterwards I was worried Mama wouldn't believe the blood on my stocking was from his stupid moccasin, so I hid the stockings in the bottom drawer and washed them out next day.

Mrs. Thing

When we left New York nobody could come down to see us off and we felt a little forlorn and neglected as we began putting our things away.

Then Jason read the card about champagne available and thought, what the hell, why not, so he rang and ordered a bottle of champagne.

Even Nikky had a sip and we drank the bottle between us.

Then Jason took the kids up on deck and I sat there feeling it was all going to be all right. A little weak with relief and excitement, definitely cheerful.

When we went down to dinner there were about a dozen fancy cakes laid out on the big serving table and we took the children up to have a look.

"Bon voyage," they said. "Bon voyage."

Mrs. Blood

In spite of the weather we seemed to be always hungry, and sometimes at breakfast we used to order nearly everything on the menu.

Except the blood puddings, of course.

George got a good laugh out of that and used to say, " 'Ere.

Wot about some of them nice blood puddins? That'll put the roses in yer cheeks."

But we wouldn't even try them and finally Rosemary told him to quit it because it made her feel sick.

Mrs. Thing

As yet I have only seen glimpses of this country and this compound. Like villages or people seen from a train window. I know nothing. I have not yet crossed the bridge.

After the baby comes . . .

Mrs. Thing

The pain began almost at the same time as the streetlights went out down our road.

"Jason." (And the other me saying, hissing, don't cry out, don't name it and it will go away.)

"What's the matter?"

"I've got an awful pain." Breathless, as though the pain were in my throat and not my belly.

"Try and relax." He lights a candle. "Do you want those pills?"

His voice is flat, disappointed. Oh God here we go again.

"No. Not yet anyway. Maybe it's nothing."

"Would you like to sit up a bit?"

"Yes. That might be nice. And maybe another candle."

"The lights will probably come back on in a minute. I'm not sure where Joseph put the candles."

"Could you find out?"

We talked like this. Formal. Middle-aged. Controlling the panic by speaking in careful sentences. A sentence is a group of words expressing a complete thought. But there are sentences and sentences. He gets up to find the candle and crashes against the wardrobe, and the pain, like a kicked animal, swipes at me again.

"Oh."

"Where're the fucking candles?"

"Downstairs. Try downstairs."

Will the lights be off at the general hospital?

180

"Jason."

His voice floats up the stairs. Softly. Please don't wake the children. "Hang on." The candlelight precedes him up the stairs. "You'd better bring the pills."

He roots through the bathroom cupboard. I can feel the sticky ooze of blood between my legs. The pain again. "Oh!"

He comes with the pills and candle, his face strange above the candlelight which molds his cheekbones, reddens his skin. We used to hold our hands in front of candles and put flashlights in our mouths.

He goes back out again.

"Where are you going?" Don't leave me, please don't leave me.

"To get you a glass of water."

"I don't need a pill yet, really."

"I think you should take one."

"It will get worse than this. I think I'd better wait."

We talk carefully, in monotones and sentences. We mustn't wake the children. For some wild reason I am glad I washed my hair.

He sits carefully at the bottom of my bed.

"Do you want me to call the doctor?"

"No. Not yet." We are relatives or lovers waiting at a terminal. Uneasy. At a loss for words. Wanting the journey to begin.

"Would you like to play a game of cards?"

"Yes. I'd like that very much."

And so, propped up on my pillows, *our* pillows, for I have his as well as mine, we play a game of Boston Whist. Another, yet another. The pills, a most innocuous-looking shape—round— and color—white, on the bed where I can reach them. We do not touch and keep the elaborate system of cards between us.

And the pain comes and goes like the voice of the man on Mr. Acquah's radio, until suddenly I am used to it, no longer flinch or cry out "oh." I can cope. I am one of them.

So that when a part of the placenta comes away quite quickly and easily with about as much sensation as pulling off a large and rather stubborn Band-aid, I say calmly, laying down my cards, "I think I'd better have a pill."

On the drive in, with nasty bits of placenta hidden like stolen liver in my sponge bag (for he told me to bring anything that

181

came away), I observe the early morning traffic, the mammy lorries, the endless rhythm of people walking to the markets. A boy with seven chairs stacked crazily upon his head. The Addis Ababa Cafe. How nice the policewoman looks in her blue skirt and yellow blouse. The statue of the President blessing us as we drive by.

"How do you feel?" Jason very quiet. But then, he always is. He looks well in shorts. Strong, powerful thighs and legs. He always looked out of place in suits. I smile at him, the pain completely under my control, like traveling with a bear cub in a tight, well-woven basket.

"Strange. Not frightened so much now it's started. A little sick."

"Don't get sick all over my new car."

I nod, smiling. He moves the white car carefully around the roundabout and starts up the long hill to the hospital.

Then I see the vultures wheeling and begin to cry.

Mrs. Blood

They have shut me in here just as surely as if the walls of my little cubicle were made of steel, not plastic. I want to be carried out into the courtyard, underneath the fierce blue glare of the sky. There my cries will be lost amid the noise of the people waiting at the clinic doors. The ward is very silent. They are all waiting for me to begin. I am so alone, so alone, so alone. My little plastic cell; my solitary confinement.

"Please confine yourself to the issue at hand," the chairman said.

"Please confine yourself."

"Fasten Your Seat Belts."

"No Smoking."

"Please confine yourself."

And the women in the sun room, long ago, two in straitjackets because they had been naughty, the others with busy fingers underneath their stiff gray dresses or hands held pink-white and silent, like skinned dead rabbits in their laps.

"There are more things in heaven and earth, Horatio."

And let my cry come unto Thee.

182

PART THREE

OWUO ATWEDIE OBAAKO MFORO
The ladder of death is not climbed by one man only.
(Free translation of the symbols seen carved on a Chief's
stool.)

Mrs. Thing

When I get to the ward the Staff Nurse says, "So," and I cling
to Jason's hand.

"Can't you stay?"

"I'll be back this afternoon. Keep your chin up."

And Esther and Grace Abounding cry out, "Eh! Madame!"
when they come in from the dispensary and discover me in my
old bed by the wall. "Eh! Madame!"

"Where's Elizabeth?"

"Tsk. She is not on until this afternoon."

. . .

I sleep, off and on, holding the pain stiffly and carefully—a
bearcub in a strong, well-woven basket. Dr. Biswas comes and
goes. They give me an injection.

"So. It has not worked out as I had thought. I am very sorry."

"I am very sorry also."

He smiles sadly, his large, womanish eyes full of sympathy.
"Everything will be all right."

"The pill made everything very quiet, very calm."

"Good. Now we will give you something to make you sleep."

"I'd rather stay awake."

"But why?"

"The baby gets no assistance of that sort."

He shrugs. "That is morbid."

"It's true."

But I agree to have the shot and fade away slowly, calmly.
No more fear. An English voice from the other side of the partition asks Alexandria or Grace or Esther, "Does she know?"

Mrs. Blood

These things you did not notice:
The dead man on the first boat.
The dead man on the second boat.
The disappearance of the cat.
The woman named Mrs. Mabee.
The lizard's wink.
The message of the fans.

Fool! Did you think I would protect you? I always say you get what you deserve, I always say.

And Richard said, in his letter, "I am thinking of applying for a post in Freetown and I know who I'd like to take with me."

The daughters of musick have been brought low and the doors shall be shut in the streets.

"You'll love it," she said. "I can tell." And then, "Do you play Duplicate?"

Mrs. Blood

It happened so quickly that afterwards it seemed a smooth unbroken movement as he walked back from the toilet and, picking up two pillows, one from Rosemary's bed and one from mine, threw them down in front of the little gas fire and flung himself down saying, "Come and lie in front of the fire." And I moving almost before he spoke, across the room from the window where I had been staring out at the snowfall, and lying down beside him—still in one unbroken movement—and then our coming together so effortlessly and right as if this is what we had both been training for, waiting for, maybe like Nureyev and Fonteyn, I told him later, practicing away in their respective companies and then finally meeting and dancing together, he lifting her effortlessly in a classic *pas de deux* just as Richard lifted me and I soared up and up, effortlessly, and he held me there at the peak and then gently brought me back to earth again, so that the act itself had no real or separate meaning—it was just part of the great fluid choreography which had begun when Richard walked back in the door and without breaking stride took the two pillows, one mine, one Rosemary's, and flung them down in front of the gas fire and said, "Come here."

So that afterwards trying to remember who said what and when, I could remember nothing but the sensation itself, and maybe Richard's voice saying, "Nice, oh nice."

And maybe my voice saying, "Richard, I love you Richard."

But it was all just part of the music and the dance.

Mrs. Blood

THE TIPS

Lucky Boy Newsboy Race

1st.	Niger Express	Tearaway
2nd.	Paris Express	Think Twice
3rd.	Chajel	Thank You
4th.	Golden Apple	So Is Life
5th.	Me and You	Keep Quiet
6th.	Paris Express	Think Twice

Ambulance in exceptionally perfect condition as new, with two beds and effective fan system when vehicle in motion or not and fully licensed for one year—£875. Phone Odonkor 77776. Akwabaa.

Scorpio (Oct. 23–Nov. 21): Give time to cultural activities and make yourself pleasant—even if matters don't work out as you wanted.

Mrs. Blood

The painted flowers beckon softly to us like sleepy whores. All things too bright and beautiful where things grow overnight like magic or like cancers. Everywhere red mouths opening and closing and the smell from the frangipani tree presses down on my face and chokes me. Lizards have knowing eyes and bellies like bloated corpses. They hang on the screens and their long pale bodies call me to come out, and somewhere a hyrax is screaming a message for me that I cannot understand.

The land is treacherous. There are snakes in the grass and the puff adder hangs waiting in the branches until I pass.

The soldier ants converge upon the compound but no one listens when I try to warn them, and the talking drums are too far away for me to untangle the threads they weave. The air is heavy with hate, and downstairs Joseph sharpens my bread knife on the stoop and if I tiptoe down he will still know I am coming and slit my throat neatly and without much effort. He is in collusion with the insects, for I have seen him open the kitchen door and turn the light on and catch them in his frying pan. He knows their language now, also the language of the flowers, for I found a plucked hibiscus, like a fresh clot, in the hall outside my bedroom and later I saw him touch his index finger to the frangipani tree.

The pain moves over me like an explorer in heavy boots. It tramples me down in its eagerness to find the child. The pain has been sent by Joseph and by the lizards and the insects and the flowers. It is looking for the child. All flesh is glass and I am a pale green bottle with a fragile bud inside me. The hyrax screams again and two fireflies wink their evil eyes above my bed. If I don't stay awake the child and I will be dead before the morning.

Mrs. Blood

And whatever possessed him to buy a white Cortina with red upholstery? He *said* it was the only thing available and I said, "Oh yes?" and gave him a straight look which he pretended not to understand. Just sat there (as though to compound the portents) pouring catsup on his fish.

Joseph is in on it too. They all are. You saw the flower outside our bedroom—in the corridor?

That was Joseph.

But why?

Mrs. Blood

> **Vulture.** (L) L *vultur,* a vulture. *OL volturus;* lit. 'tearer,'—L *vul* (*vol*), as in vul-si, *pt. t.* of *vellere,* to pluck, tear. Allied to *Vulnerable.*

> A is for Apple
> B is for Baby
> V is for Vulture
> M is for Mabee

I am vulnerable; I am allied to vulture. One hovers just above the bed. The other—smaller—one has begun his tearing from the inside. My baby, my own. When you do that you are allied to these foul-mouthed scavengers. What? Would you feed off me before your time? The heat has made you thirsty. Hush. Not yet.

Mrs. Blood

> If a tree falls in the forest
> does it make no sound if
> nobody hears the noise?
> If a child dies in the forest
> does it make no sound if
> nobody hears its cries?

V is for Vulnerable Vera, born with too many of just about everything.

Born with almost enough to make another one.

Thriving now, the doctors say.

What did they do with all that extra rest of her, those redundant arms and legs which hung around her body like the symbolic limbs of Krishna?

Why did they not leave her alone and worship her? Why, vulture-like, tear at the little thing until they reached the regulation arms and regulation legs and regulation this and that.

Does she ever say to them now (in Russian, of course—this can be only an approximate translation), "Where have you hid my arms?"

I am going to give birth to a bird. What will they do with that? Expose it on the mountains? (There are no mountains here.)

Tie stones to it and drop it in the lake? (There is one lake here—no mountains.) Burn it in the hospital incinerator? (Risky. The vultures are arranged along the rooftops; they will inhale the desecration and, maddened, may attack.) Worship it? Fall down and worship it? A white dove, a little bird, saying, "The flood is over."

Maybe they will let me take it with me in a little ivory box. Jason can run to the street of the carvers and fetch me a little ivory box to keep my birdie in.

We shall carry it back like a message, a relic from this holy land. We shall allow the people to place their washed hands on the box and receive the blessing from what lies within.

For a fee.

Mollie B's sister was home from the hospital for two weeks and just getting over it when the hospital phoned and asked her what she wanted them to do with it.

Mrs. Blood

Toot-Toot had immaculate silvery braids, done by Mrs. Karensky every morning, and rosy cheeks.

"Looks like she just came in from the harvest, doesn't she?" said Mrs. Karensky, plaiting neatly and professionally the coarse and strangely vital hair.

"I wonder what she was before she came here?" I said, handing Mrs. Karensky a rubber band.

She shrugged. "Who knows. Might've been anything. You can't tell by the way they look. There you are, sweetie," she said, patting Toot-Toot's plump little shoulder.

"Toot-toot," she said. "Toot-toot."

And I followed Mrs. Karensky up the ward, my keys tinkling like little bells against the movement of my hips and legs.

"You're a whore!" screamed Eleanor La Duce.

"You want to help me cut her fingernails?" asked Mrs. Karensky, grinning.

"No thanks. Get Nurse Primrose."

And when I took a message up to the nurse on 92 I saw the fat girl who had been chained to her bed for five years because she hadn't been a boy. And I had to wait because one of the women had packed up her suitcase and was arguing at the desk about how she wanted to pay her bill and leave.

Mrs. Blood

What I really want to know is, granted the nonexistence of a God, benign or otherwise, who is responsible for all this?

For now we see through the grass darkly; but then face to face.

Beareth all things, believeth all things, hopeth all things, endureth all things.

And upon them that are left alive of you I will send a faintness into their hearts in the land of their enemies. And the sound of a shaken leaf shall chase them. And they shall flee, as fleeing from a sword; and they shall fall when none pursueth.

And they shall fall one upon the other, as it were before a sword, when none pursueth: and ye shall have no power to stand before your enemies.

And ye shall perish among the heathen, and the land of your enemies shall eat you up.

Ye shall not offer unto the Lord that which is bruised, or crushed, or broken, or cut; neither shall ye make any offering thereof in your land.

They ought to do something about these birds.

> "Did ya ever think
> When a hearse goes by
> There's comin a time when you're
>   gonna die?
>
> They'll shut you up in a great
>   big box,
> And cover you over with dirt
>   and rocks.
>
> The worms crawl in,
> The worms crawl out,
> The worms play pinochle on
>   your snout."

For a long time I thought it was called the cement-ary because of all the stones.

All those people lying there in party clothes, pressed down like some exotic, weighted food.

To take the moisture out.

Peasants under grass.

And indifferent angels staring, like blind people, straight ahead.

Cement-ary.

But pretty when covered with geraniums or flags.

And under the long grass the worms perform the rigorous duties of their calling.

Up the board sidewalk, and along past the grocers, was the little post office. We liked to go there every week to read the *WANTED* posters. Once there was a man, Floyd Something, wanted for armed robbery. It said he had maroon eyes.

WANTED. Floyd Something. 5'10", dark hair, maroon eyes. Reward.

His sullen, thick-lipped face stared out at us from the poster. We watched carefully but never saw him. Watched all summer, and the next year he was gone. (His poster.)

But twice I caught a glimpse of him in dreams. Eyes like rubies, he wore, and two guns stuck in holsters on his hips. Both times I woke up, frightened, before he recognized me and pulled his gun.

"Listen," I said, embarrassed at having to shout over the noise of the band at the Little Budapest Cafe. "Listen, I think I am bleeding."

Everyone was very kind back there too. We had addresses of parents or friends of our friends from Calgary right through to Toronto, where we were going to change to the New York Central. Telephone numbers too. "Don't hesitate to call." But after that first gush there was no other.

And at Toronto I tore up all the addresses and flushed them down the drain.

And at home with Mama—nothing. And in New York. And on the first boat. Nothing.

We began to unclench. Jason ordered wine for every lunch and dinner. We even danced, the last night out, a tentative, slow waltz.

"Happy?" he said.

"Now I am. I was really very scared."

"Me too."

But remember, there was a dead man on that boat. And sure enough, three days before the boat sailed out to Africa it happened once again.

"Jason!"

"Hey?"

"Wake up."

"What?"

"Oh, please, wake up. I'm bleeding."

And then nothing.

And then a dead man on the second boat.

Didn't we know enough to prepare for the inevitable rule of three?

But the child rode quietly again, like a small craft in a bottle.

And the awful thing is, I was never really afraid, not really. What god would dare to thwart our high adventure?

And Pa had said, wistful at our going off into the great unknown, "You don't know how lucky you are."

Jonathan said, "Would you like to go on to the Little Budapest Cafe?"

And Jason said, looking at me to see if I was tired, "What about it? Do you think we should get an early night?"

"No. We've got a lot to celebrate. I'd like to go." And then, "Let's walk."

That's when the street photographer snapped us, laughing, the four of us going on from a good dinner to a good night out.

But Jonathan had just ordered and Jason had just asked Helen if she'd care to try a polka, when it happened.

They were very nice of course and gave us our money back. But I'll never go back there. Never. And I never want to hear a German band again.

He turneth the floods into a wilderness, and drieth up the water-springs.

The fruitful maketh he barren, for the wickedness of them that dwell therein.

Again, he maketh the wilderness a standing water, and water springs of a dry ground.

And there he setteth the hungry, that they may build them a city to dwell in.

That they may sow their land, and plant vineyards, to yield them fruits of increase.

It is very meat and write so to do.

"Birth and copulation and death. That's all there is."

> Thou who in a manger
>   Once hast lowly lain,
> Who dost now in glory
>   O'er all kingdoms reign,
> Gather in the heathen,
>   Who in lands afar
> N'er have seen the brightness
>   Of Thy guiding star.

For those in Mental Darkness

HEAVENLY Father, we beseech thee to have mercy upon all thy children who are living in mental darkness. Restore them to strength of mind and cheerfulness of spirit, and give them health and peace; through Jesus Christ our Lord.

AMEN

Me KoFi.   ME KoFi.   ME KoFi.

Once I saw George far across the crowd at the Lord Mayor's Show.

I waved and stood on tiptoe but he didn't see me. I thought to myself, "So he didn't go back to Kingston after all," and was sorry we'd lost touch and that he hadn't seen me.

Strange how I still remember his skin—after all these years and after just one time—and the way, when he was discussing something seriously at the Cosmo Club, he used to say, "now here's the thing."

Long ago I lost the little doll he gave me. It just disappeared. You know how these things happen.

Richard said, "Do you realize we've made love in four countries?"

Richard—the same Richard—also said, "Why humiliate yourself?"

Three days and two nights and on the third night I know it will be over.

I shake all the time now, and cannot eat. They say perhaps I have a touch of malaria, but I know it is from the effort needed to hold the baby in and keep the pain away.

Jason comes and holds my hand and goes away.

He has brought me two little birds made of horn and the ivory lion. I am holding it in my hand willing the strength of the carver to pass into me.

My face in my compact mirror is as gray and papery as a wasp's nest. I try to smile at him from under my pile of blankets and my wasp-nest face.

"I'm so tired."

"Hang on."

"Why am I being punished?"

"You're not. It's just one of those nasty things that sometimes happen."

"I love you."

"I love you."

"Don't cry."

Thus Jason comes and goes.

And then, the third night, it is over.

I am a flower dying from the sun. The wind passes over me and I am gone.

"Lie still."

Monkey, Banana, Cocoyam Driver. Monkey Banana Cocoyam Driver. Monkey
                    banana
cocoyam
                    DRIVER.

"Avez-vous du pain?"

I am Zacharias
I am Number One
Number One stole the meat from the cookin' pot
Who me?
Yes you
Couldn't be
Then who?
Number Two
I am Zacharias
I am Number Two
Number Two stole the meat from the cookin' pot
Who me?
Yes you
Couldn't be!
Then who

The mandrakes give a smell, and at our gates are all manner of pleasant fruits, new and old, which I have laid up for thee, O my beloved.

Come, come, come, come.

Then was I in his eyes as one who had found favor.

The night, like a murderer's sweaty palm, comes down against my face.
"Elizabeth!"
"Sah."
"I cannot breathe."
"Sah. Tonight it is very heavy. Soon it will be better."
And I remember, "It will be rain tonight."
"Let it come down."

"Dr. Biswas. Where is Dr. Biswas?"
"Lie still."

I am not what I am.

A deed without a name.

"Do you know Richard?"

"Elizabeth, give me your hand. You are black and comely. Come, come, come, come."

"Lie still."

"Do you play Duplicate?"

Jason, there is no nice way of saying this.

The eye of the moon is full of blood. I say the moon is full of blood.

They've got to do something about all this blood.

"Lie still."

And I said to the watchman,
"Saw ye him whom my soul loved?"

"Dr. Biswas. Where is he? Where is Dr. Biswas?"
"Lie still."

We didn't pay attention to the signs.

"The milk will go off, worse luck."

Over the falls. We are going over the falls. Over.
Elizabeth! I am so steeped in blood.

"Elizabeth. What are the vultures doing in my room?"
"Lie still."

Oh God, you have broken down all my hedges; you have brought my strongholds to ruin.

There's rosemary; that's for remembrance.
Come, come, come, come, give me your hand.

O, who hath done this deed?

Jason!

On the back of the air letter: *Ne rien insérer.*

Jason, my love, I am in blood steeped in so far that, should
I wade no more
Returning were as tedious as go o'er.

And somebody said, "Have you met Richard?"

The wolf hath seiz'd his prey,
   the poor lamb cries.

A deed without a name.

Come, come, come, come, give me your hand.

Ne rien insérer.

I am the Duchess of Malfi still.

Jason, my love. I have deceived my father, and may thee.

Love, *L'oeuf.* Nothing. Nothing will come of nothing.
Speak again.

We held hands in a movie called "The Man Who Never
Was."

All flesh is glass.

"Lie still!"

I am so steeped in blood.

"Shortages? . . . What shortages?"

The child lived, like a hermit crab, within my rotting shell.

Jason!

And every thing that she lieth upon in her separation shall be unclean; every thing also that she sitteth upon shall be unclean.

I am one who is sick of her flowers.

"Look," he said. "You've cursed my pajamas."

Press Button B.

Someone said, "Do you know Richard?" and I looked up through the smoke and sound and there he was.

There was an hibiscus flower, like a clot, outside the bedroom door.

And then they took my crimson soul and crimson lining. And then they let me go.

Why else would he buy a white car with red upholstery?

Jason, my love, I am not what I am.

Look to your house, your daughter, and your bags. Thieves! Thieves!

Jason, my love, I have done a deed without a name.

Rex. 8:30 Tonight
PAY UP OR DIE

"Do you play Duplicate?"

Richard.

Jason, my love. I am not what I am.

My salad days.
When I was green in judgment,
cold in blood,
To say as I said then.

Press Button A.

O, well done! I commend your pains.

Friends come hither.
I am so sated in the world, that I have lost my way forever.

Jason, my love, I am not what I am.

"Richard?"
They are taking the thing away. Elizabeth is weeping.
"Richard!"
My child. A Something in a silver bowl. A Nothing. It felt like a fish.
"Richard."
My child is dead. It gave a little "mew" and then it died.
"Richard."
Jason. Oh, Jason, I'm so sorry.
"Richard."
They are taking it away now; and the bloody sheets; and a black soft hand wipes my thighs.
"Richard. I've got to talk to you."
Jason. Forgive me, I was not strong enough. The child is dead. They are washing my face now with soft cloths, and Elizabeth holds me, weeping.
"Press Button A."
"Oh, God. Yes. Richard, I've got to talk to you. I'm pregnant. *Auntie Mary has she been here all along?—begins her high thin web of song to lift her up to heaven. Esther rubs my belly.*
Only silence. "Richard!"
Oh, Jason, I'm so sorry.
"Get rid of it."